ADVANCE PR.

When Mercy Seasons Justice:
Pope Francis and a Story of Migration

"This book is an expression of David Bonior's compassion and his life of selfless public service. He has painted a beautiful and deeply moving portrait of Pope Francis and of the Pope's extraordinary, holy spirit of mercy, justice, and goodness, which has uplifted and inspired millions around the world. *When Mercy Seasons Justice* is a powerful and important story of how Pope Francis continues, in the spirit of his namesake, St. Francis of Assisi, to heed the call to 'Preach the gospel; sometimes use words'—whether advancing women's equality, protecting the poor and needy, or promoting justice and dignity for all. During this difficult moment, this special book is a source of hope: reminding us that hope is where it always is, between faith and charity."

> – Nancy Pelosi, Speaker of the U.S. House of
> Representatives

When Mercy Seasons Justice is two stories and one journey. It is the story of Father Juan Soto, trusted aide to Pope Francis, who is grappling with the priest abuse scandal and the direction of his beloved church. It is also the story of Maria Elena Gonzalez and her family—migrants who are forced to flee Honduras to escape certain death.

The journeys of Father Soto and Maria Elena Gonzalez are worlds apart yet parallel. In both, we see the Catholic Church at work—at its worst and at its best. When their lives ultimately intersect, we see a path to its redemption.

In his novel, Bonior has combined great storytelling with

intense research and a behind-the-scenes exploration of the inner workings of the Catholic Church that led me on a cathartic yet spiritual journey.

Importantly, *Mercy* provides a keen examination of the crucial yet mostly invisible role that women have played in the Church's past—and a reminder that, if we are to succeed as a faith, that must change. The dream of devout women to be recognized as true leaders must be realized, and nothing less than a movement is required to make this vision come to light. *Mercy* is a first step in that direction.

When Mercy Seasons Justice led me to a new relationship with the Church and with my faith. If you are looking for a path back to the Catholic Church, this story will show you the way.

– Jeanne Zulick Ferruolo, Author of *Ruby in the Sky* and *A Galaxy of Sea Stars*

David Bonior's tale of the immigrant's northern journey from Central America to the Texas border makes ingenious side trips to the Rome of Pope Francis, the Washington of Donald Trump, and the Mediterranean island of Lampedusa, weaving in the bigger story of the Catholic Church at this moment in time. The men and women who run the shelters and churches that provide sustenance and a bed on the migrant's journey are aptly juxtaposed with Pope Francis's leadership of the Church in Rome struggling with the weight of history, a changing world, and a fast-growing sexual abuse scandal. Can Pope Francis, a man with affinity for the poor and the displaced, steer the Church through its biggest crisis in centuries? Might women be the answer?

As Bonior explores those questions, he also elevates the oft-told story of immigrants making the journey north with intimate and telling details such as Maria Elena, the head of the

Gonzalez family, consoling her children one evening by describing an early outing with her future husband and their father: "He gently reached for my hand. We both knew it would happen someday." And Jesus, another young Honduran immigrant, knowingly reflects, as he ambles through his hometown on the morning of his departure for the north that he is "tearing himself away" from the women "who make up his whole life." Such emotions bind us to the journey that will become terrifying but also surprising. New bonds form, friendships develop. A reporter for the *New York Times* captures some of that journey, but—like any good reporter—never becomes dominant.

The story in Rome and Central America come together where the best of romps end—on a soccer field.

> – Lydia Chavez, former reporter for the *New York Times* and professor emeritus at UC Berkeley's Graduate School of Journalism. Now running Mission Local.

"Now faith is the assurance of things hoped for, the conviction of things not seen . . . By faith Abraham obeyed when he was called to set out for a place that he was to receive as an inheritance, and he set out, not knowing where he was going." Hebrews 11:1,8

When Mercy Seasons Justice is a story of things hoped-for in the depths of our souls, yet dismissed in conventional political wisdom as unrealizable fantasy. David Bonior is well-acquainted with that conventional wisdom and well-known for his capacity to transcend it throughout an illustrious political career. Sustained by the *conviction* of things not seen, his characters set out for a place in both church and society they trust to be an inheritance of their faith. They travel treacherous territory along the way, sometimes not knowing where they are going. They draw clean water from wells of authentic piety. They arrive in a truly new land congruent with the best in their hearts. Prepare to be inspired, strengthened, and fascinated by this story of migration, mercy, and justice.

> – Reverend Doug Tanner, founding director of the Faith & Politics Institute, Washington, D.C. The institute is best known for its Congressional Civil Rights Pilgrimages to Alabama, led from 1998 through 2020 by the late Congressman John Lewis.

This is a very hopeful book about some very difficult problems that test the character of both the Catholic Church and the American government. The question of whether we will be a church and state that welcomes the stranger and hears the cry of the poor is going to be measured by our souls and our societies.

> – Father Peter Daly

Reading this book, you can see that David Bonior knows of what he writes. His Catholic roots in Detroit, his understanding of Church politics, and his deep knowledge of Catholic social justice activists, from Sister Joan Chittister to Saint Oscar Romero, shine through. His understanding of the realities of Central America and Mexico, of what drives migration, and of the challenges that migrants encounter come from his deep engagement with the region as a leading member of Congress, including in the battle against Contra aid, his support for peace in Central America as chair of the Democratic Task Force on Central America in the 1980s, and his role in creating and supporting the commission that investigated the murder of six Jesuit priests and two women in El Salvador in 1989.

The book reflects not just his knowledge of the politics of

the region, and of U.S. policy, but his on-the-ground experience. You can see in his book that David Bonior has seen close-up the barrios of San Salvador, the towns that migrants pass through in Guatemala and Mexico, and the selfless work of those who work with migrants at the U.S./Mexican border. This book is informed by those experiences.

– Geoff Thale, President, Washington Office on Central America

Other Books by David Bonior

The Vietnam Veteran: A History of Neglect
(co-author)

Walking to Mackinac
(travel)

*Eastside Kid: A Memoir of My Youth
from Detroit to Congress*
(memoir)

*Whip: Leading the Progressive Battle
During the Rise of the Right*
(memoir)

WHEN
MERCY
SEASONS
JUSTICE

Pope Francis and a
Story of Migration

A NOVEL

David Edward Bonior

City Point Press

Published by:
City Point Press
P.O. Box 2063
Westport, CT 06880
www.citypointpress.com

Paperback ISBN 978-1-947951-32-7
eBook ISBN 978-1-947951-33-4
Book design by Barbara Aronica
Cover design by Miggs B and Barbara Aronica
Original drawing of Pope Francis by Bill Murphy
Maps by Nancy Bonior
Manufactured in the United States of America

But mercy is above this sceptred sway;
It is enthroned in the hearts of kings,
It is an attribute to God himself;
And earthly power doth then show likest God's
When Mercy Seasons Justice.

William Shakespeare
The Merchant of Venice,
Act IV, Scene 1

CONTENTS

FATHER JUAN SOTO AND POPE FRANCIS

Pope Francis is meeting with a group of grammar school students at an outdoor gathering in one of Rome's working-class neighborhoods. It is April, the world easing into spring, on the fifteenth day of the month, and everyone is in a celebratory mood.

Francis begins with a few words about how important it is for the students to study diligently and to treat each other and their teachers with kindness and charity. Then he asks if any of the students have questions for him. The first person to come to the microphone stand is a boy named Emanuele, who appears to be about 9 years old. He stands while the pope has now seated himself thirty feet away.

Cameras around the gathering are filming the event and showing it on a large outdoor screen so that the others seated farther back in the crowd can share in it. Everyone is waiting to hear what this boy will ask the pope.

Francis's appearance before the students was arranged by Juan Soto, a 58-year-old Jesuit priest and the pope's closest confidant going back thirty-five years. Nobody knows the pope better and knows what his priorities are than Father Soto.

As a young seminarian, Juan was a brilliant scholar who also cared deeply for those who had little—the poor, the lonely, the homeless, and the persecuted. He spent a good part of his day crafting new strategies to engage these communities. Soto organized other seminarians, prompting them to unleash their emotions and talents on behalf of his causes.

He rallied them to collect, assemble, and deliver food baskets to the hungry. Juan Soto pulled together squads of carpenters in the community to build small houses for homeless families. He found skilled musicians who serenaded the sick and lonely in hospitals, and the forgotten seniors living in solitude.

During the early 1980s, the repressive Argentinian authorities came in search of members of Soto's flock who had been labelled "political subversives" because they had been aiding these communities. Soto and his colleagues found sanctuary for them and saved their lives.

Father Soto first met Jorge Bergoglio in 1983, at a closed discussion at the Buenos Aires Seminary, Villa DeVoto. Jorge Bergoglio was at that time a bishop and the Provincial Superior of the Argentinian Jesuits. A handful of seminarians at the discussion asked Bergoglio why he was not speaking out publicly against the murderous military regime and their Dirty War.

Before Bishop Bergoglio was even given a chance to respond, Soto interrupted his brother seminarians and began telling them how often Bishop Bergoglio had arranged sanctuary and exile for those whose lives were threatened. Indeed, Soto went on, a good part of Bergoglio's day was spent alerting those targeted and finding ways to help them hide or escape.

Soto's defense of Bergoglio at this meeting was the beginning of a long and close working and personal relationship. The Bishop needed someone like the unassuming Father Soto to help him extradite those besieged by the morally corrupt generals who ran the government and terrorized its citizens.

Soto's ability to be everywhere for Bergoglio, yet sometimes not even noticed, was helped by his slight five-foot six-inch frame. He was an "under-the-radar guy." His bookish look was accentuated by wire-rimmed glasses and a knitted brow. His eyes telegraphed a "can do" optimism, and there is the occasional quiet smile that ingratiates him with others. Nothing about him was obviously threatening, and he capitalized on his appearance and demeanor as an advantage. He used it to assist Bergoglio's efforts to save others from death at the hands of the Argentine government. These efforts formed a close bond of trust between them that, decades later, had Father Soto still serving the same man, who was now Pope Francis.

Emanuele stands frozen at the microphone. He has been told about Francis's goodness and kindness, but that doesn't stop Emanuele from being intimidated by this robed man seated in front of him. He cannot seem to get his question out, and there is a quiet tension building among all who have come to see the pope.

Suddenly, it all becomes too much for young Emanuele, who becomes overwhelmed by the moment. He breaks down and starts to cry into his hands. A priest who has been assisting and encouraging him to ask the pope his question, reaches out to comfort the boy, but with no results.

Finally, Francis speaks out and says to the boy, "Come—come to me."

Emanuele, hesitantly and with the help of the priest, walks toward the pope, who instantly embraces Emanuele. They stay in this embrace for a long while, whispering to each other.

The pope is dressed in his whites and, on this cool crisp morning, Emanuele wears a hip-length blue hooded winter coat that falls a little below his waist. Francis is fatherly and tender with the young boy.

Soto, in consultation with Francis, had already chosen two cardinals to join the pope on stage. Dressed in red zucchettos (beanies), they sit on both sides of the pope and are entirely enthralled with the exchange the boy and the pope are having.

As the manager of the event, Soto knows the child's behavior has thrown everything off script. He also knows that these are the times when Francis is often at his best. Father Soto patiently waits for the drama to play out.

Now that Francis has consoled Emanuele and put aside his fear, the boy whispers again into the pope's ear, asking his question and then hurriedly returns to his seat with his classmates where he once again buries his head in his hands.

Then Francis, in a slow and compassionate voice, speaks to the crowd.

"I asked Emanuele's permission to say publicly the question he asked me. And he said 'yes.' So, I will tell you. Emanuel asked, 'A little while ago my father passed away. He was a nonbeliever, but he had all four of his children baptized. He was a good man. Is Dad in heaven?"

The pope pauses and lets the significance of Emanuele's story and question sink in for the crowd.

"His father was not a believer, but he had his children baptized," Francis repeated. "He also had a good heart, and Emanuele wonders, because he was a nonbeliever, is he in heaven?"

It is time again for Francis to wait a moment before he continues past the boy's heartbreaking question.

"The one who says who goes to heaven is God. But what is God's heart like, with a dad like that? What do you think?"

This time the pope does not pause for the crowd to attempt a response but goes on to answer his own question.

"A father's heart. God has a dad's heart. And with a dad who was not a believer, but who baptized his children and gave them that bravura, do you think that God would be able to leave him far from himself? Do you think? Speak up, come on"

With Francis's encouragement the crowd begins to yell out, "No, no."

The pope responds by asking another question. "Does God abandon his children?"

To that, the crowd screams out again, "No, no!"

This leads the pope to turn to Emanuele and say, "There, Emanuele—that is your answer. God surely was proud of your father, because it is easier as a believer to baptize your children than to baptize them when you are not a believer. Surely this pleased God very much. Talk to your dad, pray to your dad."

All present at this simple gathering, on an ordinary spring day, had witnessed a stunning papal exchange, because such an answer of inclusion would have been inconceivable before his pontificate.

The thoughtful and loving way Francis reacted to Emanuele was moving for all who witnessed it, but not unprecedented. What was most significant, and groundbreaking, was that the pope's answer to Emanuele's question was one of mercy, and mercy underscores Francis's papacy. It was an answer that built upon the teachings of Vatican II.

Francis's papacy was leading the way for the next phase of a reformed and open church. It has been part of Francis's mission to find goodness in each of us, including the unbeliever. It was a bold and courageous assertion of mercy to reach out to them, a first among many firsts Francis has initiated.

Father Juan Soto knows that nothing that occurred at this gathering had been planned. Also, in his role serving Pope Francis, he has acquired enough knowledge about the internet to know this filmed exchange will go viral around the globe.

He also knows, as the pope's closest assistant, that Francis's break with church policy about nonbelievers will cause him to be inundated with questions about what this all means.

Father Soto often finds himself trying to answer questions about his boss's beliefs and the pope's generosity of spirit. The scholar within Soto equips him to find a defense of the pope in scripture. Beyond the scriptures, though, are those life experiences that factor into Francis's character, and Soto has near-encyclopedic knowledge of those too.

Father Soto spends a great deal of time ruminating on questions such as: Where does such a man learn mercy? From his family's migration from Italy to Argentina? From the lessons of the Great Depression—avoiding waste, practicing thrift, being generous to friends and neighbors? Or perhaps living at the edge of poverty and being fearful of slipping into it? The Depression and the fear of want imbued Francis with the notion that it would be best to put more emphasis on the spiritual, rather than on the temporal satisfactions of the moment.

Soto recognizes that Francis's papacy is different from that of his predecessors. He also believes it can continue to grow and evolve into a liberating force away from many of the habits and indulgences that have plagued the Church. Soto feels honored to be a part of these long overdue reforms.

He also appreciates the prominent role he is being allowed to play in designing and orchestrating those reforms, and that makes him all the more careful about being smart and skilled in the advice he shares with Francis. Much depends on his counsel.

Though Soto carries no higher title than "Father," he knows he has Francis's confidence and respect. Together they are making history.

On the evening after the gathering with the students, Francis made his way to his private quarters in the Vatican. He was weary from the day's activities, which also included meetings with Father Soto and Cardinal Marc Ouellet to review new appointments to the position of bishop, interviews with several media outlets, and an audience with a group of nuns from India.

Francis is a cool breeze in a church that had become stodgy and corrupted. So many of his "firsts" have been revolutionary. He is the first Jesuit to be pope, the first pope from South America. He is the first pope to say he does not judge gay people. He is the first pope to have washed the feet of a woman and to have appointed a woman's commission on deaconess. He has invited all Catholics to voice their opinions on divorce.

He was the first pope to build a shelter for the homeless and spend his birthday with them. And he was the first pope to rescue an immigrant family from Syria and then shelter them in the Vatican.

Francis has been courageous in critiquing global capitalism. In his apostolic exhortation *Evangelii Gaudium*, Francis directed his criticism against the twin evils of inequality and exclusion found in the financial and economic system: "Global capitalism fails to create fairness, equity, and dignified livelihoods for the poor." He called these gaps in capitalism the "dung of the devil."

The pope was equally forceful in his encyclical on ecology, "Laudato Si" (On Care of Our Common Home). He called for a broad cultural revolution to save our planet, our home. At Soto's suggestion, he even invited the executives of the oil industry to the Vatican for a chat.

Francis lives his faith and his exhortations. As a cardinal in Buenos Aires, he took the subway to meetings and to his pastoral missions in the city. Soon after he was elected Pope, he formed a commission to reform parts of the Curia and the Vatican Bank. He lives simply without pomp or luxury—answering his own phone, carrying his own bags, and sometimes earning Soto's and security officials' concern by walking around Rome and the Vatican without a bodyguard.

Francis knows how much the Church is in need of strong

and radical leadership. The pews are empty and the vocations for a religious life have dwindled. The sexual scandals involving priests and bishops all over the world have battered the Church's credibility when it comes to matters of moral teachings and have exposed the disgusting side of the Church as an institution.

For Francis, the road back to righteousness is pastoral. *Go to the people. Be with your flock. A shepherd must smell like his flock. Embrace the poor and the immigrants. This is where redemption and salvation reside. This is where the lessons of the gospel should take us.*

Soon after Cardinal Bergoglio was elected Pope, he expressed his horror that 25,000 migrants had been lost at sea while trying to reach a safe refuge from the ravages of war and economic deprivation in Africa and the Middle East.

Locking the gate to poor immigrants was increasingly dominating the political discourse in Europe and then America. Francis was determined to fight back against this xenophobia.

It began with a visit to a small island in the Mediterranean.

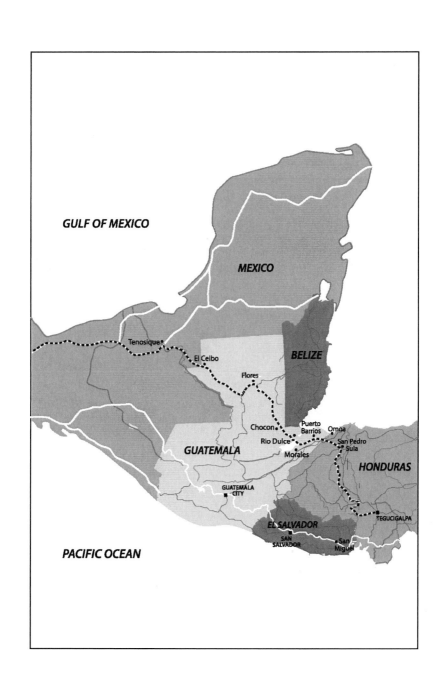

GULF OF MEXICO

MEXICO

Tenosique

El Ceibo

Flores

BELIZE

Chocon

Puerto
Barrios

Omoa

Rio Dulce

San Pedro
Sula

Morales

GUATEMALA

HONDURAS

GUATEMALA
CITY

EL SALVADOR

TEGUCIGALPA

SAN
SALVADOR

San
Miguel

PACIFIC OCEAN

UNITED STATES OF AMERICA

Austin
Houston
San Antonio
Galveston

Dilley
Family
Detention
Center
Corpus Christi
Laredo
Nuevo
Laredo
Humanitarian Respite Center
US Border Patrol Processing
& Detention Center
McAllen
Reynosa
Brownsville
Casa Padre Center
Saltillo
Monterrey
Matamoros

MEXICO

San Fernando
Site of Massacre

GULF OF MEXICO

S. Luis
Potosí
TAMAULIPAS
STATE
Tampico

MEXICO
CITY
Córdoba
Veracruz
La Patrona

The Vatican

Pope Francis: Jorge Bergoglio, also known as Francis.

Father Juan Soto: top confidant and assistant to Pope Francis.

Sister Mary Vernard: also known as Dr. Mary. Medical missionary in Haiti. Then medical doctor in Lampedusa and in the Vatican.

Cardinal Marc Ouellet: powerful Canadian cardinal and defender of Francis. Papabile.

Cardinal Joe Tobin: also known as Padre Joe. Progressive advisor to Francis.

Cardinal Blase Cupich: progressive advisor to Francis.

Sister Joan Chittester: preeminent Catholic writer, theologian, and activist for women in the Church.

Archbishop Vigano: conservative accuser of Francis.

Honduran Family

Maria Elena Gonzalez: mother and central character.

Jose Gonzalez: son, age 13.

Teresa Gonzalez: daughter, age 11.

Camilla Gonzalez: daughter, age 9.

Dionysia Gonzalez: daughter, age 8. Also known as Dio.

Central Americans

Miguel Cabrera: security escort for refugees and asylum seekers. Formerly agricultural worker and landscape artist.

Rocia Marquez: *New York Times* reporter and journalism professor at University of California, Berkeley.

Father Ismail Moreno Coto: also known as Padre Melo. Human rights activist from the Northern Triangle (Honduras, Guatemala, and El Salvador) and advisor to Pope Francis.

Captain Arturo Lopez Menendez: Guatemala military officer.

Jesus Aguilar:15-year-old Honduran boy, traveling solo to cross into the United States.

Carlos: teenage friend of Jesus. They meet in Matamoros, Mexico.

Father Peter Daly: formerly Pastor of Saint John Vianney Church in southern Maryland. Also advisor to Pope Francis and an immigration attorney.

Sister Norma Pimentel: also known as Sister Norma. Director of Catholic Charities of the Rio Grande Valley and activist for immigrants and asylum seekers.

BOOK ONE

Migration

CHAPTER ONE

Peter the Shepherd and
Miguel the Artistic Gardener

Father Peter Daly is a Catholic priest and a good shepherd as pastor of his flock in Calvert County, Maryland. He also writes a column for the *National Catholic Reporter*, and in one of them he tells a 2002 story about Cardinal Theodore McCarrick, the former archbishop of Washington, D.C., whom Pope Francis would expel from the Church in 2019 when he was found guilty of sexually abusing minors and adult seminarians for decades.

That year Pope John Paul II summoned all the cardinals to Rome after the first announcement of sexual abuse charges against Catholic priests in America. When McCarrick returned to the United States, he summoned all the priests of the archdiocese of Washington, D.C., to a mandatory meeting at the Franciscan monastery near the Catholic University of America.

"We were eager to go," Father Daly recalled. "It would be our first chance to discuss the clergy sexual abuse scandal with our archbishop. There were more than 200 priests present. It was a typical hierarchical meeting. The cardinal and the bishops sat up front."

Daly also recalled that McCarrick spent a long time discussing what would become known as the "Dallas Charter" (Charter for the Protection of Children and Young People), which described how priests were to be treated henceforth when accused of sexual abuse of a minor. There was a zero-tolerance policy and a mechanism to handle accusations against priests. But a part of the charter also exempted bishops from accountability if they had attempted to deal with the issue by moving offending priests to other parishes.

Father Daly is in his late sixties. He is of average height and has a twinkle in his eyes. He mixes his Irish sense of humor with the debating skills of a clever and thoughtful lawyer, which he also is.

In addition to writing his column, Father Daly also co-authored a terrific novel of Vatican intrigue, entitled *Strange Gods*. For thirty-one years, Father Daly devoted his life to his parish of Saint John Vianney in Prince Frederick, Maryland, but he is retired now and lives fifty miles away from his parish on Capitol Hill in Washington. But he does not seem to understand what "retired" means because he is so fully engaged in his new ministry: putting his legal skills to work on behalf of migrants coming to the United States.

Father Daly is the kind of priest Pope Francis wants in the Church—someone who bonds with his flock like St. John Vianney did in France 200 years ago. In the Catholic Church, John Vianney is titled the patron saint of parish priests. There are Catholic parishes throughout the world named after him. Father Daly walks in his footsteps and is revered by his parishioners.

As a parish priest, Peter Daly treats each confession, baptism, and funeral with reverence and specificity. His homilies at Mass touch on the everyday concerns of his parishioners and the ways their faith could strengthen their lives and communities.

When he marries a couple, he takes the time to know them and to tailor his remarks around their lives together. His funeral eulogies are personal, and the congregation has a warm feeling that Peter Daly was concerned about a person's life on earth as well as in the hereafter.

You can laugh with Father Daly, pray with him, sing with him. He is of the people. One characteristic sets him apart from many of his fellow priests and his religious superiors; one attribute that Peter Daly possesses is in short supply in the Church: courage.

Father Daly's courage was what seemed to shine through as he continued to tell the story of his encounter so long ago with Cardinal McCarrick.

"McCarrick gave us all the usual hierarchical perspectives on the scandal," Father Daly recalled. "They (the bishops) said the problem is serious, but not as bad as what is accused. The press is anti-Catholic. Zero tolerance puts innocent priests at risk and takes away bishops' discretion. Bishops cannot be accountable to anyone but Rome. Every bishop is autonomous in his own diocese, so they can't be accountable to each other."

After McCarrick's statement, he opened the meeting to questions, and the first ones were a couple of softball questions. Father Daly waited his turn at one of the microphones, all the while frustrated that they were not dealing with the real problems.

"I remember it vividly," he recalled. "I had made notes on my legal pad. I was nervous as a cat. When my turn came, I was visibly shaking.

"I faced into the microphone and said, 'Today Cardinal Law (of Boston) is answering a subpoena for a disposition in a civil lawsuit in the sexual abuse scandal in Boston. Instead he should be answering an indictment for suborning the felony of child molestation.'"

Father Daly recalled that Cardinal McCarrick looked at him with complete shock, as the presbyterate engaged in a sort of inward taking of breath.

"I remember that my voice quaked, and my hands shook so much I could not read my notes," Father Daly said. "I went on to address the Dallas charter and its zero-tolerance policy. I noted that the charter held priests to strict account, but there was no accounting for bishops, archbishops, or cardinals. They were exempted, I said, and they shouldn't be. We should all be held accountable to the civil law, to public scrutiny and to our people."

As Father Daly recounted this important day and event, he recalled that his next words were said with anger in his voice. "Our people understand sin," he said. "Everybody sins. What they don't understand is cover-up and the failure to protect children. Everybody, including cardinals, should be held fully accountable."

Cardinal McCarrick was clearly uncomfortable with Father Daly's pointed reference to cardinals and to the priest's display of emotion.

"I'm not sure this is the time or place to have this discussion," the cardinal said, interrupting Father Daly's impassioned speech.

Father Daly shot back at him immediately. He said he still remembers what he said word for word: "If a closed meeting with our brother priests, in the midst of the worst scandal to hit the American church, is not the time and place to have this discussion, *then you tell me the time and place, and I will be there!*"

Father Daly said he then sat down, shaking, and he continued doing so as only one priest, Fred MacIntyre, stood up to defend him. Everyone else was silent.

Father Daly's courage to speak truth to power is an attribute that is in short supply in Washington, D.C., and in the Catholic Church.

· · ·

Call it luck, call it kismet, or call it the Holy Spirit. Whatever you call it, and whatever it is, when it happens, it is like magic.

When two saintly people from different cultures and distant places come together, there should be no surprise when they create opportunity for others.

This is what happened when Father Peter Daly and Miguel met in a small Southern Maryland town.

Miguel Jimenez Cabrera is a handsome man with a solid body on his six-foot frame. He is from Guadeloupe, Mexico, a small rural community about an hour and a half by car from Mexico City. His village offered little opportunity for young men like him to earn a living. In his mid-20s, Miguel, along with a brother and uncle, decided to seek employment in the north. They eventually obtained temporary work visas and travelled to Ontario, Canada, to harvest cigar tobacco on Canadian farms bordering Lake Erie. Their goal was to provide a better life for their wives and children.

After several years in Canada, Miguel looked for a better working situation and found landscape work in the United States, in Southern Maryland.

It was hard and grueling work, labor that locals didn't want to do. Their employers were happy to have Miguel and his brother and uncle, and they were given temporary work visas to come each year in April to work for a nursery for eight months and then return back to Mexico at the end of November. These visas are called H2B.

Miguel's work in the U.S.A. allows him to send healthy remittance checks back home to his family in Mexico. He earns nine times more in the United States than what he would be paid for similar work in Mexico. Over the years, this money has been enough to pay for one son's medical education and another son's education to become a teacher. His two youngest, both girls, are also getting college educations.

Miguel met Father Daly when the parish hired Miguel's

employer to do some landscape work and maintenance on the church grounds. From time to time, Father Daly brought cold drinks and energy bars outside to Miguel and the rest of the crew. The priest also welcomed them to the services held at the church, and on Sunday after Mass, Peter Daly invited Miguel to have lunch at the local Mexican restaurant in Prince Frederick.

Their relationship grew from there, as Miguel told Father Daly about his family and how negatively they were being affected by the brutal U.S. immigration policy and the corrupt governments in Mexico. It was impossible for them not to discuss the recent election of Donald J. Trump.

During a speech in 2015, when he announced that he was running for president of the United States, Donald Trump said about Mexicans: "They are not our friends, believe me. They're bringing drugs. They're bringing crime. They're rapists. And some I assume are good people."

He then promised to build a wall along the Mexican border and said he would make the Mexican government pay for it.

Once Trump was elected president, he and his administration made every effort to close the border and to drastically reduce the number of refugees allowed in the country. The president also did all he could do to slam the door shut on those seeking refugee status from the economic deprivation and violence in their countries. In an act of international cruelty, Trump and the cohorts in his government began separating children from their parents, and this went on until the number reached as high as 5,000. Many of these families have never been re-united.

Trump's actions led to declining work visas into the United States, and Miguel became a victim of these denials. He was not able to return to the landscape work he did in Maryland. No such jobs existed for him in Mexico, and he could barely eke out a living. Without that money, his daughters' education had to be put aside. Miguel had made it his life's work to educate his children in order to give them a chance at a better life. He was devastated.

During Miguel's conversations with Father Daly, the priest had said he had friends in Mexico and other Central American countries who could help those seeking political asylum in the United States. Over the years, Peter Daly had developed a close relationship with the immigration community and with Catholic Charities, an organization that supported migrants and refugees. One of Father Daly's contacts was a Honduran priest, Father Ismael Moreno Coto, popularly known as Padre Melo.

Padre Melo is an Afro-descendant Honduran and a champion of the oppressed in Honduras and other Central American countries. He has not lost touch with his pastoral work and has been hands-on with his parishioners from the poor parish of Our Lady of Guadeloupe in Tegucigalpa. Padre Melo's views are very much in keeping with Pope Francis's beliefs in this quote about staying close to the poor: "God anointed his servants so that they would be there for others—the poor, prisoners, the sick, those who are sorrowing and alone. Priests should be shepherds living with the smell of the sheep."

Miguel knew that if he intended to make his way back to America under its new rules and laws, he would need to ask Father Daly for his help—if not for a visa back to the United States, then perhaps help in getting a job in Mexico.

• • •

Jose Gonzalez received his first beating when he was just 13 years old. It occurred in an alley, in his Comayaguela neighborhood in Tegucigalpa, Honduras. The Barrios 18 gang regarded this as an "introduction beating."

Jose left school on that afternoon, followed his usual route home through the city, and was nearing his home, where he lived with his mother and three sisters. He was aware of the gangs, and his mother, Maria Elena, had warned him to stay out of their way.

He was rounding a corner when one of the four older gang members, who wore a red bandanna around his forehead, pulled him into the alley.

"Jose," he yelled." You join us, or you and your family will end up like your papa—dead."

Before Jose even had a chance to respond, the others descended on him, punching and kicking him until he was left battered on the ground in pain and gasping for air. Seconds later, it seemed, the gang members jumped up and were running away, leaving Jose where they had dropped him.

After a short while, Jose gathered himself, and standing up, brushed away the dirt from his clothes. He could feel the pounding and heat in his swollen, red face, as if he had just been in the ring with Oscar De La Hoya. He staggered the four blocks to his home.

He hoped he could hide what happened from his mother, to keep her from worrying, but through the disappearing daylight the other neighborhood children stared as he passed by, and he knew already he wasn't keeping this from anyone.

Maria Elena was just finishing up her sewing when her oldest child came through the door, looking like she had never seen him before, his face streaked with blood and tears. Jose collapsed into her arms, this boy she had raised from birth, the pride of her life, now appearing to have had all his innocence pounded out of him in one afternoon—and painfully so.

She had been through this once before. She would not endure it again.

Later that evening, after Maria Elena tended to Jose's wounds and gotten him and his sisters—Teresa, age 11, Camilla, age 9, and Dionysia, age 8—to sleep, she made the excruciating decision that she and her children must leave their home in Tegucigalpa. She had made Jose tell her what the gang had said to him just before they started beating him, and Maria Elena knew they were connected to the narcotics trade. They were not just boasting when they told Jose they would kill his family if he refused to join them.

In Honduras and El Salvador, those threats are often carried out. Maria Elena's husband—the children's father—disappeared just after Dionysia was conceived. And police protection for poor families like Maria Elena's is rare. The young sons of several of her neighbors have received similar threats, and many of them have fled to the north, seeking asylum and safety.

The violence that has grown up in Central America over the last half century can trace its origins to the United States' policies in the region. The gangs in Honduras, like MS13 and the Barrio 18, have evolved out of this violence.

Since 1970, more than 300,000 Central Americans have died in the wars that have broken out in the region between the existing U.S.-supported conservative governments and the liberation armies that have sprung up in an attempt to overthrow them. Human rights organizations, along with the United Nations, have laid the blame for the violence overwhelmingly upon the military and the right-wing dictatorships that have been supported by the United States.

In El Salvador, more than 80,000 have been killed by their government's military or state-supported death squads. Those murdered and massacred were mostly poor and indigenous people, and they included nuns and priests.

In Guatemala the number reached a staggering 200,000

deaths at the hands of military rulers and right-wing, U.S.-supported leaders during that country's decades-long civil war. Native Mayan communities bore the brunt of the massacres. A Guatemalan court for genocide convicted former general and president Rios Montt of committing genocide against his own people during his eighteen-month reign from 1981 to 1983. Even so, the American president at that time, Ronald Reagan, rushed to Montt's defense, proclaiming that the general "got a bum rap." Reagan called Montt "a man of great personal integrity and commitment," despite overwhelming evidence to the contrary.

In neighboring Honduras, Reagan and his CIA operatives turned parts of Honduras into an armed camp to train and house the Contras, a band of rebels fighting to overthrow the democratically elected Marxist-Leninist government of Daniel Ortega in Nicaragua. Many of the military leaders of these countries that committed atrocities against their own people were trained in the United States at the Army School of the Americas in Fort Benning in Georgia and Fort Bragg in North Carolina.

When the wars ended in the late 1980s, the violence did not stop. A culture of violence that had run rampant for so many decades could not just be turned off like a spigot on a water pump. Murderous gangs, affiliated with drugs and other contraband, terrorized the innocent and war-weary populations. The gangs' pressure, their rapes and murders, became so pronounced that these small Latin countries were labelled international murder capitals.

Fearing for their lives, people like Maria Elena began to seek refuge and asylum in other countries, most often in the United States, which ironically was the country chiefly responsible for fostering this culture of violence and instability.

• • •

Maria Elena has gorgeous dark hair, an inviting oval face, and lovely features. Her eyes are alive and bold, filled with determination, and her rare smiles can light up a room. She carries ten pounds more than she wants or knows is healthy, and she cannot mask her worried look. Yet hidden beneath that concern is her indomitable spirit for survival.

Maria and her children lived a life of poverty in her two-room adobe house with a dirt floor. There she worked sewing garments and was paid an unlivable wage for piecework. Only within herself did she brighten at the joys her children presented her. Their laughter, hugs, and messages of love, given mostly on holidays and religious feasts, brightened her day. Maria Elena's overriding thought was to protect and love these children and to provide them with a better way.

Despite this life of poverty, it followed the structure and order of Maria Elena's Catholic faith. The popular Jesuit priest Padre Melo had befriended Maria and her children a few years ago. He said Mass at Our Lady of Guadalupe Church, where the family attended services.

For the past three years, Jose had faithfully served Mass for Padre Melo. During that time, the famous priest made a special effort to look after Jose's family. Maria Elena had seen the confrontation between Jose and the gangs coming, just waiting for him to be a little older, and she had been discussing this decision to leave and go north for some time, during intense prayer and consultation with Padre Melo. The priest gave her a rosary so that she might pray to the Blessed Mother that, when the time came, their journey would be a safe one.

Now that they had decided to leave the next day, Padre Melo gave a scapular to Jose. Maria's neighbor in the barrio and parish provided her with a holy card picture of St. Christopher, who was once regarded as the patron saint of safe travel but whose beatification has since been abandoned by the Church in Rome. Another parishioner gave Maria Elena a holy card picture of the new saint from neighboring El Salvador, Archbishop Oscar Romero, a champion of justice and the poor.

The scapular that Padre Melo gave to Jose carries the image of his namesake, Joseph, the father and carpenter who cared for Jesus and Mary. Padre Melo had been tutoring Jose on his reading and writing and asked his young student to start each page or note he wrote with the initial "JMJ" in the upper right-hand corner of the paper. The letters stand for Jesus, Mary, and Joseph—the holy family.

Jose was only 5 years old when his father went away, and he never had the chance to know him well. Padre Melo in his work with families too often was confronted with young teenage boys who were the only males left in their homes. He was preparing Jose for the added responsibility that was now his. Jose became "the man of the house" at a young age, his childhood considerably shortened. He often cared for his three sisters.

When Jose wasn't working with Padre Mello at the church, his passion was soccer. Whenever he had the time, he could be found in the barrio near the church playing a pick-up match with other boys and sometimes girls. Soccer balls were too expensive, so their games were played with a self-made ball of tightly bound rags.

Jose excelled at soccer because he was a natural athlete, fast and well-coordinated. His success among his peers gave him confidence and stature. Even at such a young age, he was quickly developing leadership skills and confidences that he would need to help his mother navigate their dangerous journey north.

• • •

Maria Elena prays for the strength to endure. She must get through hundreds of miles on foot with children in tow, and she has heard that, along the way, they are likely to encounter many who will most certainly try to exploit them—the narco gangs, the corrupt police authorities with their hands out, the coyotes they must trust to get them across the border into the United States without being apprehended, and those who will transport them and house them, some of whom rape and murder the migrants.

She expects to encounter Samaritans as well. They will provide shelter along the way. They will give food to eat and drink to quench parched throats and dried lips. They will be filled with the Holy Spirit, and that hope shall carry Maria Elena and the children one step farther each time their bodies scream "no más." She expects that, when they most need it, people of mercy and compassion will find them. Most of all, when all seems lost, Maria Elena will be comforted by the words from Galatians that she has lived by during her impoverished and righteous life: *Let us not lose heart in doing good, for in due time we shall reap if we do not grow weary.*

Our Lady of Guadeloupe Parish, though impoverished economically, is nonetheless a true community, and its members look out for one another. For Maria Elena and her family, they have collected enough pesos, matched by a contribution from Catholic Charities, to help Maria Elena buy bus tickets to take them as far as Mexico—a most generous and unexpected gift. Once in Mexico the degree of danger will rise. There is no plan yet for how they will cross into the United States. Swimming across the Rio Grande, scaling a thirty-foot fence, and then navigating in the dark scrub land or a deadly desert with four children under 14 seems incomprehensible to her.

Maria Elena carries this uncertainty heavily in her mind. Does she risk losing her children by separation at the U.S. border, as she has heard happened to other Honduran parents who were there recently? She is haunted by all this.

The family's last night at home is centered on a simple meal of flour tortillas and red beans with water. As they are finishing dinner, they hear a knock on their door. Jose opens it to find Padre Melo, who greets each of them with a hug.

Padre Melo asks Jose to listen carefully as he shares with Maria Elena an envelope and four light backpacks that he was able to get from Catholic Charities. The packs will be for the children and will have just enough room for a change of clothing and a few personal possessions.

Then the Padre slowly explains the contents of the envelope to Maria Elena while he looks back and forth toward Jose, to be sure he understands the significance of the gift his mother is about to receive.

Inside the envelope are five visas into Mexico—or at least they are perfect facsimiles of visas. They should keep them safe on their bus journey to Reynosa. "Only surrender them to the proper police or border authorities," Padre Melo says, with a serious tone. "I have made duplicates which, Jose, you will carry in a waterproof pouch."

Also in the envelope are the names, addresses, and phone numbers of Catholic Charities shelters and Catholic churches where they may find sanctuary en route, along with the name of a man that Catholic Charities has employed to assist people traveling to the United States to seek refuge or asylum assistance. And finally, the address and phone number of the Catholic Charities of the Rio Grande Valley in McAllen, Texas, and the phone number of Sister Norma, who runs the center there.

Before Father Melo leaves, he asks the family to kneel on their dirt floor, and the priest anoints each on the forehead with oil, signifying the Holy Spirit within them for their journey.

"Go with God, in peace." Padre Melo embraces each one before he leaves and smiles into their eyes. He wants them to remember that smile as they make their way.

When Padre Melo is gone, Maria tells each child they can bring one personal item with them to remember their home. She explains what each child already knows.

"It is not safe to remain here," she says. "Perhaps one day we will be able to return and visit our friends and family. But tomorrow we will go and make our way to hopefully a better life. With God at our side and angels of mercy lighting our path."

Jose packs his bag and takes with him a photo of his family together—his pregnant mother, two sisters, Jose, and his father. It is his most prized possession. Carefully he wraps the photo in cardboard and a used plastic bag and tucks it between an old pair of jeans and a T-shirt emblazoned with the image of the great Brazilian soccer star, Pelé.

He then curls up on a ragged old couch for what will turn out to be a fitful night's sleep. He feels the heavy burden the morning promises.

In the bedroom, Teresa and Camilla share a small mattress, while Dio and her mother are on the other one.

Maria Elena continues to roll over in her mind the fact that she is about to leave the only place she has ever known. Tears well up in her eyes. She senses a betrayal accompanying her migration. She is leaving family, friends, her culture, the only certainty in her life.

She sees the four backpacks lined up near a small window in the bedroom. They will be her children's suitcases, pillows, and inanimate companions on this journey. She is saddened by what little they will carry with them in their packs, but she knows the most important thing they will carry in their hearts is their love for one another, their love of family.

CHAPTER TWO

The Journey from Tegucigalpa to the Guatemalan Border

Tegucigalpa has no central bus station. The best bus service for this city of one million people when they travel north is the station in Maria Elena's neighborhood, Comayaguela. Her family will take a Tica bus that travels to Guatemala and then to the Mexican border where they will transfer to another bus.

The switch may be difficult, depending on how the Mexican border authorities are feeling about the United States. President Trump and his administration want the Mexican government to stop other Central Americans from coming into Mexico at its southern border, and the Mexican authorities can be lenient or difficult with these passengers depending upon how much pressure the U.S. government is exerting at any given moment. Today they are not feeling any warmth for Mr. Trump and his government.

• • •

None of Maria Elena's kids sleep well, and neither does she. They are up early, at the rooster's crow. The girls are teary and sad because it has hit them that they are leaving friends, their *tios* and *tias* and cousins, their friends at school, their teachers, and Carlos, the handsome young man who works a fruit stall at the mercado and who from time to time treats them to bananas or mangos.

Maria Elena feels guilty about taking her children from their home, but that is tempered by her vision of a safer and better life for them. She is determined, and knows she is making the right decision.

Groggy from not enough sleep, Jose is ready for a difficult journey if things go badly. He feels the challenges will be worth it to get away from the drug gangs that beat him and threatened his family.

Maria Elena has to help the little ones gather the things they put out last night to take. They say goodbye to their house, followed by the streets and neighborhood where they have lived all their lives. Slowly the family walks the four blocks to the bus terminal, only to discover that their 9:00 a.m. bus is running a little late.

They wait nervously in the station. Dio is fidgeting about while Maria Elena tries to calm her. Finally, when the bus arrives, most of its passengers get off , though a few remain on board.

With nothing more than the clothes on their backs and a few possessions in their new backpacks, Maria Elena, Jose, and his sisters climb the steps of the bus and begin searching for seats close together.

They are among the first to board, and they get four seats in a row with only the aisle separating them. Dio sits next to her mother and her sisters sit together across the aisle. Jose finds an unoccupied seat in the row in front of his mother. The seat next to him is empty, but a man in his forties moves from the back of the bus into the empty seat next to Jose.

The man nods to Jose and with a smile introduces himself as Miguel Cabrera. He waits a moment, then jokingly adds that he is not the baseball player of the same name.

"Hola," Jose nervously responds, not really understanding

Miguel's reference to the great Detroit Tiger.

In a low and barely audible voice, Miguel says to Jose, "I am a friend of Padre Melo, and I am here to help you and your family travel north. Please quietly tell your mother who I am and that I would like to speak with her.

Jose does as Miguel asks, and he and Maria Elena trade places with Jose so she and the mystery passenger can talk.

Miguel begins again and introduces himself to Maria. As they reveal facts about themselves, he figures out that he is ten years older. He notices the black and white rosary beads laced through her fingers. Miguel too is a Catholic, and he takes this connection as a beginning to speak about the saintly Padre Melo who has created opportunities for both of them. She nods in agreement that Padre Melo has breathed new hope into her life and the lives of her children.

"I had almost no money," Miguel tells her, "and with a family to care for, I was desperate. Then I get a call from Padre Melo to come to Mexico City to interview for a job escorting migrants back to their homes, or in your case to the Mexico or U.S. border. Often, they are unaccompanied children and teenagers. Sometimes a mother like you will be with the children, sometimes a father. Like you, I have four of my own. I am their only hope for an education that will allow them to escape a hard life."

Maria listens intently, saying nothing, though she nods slowly to the rhythms of Miguel's story.

"I am used to long bus trips in Mexico," he continues. "I was an agricultural worker in Canada and then Maryland in the United States. For twenty-five years, I rode the bus from my home near Mexico City in the spring and then back home again from Maryland in time for Christmas with my family. So, for most of my working life, I have been away from home earning good money for my children's education. One son is now a doctor, and the other boy is a teacher. I have two girls. One in college and the other getting ready to go."

Maria finally responds, "It is good that you love your children so much that you would sacrifice being away from them, so you could afford their education. Your family must miss you, no? And you them?"

"Si" he said. "That is the price we are all paying for them to have a chance for a better life. It is both our gift to them as well our sin for being absent."

There is a long pause in their conversation. Maria looks out the window and realizes that she is now seeing the countryside, and that means they have left the city of her birth.

"My whole life has been in the city of Tegucigalpa. This is the first time to really see my country. It is most beautiful, no? The hills, mountains, green fields filled with beans. How wonderful is the Lord!"

Miguel smiles at her, recognizing that even though she is a grown woman she is naïve to the world outside the place where she grew up.

"I am now scared," Maria Elena says. "Most days I am up with the roosters, to cook a simple breakfast for my children." She points to Jose. "That one eats like a horse but is respectful of the others' needs. I send them off to school, and then I work ten hours sewing. I earn a small wage, but it is enough for food, clothing and shelter, and in that I feel secure. But we have left that now and have nothing. The future is murky, like that fog in the valley I am seeing through this window."

Miguel looks out the window to the murky distance she is seeing.

"Nothing is clear," she says. "I am frightened by gangs and corrupt authorities who will try to exploit us and by the gringos on the other side up north if we are able to get there."

Miguel grasps her hands, still entwined in her beads, and assures her that he will guide them and stay with them until they reach the shelter in Reynosa.

"We will all arrive safely," he says.

Maria responds with one of her rare smiles. "There is an old Honduran saying," she says. "Grief shared is only half grief. Joy shared is double joy."

"Ah, yes, I know that saying," Miguel says.

"We are lucky to be on a bus and to have your company and guidance," Maria Elena says in reply. "I will say three rosaries today for you and your family. And will offer thanks to Our Lady for the miracles of kindness that Padre Melo and our neighbors of our parish have given us."

Miguel laughs, glad she is seeing something positive.

"That is a lot of Hail Marys, Our Fathers, and Glory Bes!" he says. "More than I get from the priest when I go to confession."

This draws a small smile from Maria Elena.

The bus is comfortable, and there are maybe forty-eight seats. It is full, with other families and small children. Babies cry, and the smell of food permeates the bus. Some passengers sleep, others listen to music, a few read, while others engage in muted conversations and the rest are silent, lost in their thoughts. The heads of forty-eight people are choreographed in ups and downs and left and right, as the bus makes its way, rising and falling down the spiraling two-lane mountain road.

The driver makes numerous stops along the way, and passengers get off and on. The bus is used by the working poor. The truly destitute who are escaping Central America are often on foot, begging for food along the way and hopping northbound trains that are called *tren de la muerte*, "Train of Death."

After traveling all day, they reach the mountain village of

Trinidad, which is bathed in a magnificent sunset of golden tones of light as if a blanket of celestial grace were rolled over the entire area.

During the night, the bus will cross Honduras into Guatemala. At the border, there will be a check of identity. Miguel has told Maria and Jose what will likely happen. Miguel also tells Maria Elena that during the night, he usually sits on the step near the bus driver to make sure the driver has someone to talk with, so he stays awake. Safety first.

Over the years of traveling back and forth by bus, Miguel, his brother and uncle took turns during the night talking with the drivers.

Maria Elena has not thought of this problem, and she adds it to her growing list of worries as the bus winds its way toward the Guatemalan border.

When they are about an hour away from the border, the bus starts making a series of jerking motions that causes it to buck like a bronco and wake up many of the passengers from their late afternoon naps.

A baby starts to cry, and many of the passengers look out their windows, hoping to solve the mystery of their lurching bus. Finally, the bucking motion stops, but a few minutes later, the bus almost feels as if it's being lifted by strong winds, like an airplane moving through ominous storm clouds, as it makes its way through a mountain pass. Anyone sleeping is awakened from the false security of their slumbers. When the bus descends through the pass, it begins to buck and lurch again.

Alarmed, the bus driver announces that the bus is damaged, and, instead of driving to the Guatemalan border, they will stop in nearby San Pedro Sula. He says they may need to stay the night in San Pedro Sula while a new bus is dispatched to the station. This sets off a chorus of sighs and disappointments because, for most, this means they will be sleeping in the bus station.

Miguel confers with Maria Elena, Jose, and Teresa while Camilla and Dio crane from across the aisle to hear their conversation.

Miguel tells them that he will use his cell phone to call the La Lima Migrant Center in San Pedro to see if their shelter has room for them for the night. But it is already half past 8:00 p.m., and the bus is still a few miles from San Pedro.

Miguel reaches the migrant center near the airport and is told by Sister Clare of the Catholic sisterhood of Las Hermanas Scalabrinians, that the center is full.

Since Trump has ordered the Salvadorans and Hondurans in the U.S. Protective Custody Program to return to their countries," she explains, "the shelter has been packed with returning citizens. In addition, the newly formed refugee caravans that are moving from San Pedro into Guatemala, and then to Mexico, have taxed their resources. But I know a priest at a new small parish near your bus station who has a church that might have some room."

Ten minutes later, Miguel's cell phone rings, and it is Sister Clare, who gives him instructions on how to get to Saint Oscar Romero Church.

"It is six blocks from the bus terminal," she says. "It is a dangerous neighborhood so be smart and move quickly to the church once you depart the terminal. Father Ramirez will meet you at the main church door facing the boulevard."

"*Muchas gracias*, Sister," Miguel responds. "It will be an honor to rest in the church of the martyred Romero."

As the bus pulls into the terminal, the driver apologizes, but he promises that a new bus will be available at noon tomorrow to resume their journey. "Passengers are welcome to sleep in the station," he says.

Almost half the passengers head into the station, and it is clear that the others have also heard about sleeping in the church. Miguel assumes the role of leader and tells them there is room for only twenty. He instructs them all to form a single line for the brisk ten-minute walk to the church. Miguel places two adult male passengers at the rear of the line, and he and Jose lead the march at the front. They proceed briskly along these six unknown and frightening blocks.

Even with their fear of who-knows-what, it feels good to walk and stretch their legs. As nervous as some may be, they take comfort in knowing that their destination is the House of the Lord. Even so, the ones who know the story of Oscar Romero also know that the sanctuary of a church does not mean you are entirely safe.

San Pedro Sula is the second largest city in Honduras with 750,000 people. It is also reputed to be one of the world's most crime-infested cities. The gangs and drug trade have brutalized the population, and, just last year, the police department was disbanded because of corruption.

A half-moon lights their walk to the church, and they are happy to see Father Ramirez, waiting to escort them into the church's vestibule. He welcomes them and reminds them about Jesus's story of the traveler by the side of the road—and how the Catholic Church teaches its followers to take in those who need shelter.

"It is what Saint Oscar Romero would have done," Father Ramirez says.

He tells them they may sleep on the pews or on cardboard sheets left over from other migrants who were part of a caravan and slept here a few nights ago. Privately, Father Ramirez tells Miguel what has happened after the Trump Administration expelled Hondurans from protective custody in the United States.

"They were allowed into the United States because Hurricane Mitch devastated Central America," the priest says, "especially from Honduras, where 7,000 died and hundreds of thousands were made homeless. Now these refugees are sent back to conditions of extreme poverty, corruption, drugs, gang intimidation, rapes, and God knows what else. It is no wonder that so many want to escape their nightmare here and travel to either Mexico or the United States. To be safe on their journey, they have wisely concluded that they must travel in a caravan, as you have just done from the bus station. For some, their journey will be a thousand miles, not a thousand steps."

Miguel has been doing escorting for about a year, and he has learned a lot about the dynamics of the United States/Mexico relationship.

"Father, we are most grateful for your courage and hospitality," he says. "I have been reading that the gangs and drug cartels have exploited the porous borders and smuggled 250,000 guns into Mexico each year. And once the guns get to Mexico, they are acquired by the drug cartels and gangs in Honduras, Guatemala, and El Salvador, countries that are experiencing an infestation of gun violence."

"And, of course," Father Ramirez laments, "the bloodshed of violence in our small countries drives immigration into the United States."

Father Ramirez points to the statue of Saint Oscar Romero and says, "Nobody understood this more than our new saint, who was shot to death on the altar while saying Mass in 1980."

Maria Elena and her children at first find it eerie to sleep in the church, as if they are being disrespectful, but they also feel safe in this sanctuary. They feel His presence and protection.

At daylight, the new morning is fresh with hope. Dio walks over to the small side altar with a statue of Saint Romero. She deposits a small coin and lights a candle and then quietly bows her head in prayer for her family.

In smaller groups, they wander back to the bus station. At food kiosks next to the station, they find tortillas and coffee and look for places where they can quietly wait for the new bus to arrive. Miguel surprises the Gonzalez family with a fresh box of baked goods. Included in the box are *semitas* and *rosquilla*. With a smile Miguel opens the box and offers the freshly baked and sweet-smelling pastries to each family member. All present know that this is a special treat. "They tell me," Miguel says, "that *semita* is a sweet bread that drives Hondurans mad with pleasure. And the other one that looks like a donut is called a *rosquilla*. It's a slightly savory corn cookie." Maria is smiling at her new Mexican friend as if to say, "Miguel, we know, they are our national sweets. And how 'sweet' of you to treat us."

• • •

While they continue to wait for the new bus, Miguel spends some time talking to Jose and gets to know the boy a little bit better.

"Once we depart the terminal here, we will be at the border crossing in forty-five minutes," Miguel says. "When the authorities approach us on the bus, you must stay calm and let your mother and me do the talking."

Jose nods in agreement and looks over at his mother.

"There is a law between Honduras, El Salvador, and Guatemala," Miguel continues, "that allows citizens to cross from one country to the other without special documents. But with President Trump pressuring these governments to curb migrations into the United States, the authorities may ask questions. Remember, I am your *tio*, Miguel, and we are traveling to visit relatives in Reynosa, Mexico. It is a big city, even bigger than San Pedro Sula."

Jose asks, "How long before we will be in Guatemala?"

"Not long," Miguel replies "If all goes well, we should be at the Mexican border tomorrow. We will stay in a shelter there overnight and then catch another bus that will take us to Reynosa. When we leave the bus today, let's stay close to each other in a group. Perhaps taking short walks to exercise our legs—too much sitting is not healthy without stretching."

Finally, the bus arrives, and the passengers board as usual, and everyone seems to sit in the same spots they were in on the first bus.

Maria Elena and Miguel are again seat mates, and a gringa comes over to them. She is an attractive older woman with stunning white hair. She dresses casually but well, like a professional. With a friendly open smile, she introduces herself.

"*Perdon. Mia llama es* Rocia Marquez. I am a newspaper reporter for the *New York Times*. I am doing a story about migrants and caravans and would like to talk with you. I will respect your anonymity. But I would like to hear your story if you have one to share."

Miguel and Maria Elena are both taken aback by her inquiry, and it makes them nervous. Miguel suggests that he and the reporter trade seats with Jose and his sister, who are seated in front of them. Everyone agrees.

Rocia shows Miguel her passport, driver's license, and several articles in the *Times* with her byline.

Miguel says kindly, "*Un momento, por favor*," and begins to read the articles after studying her identification. After a while, he is satisfied that she is who she says she is, and that her articles reflect an understanding of the plight of the migrants and asylum seekers. He also believes he can get information from her that will help him and Maria Elena make better decisions as they proceed north.

Still, Miguel wants to be reserved about how much access they will give Rocia Marquez. "I will talk with you," he says. "But first I need to consult with my friend, Maria. How far are you traveling on the bus?"

"I am writing a story about my trip up to the border at McAllen, Texas," Rocia says. "I will need to spend a little time talking to people at our stops and then will continue to travel north to the border."

"Give me some time to talk with my travel companions," he says. "I will be back soon."

Miguel then speaks privately with Maria Elena. "I checked her identification papers," he says, "and then read two stories she has written for her newspaper. I think she can be helpful to us. If you agree, I suggest that you share your story with her, yet insist that our names and those of the children are changed. If she writes a good story, even with anonymous names, you may be able to use it in your efforts to get asylum in the U.S.A. or, if that fails, then asylum in Mexico. What do you think?"

Maria Elena is unsure. This is all so new for her. How can she know what is best? In just one day, she has come to trust Miguel—but she did so because she knows that Padre Melo trusts Miguel. Now she reasons that her trust in Miguel should lead her to follow his advice. Except how can she tell this strange woman her complete story, when even her children do not know it.

"I need a little time to think about sharing my story," Maria Elena tells Miguel. "I will think and pray about my decision, and after our stop at the Guatemalan border, I will let you know."

Miguel understands, and he lets Rocia know that she must be patient until after the border check, which is coming soon.

Maria Elena closes her eyes and opens her heart to Jesus and

Mary, her most admired and trusted confidants, asking them for guidance and wisdom.

The border crossing is between the coastal towns of Omoa in Honduras (at the Caribbean Gulf) and Puerto Barrios in Guatemala. The bus driver slows down because he knows they will be undergoing an inspection.

• • •

Captain Arturo Lopez Menendez is a tall man with a trimmed mustache, and he wears a neatly pressed uniform, giving him an air of authority. Achieving the rank of an officer in the Guatemalan armed forces is often the route up the social and class ladders. Historically, many young officers have believed that the way to please their superiors is by being tough and at times ruthless with the ordinary citizens—many of whom are part of the indigenous population—they encounter in the course of their duty.

Captain Menendez climbs the three steps up into the bus, greets the driver, and asks for his transportation papers and driver's license. The two men know each other from their frequent interactions, and this exchange is just a formality that gives the captain time to get a sense of who is on the bus.

The captain's posture is straight and commanding, his shoulders square and set firmly in an erect locked position. He does not smile, but there is no frown either. He is all business.

Most of the passengers on the bus are looking directly at the captain, sizing him up and trying to figure out what he is going to do. After all, the military in this country had been responsible for killing nearly two hundred thousand of its own citizens during their recent civil war. The tension on the bus is taut.

The captain understands that a good number of those on the

bus are headed north to the Mexican/U.S. border, with hopes of crossing. He also knows his government, run by Jimmy Morales, a former comedic actor, is corrupt and under immense pressure to stop its own citizens, as well as those from Honduras and El Salvador, from migrating north to the United States. President Trump has threatened to end hundreds of millions of dollars in aid to these countries—money that is desperately needed.

Captain Menendez may be all-military in his uniform and bearing, but he cannot do anything to hide his soft and kind eyes. If they are windows into his soul, a different story must be told about Captain Menendez—one of growing up in a family so poor that his older brothers had to migrate north to the United States. Part of their story was being caught at the border and incarcerated for six months before they were released.

The captain is also a devout and practicing Catholic. Mercy and justice have deep spiritual meaning for him, resulting in a man with a cool military exterior who also stops to aid the struggling family at the side of the road. He possesses a Samaritan's tender heart for the poor, and as his eyes roam the interior of the bus, they lock onto Maria, Miguel, and the four children.

With an aide at his side, the Captain moves up the aisle checking identification papers. He is firm but respectful, and when he approaches Miguel and Maria Elena he asks if they are together.

"Si," Miguel responds.

The captain then points to the four children and says, "And they as well?"

Miguel nods yes.

Rocia from her seat several rows back, watches intently, hoping to patch together any clues that might reveal the family's story in advance of what she hopes will be an interview with Maria Elena.

Miguel hands the captain the travel documents Padre Melo gave Maria Elena as well as his own. Miguel holds back a travel letter that Catholic Charities provided him for his safe travels. The letter is signed by Catholic cardinals from Central America. Like a wise poker player, he plays his cards carefully and will only use his ace when necessary. Something tells Miguel that this is not yet the time.

The captain looks over the documents and then with a smile looks at Miguel and Maria and uses the same words Padre Melo used when he sent them off: "Go with God in peace."

They were fortunate to have had Captain Menendez as their inspector because after a few more minutes of questions, he informs the driver to move his group on ahead and into the interior of Guatemala.

• • •

The beauty of the countryside in Guatemala can take your breath away. The country's majestic mountains, lush green valleys, the exotic jungle territory of the Petén, and the tropical serenity surrounding the Mayan ruins are awe-inspiring. The bus carrying Maria Elena and her family rambles through the Petén on its way to its capital, the island/city of Flores.

In 1960, the Guatemalan government opened the remote Petén for tourism, offering its ancient ruins, lakes, and tropical bounties. A road, three hundred miles long, was built but never paved. It took twenty-four hours to reach Flores from Guatemala City. Today the road has been upgraded and plays host to the passengers on the bus as they sail along through the verdant jungle environment, absorbing the splendor of the tropics.

Camilla and Teresa think the holler and spider monkeys in the *caoba* (mahogany) trees along the side of the road are very funny. When it gets dark outside, Miguel tells them to watch carefully to see if they can get a glimpse of a jaguar or puma, two of the fastest mammals on earth.

Every time Rocia finds herself outside the cities of this region, she is captivated by what she sees and wonders how a place so magnificently terrestrial can be where tens of thousands of its citizens were slaughtered by their own government. She recalls the words of James Madison, who said that "if tyranny and oppression come to this land, it will be in the guise of fighting a foreign enemy."

Rocia has covered Central America off and on for almost thirty years and has been recognized for her outstanding reporting, especially her work in the Northern Triangle countries. Her coverage of the murders in San Salvador of the Jesuit priests, their housekeeper, and her daughter was awarded a Pulitzer Prize. Her coverage of the contra war in Nicaragua and Honduras received plaudits from the Washington Office on Latin America, and she was awarded the Shaiken/Manse prize from the Center of Latin American Studies at the University of California at Berkeley. Retired from the *New York Times*, Rocia now holds a position at Berkeley of professor in the School of Journalism. From time to time, the *Times* will ask her to do a special story, and that's how she finds herself on a bus from Tegucigalpa to McAllen, Texas, covering a story that has captured the attention of the world.

The lives of the people on the bus fascinate her. This makes her a superb journalist and an excellent teacher. She believes that "everybody has a story and capturing the core of who 'they' are is key to the telling of that story." Rocia is a mother herself, and she tries hard to feel and understand the strain of women on the run with their children. She recognizes in Maria Elena someone with a story to tell.

Maria Elena decides, after some thought, that she will talk with the woman reporter and tells Miguel to let her come to where Maria Elena is sitting. The women begin to talk while Miguel hovers over them in the aisle of the bus.

It occurs to Miguel that he too is eager to hear her story.

Maria Elena begins by saying that this is hard for her to share because she has not told her complete tale to anyone except Padre Melo. She clutches a tissue, kneading it in her hands. Slowly, looking up from it, she begins.

As Maria Elena speaks, she alternates eye contact from her hands to Rocia, who she can tell is a caring woman. Rocia does not take notes but listens intently, and with her own facial expressions reflects the grief Maria has been carrying these past ten years. She feels the weight of Maria Elena's anguish.

"My husband, Juan, was a good husband and father," Maria Elena says. "He loved his family more than anything else. We met first at school. When I was Jose's age, Juan walked me from school to catechism at our church. He was quiet, almost shy, and a year older than me.

"One day after many walks to catechism, we were on our way home, and he gently reached for my hand. We both knew it would happen someday, but when it did, we shared this happiness of belonging with each other. Our worlds were identical— same school, church, and friends. We had the same hopes and dreams, and our lives centered around a small area in our neighborhood. Then we had each other, as we were falling in love.

"When Juan turned 18, and I was 17, we were married at Our Lady of Guadeloupe. Like everybody in our parish, we had little money. Juan got a job at the mercado, and I found work sewing garments. With our savings, we had enough for a small two-room house, and not long after that the children came."

Maria Elena, with a sly smile on her face, looks up at Rocia and says, "You know, we were very fertile. First came Jose, who we named after our Savior's father, then Teresa after Mother Teresa, and then Camilla, just because we liked the name. We had little, but we found joy.

"When I was pregnant with Dionysia, Juan faced his first threat by leaders of Barrio 18. They demanded he peddle drugs in the market where he worked, but he instantly refused. They kept after him, telling him that if he did not comply, bad things would happen to him and his family. We were all scared because we knew how brutal these gangs could be. We talked about what to do and where to go. At first Juan went to the police for help, but they did nothing and may have told the gang that Juan was seeking police help."

"How did your children feel about the threats from the gangs?" Rocia asks.

"Our children were nervous. They did not want to go outside, and when they did, they always stayed close to each other. The gang threats planted fear into our family, as strong and evil as the dope they were injecting into the veins of residents of our community."

Maria Elena pauses to gather her thoughts and strength, but tears well up in her eyes. Rocia offers her tissues, and Miguel hands her a bottle of water to sip. She takes both. "Gracias."

"When did the gang physically confront your husband?" Rocia asks.

"One day eight years ago, after work at the market, Juan was attacked on his way home. They beat him, then shot him in the back of the head as he lay face down on the ground."

Maria Elena pauses to wipe her eyes and stares out the window as if trying to imagine her husband's last seconds. "They murdered him. They murdered our dreams."

Rocia puts her arm around Maria and gently draws her

close. Miguel, who has been shielding this conversation from her children, makes the sign of the cross while taking a deep breath.

Maria Elena then turns her attention to her children as the bus heads toward the Mexican border. She watches Teresa and Camilla read and sees Dio staring out the window. Maria Elena wonders what her baby is thinking.

The children know about their father's murder. They have known for years but not how he was killed. His life and death have only occasionally been talked about in the home. The girls hardly knew their father before he was killed. Teresa was 3, Camilla not yet 2, and Dio in her mother's womb.

In the evenings, one of them might ask, "What was he like?"

They knew from Jose's photo that he was handsome and taller than any of them, with dark wavy hair, and a kind face and demeanor. At the market, Juan unloaded carts and trucks that brought produce from the farms. He was physically strong, a nice combination with his sweet nature. People love a gentle giant.

Jose missed Juan terribly, asked a lot of questions about him and dreamed about him. Some of this led to Jose being confused and withdrawn for a while. Maria assured Jose that his father was in heaven with Jesus and that Jose would see him someday when he went to heaven. This seemed to ease the ache in the boy's broken heart.

In the row in front of Maria Elena, Jose and Miguel strike up a conversation about soccer now that the boy is more comfortable with these strangers.

"I think the best player today is the Portugal star, Cristiano Renaldo," Miguel says.

"No way," insists Jose. "The best is the Argentinian, Lionel Messi. He is so good—fast, quick, with a powerful leg."

Maria Elena listens with joy. How wonderful to see her son

engaged with an adult male over a subject he loves. And how terrible that he was robbed of this experience with his own father. She recalls fondly how tender Juan was with little Jose. Juan was in love with his son, teaching him everything he could absorb at such an early age.

Maria Elena especially cherished the image of her husband carrying their son on his shoulders through the market on their shopping days. Maria is proud of how much Jose has grown, and of the role he has assumed in the family since his father's murder—caring for his sisters, being a leader in school and his church, and doing anything his mother asks of him.

The crossing into Mexico will be more of a challenge than entering Guatemala. The Northern Triangle countries of Guatemala, Honduras, and El Salvador have a reciprocal treaty with each other that permits an easy flow of human beings across their borders. No such treaties exist with Mexico or the United States.

Mexico's southern border is busy primarily with people like Maria Elena and her family, who are coming into Mexico because of personal safety concerns. Also, repeated occurrences of hurricanes and other natural disasters, and of course the lack of economic opportunity in Guatemala, El Salvador, and Honduras, have caused people to flee north.

As the bus carrying Maria Elena and the others slows and approaches the border, they ready themselves to be interrogated by the Mexican authorities. Everyone is hopeful they will not fall victim to some new regulations, fees, or taxes.

The pressure that the U.S. government under Donald Trump has placed on the Mexican government to close their southern border to migrants and asylum seekers has made the crossing more difficult. The increase in migrant caravans, as well as their growing numbers, has also created a backlash from some

Mexicans who see them as taking their jobs. Yet, despite this, many ordinary citizens of Mexico show concern for the migrants and their families because they know how easily they could find themselves in the same place.

Just a few days ago, Mexico closed its end of a bridge leading into the Mexican state of Chiapas from Guatemala because a caravan that had originated in San Pedro Sula had grown to several thousands. But the migrants were not deterred by this closure, and instead they made international news by swimming across the river or floating to the Mexican side on dangerous home-made rafts.

The Mexican government sent two plane loads of federal police officers to stop them, but the migrant caravan pushed by them and continued unimpeded. Those observing credited the presence of foreign journalists and human rights monitors with preventing the federal police force from using harsher measures to stop them.

Maria Elena's daughters have named their bus "Justice," and the plan is for it to cross into Mexico at El Ceibo in the Guatemalan Department of Petén. It will enter the country at a town with the same name, El Ceibo, in the Mexican state of Tabasco. This is the northernmost crossing along the border, one of ten from the south to the north.

As the bus comes to a halt at the border, the passengers are instructed to get off and take any luggage or packages. Miguel, Maria, and her family go down the bus stairs, and the security border agents tell the passengers to place their luggage, backpacks, and packages on the ground and step away from them. Sniffing dogs then descend on the bus and around the luggage and packages looking for food or drugs. This process takes about forty-five minutes.

The travelers then enter a modest building where they queue

up. When they reach the agents, they are asked for their passports, visas, tourist cards, and the reason for their visit.

There are only two agents working the document check. Tension fills the air. In a harsh voice the male document checker asks, "Where is your destination?"

"Reynosa," Miguel responds.

The agents' job is to filter out illegal agricultural products, drugs, and migrants. He is now curious about their trip to Reynosa.

"Who will you be visiting and how long do you plan to stay?" he asks.

"We are a unit," Miguel says, "all together, and we will be visiting family."

The agent looks puzzled. With a furrowed brow he pursues his inquiry. "Señor, I do not understand. This is just a family visit? No business? For how long will you be visiting 'family'? Do your children go to school?"

Miguel senses trouble and points to Maria Elena and the children. "This is my family and I am their *tio*," he says. "Certainly, you understand the unsafe conditions in Tegucigalpa. It is not safe for them. We are going to Reynosa to stay with our family and make a decision whether or not to seek asylum. I work for Catholic Charities and help to escort a safe passage for families who are seeking a better life for themselves and their children."

"How do I know you work for Catholic Charities?"

Miguel takes out the letter signed by the three cardinals and hands it to the border agent who reads the letter. The agent acknowledges that, yes, it is their international right to apply for asylum.

The agent then asks the group if anybody has been on an agricultural farm these last two weeks. They all say no.

He hands all the papers back to Miguel and Maria.

"You may pass." And with a wave of his hand commands, "All of you—go.

CHAPTER THREE

Jesus Aguilar—A Kid on the Run

Jesus Aguilar has just finished serving Mass for Father Ramirez at his new parish church, Saint Oscar Romero, in a tough barrio in San Pedro Sula. This is the same barrio where Sister Clare helped Miguel when their crippled bus entered San Pedro on the first night of their journey. The murder rate in the city of San Pedro Sula is among the highest in the world, and this barrio is often the most violent.

Jesus Aguilar turned 15 years old six weeks ago, and he has been struggling with a decision to migrate to the United States like so many others his age. But that also means leaving his home and his family. Jesus is quiet and contemplative by nature, but his reticence should not be confused with shyness or stupidity. Figuring out what to do is weighing heavily on his young shoulders.

Jesus is also an extremely observant kid who instinctively understands that the way to survive and help his mother and sisters is to think strategically, plan well, and be cautious before trusting anyone. Serving Father Ramirez as an altar boy has given Jesus confidence, and the church sanctuary provides him with solace. The church is where he goes to pray but also where he can think and plan. It is his refuge.

Jesus first became aware of the migrations north when his father left home for the United States four years ago. The family has not heard from him since then. Jesus lives with his mother and two younger sisters in poverty so deep that sometimes they do not have enough to eat during the last week of each month.

Young fatherless teenage boys most often take one of two routes. The first is a type of rebellion that can lead to social and legal problems. The other is for them to step up the best they can for others in their family. They seek responsibility and solutions to what may appear to be hopeless situations. Courage and resilience find their way to the fore and amazing results sometimes happen. Probably without even realizing it, Jesus has chosen the second route.

His mother and her brother have always been close, and he regularly sends them a remittance check from Houston. Jesus's uncle is a foreman for a road construction company, and over the ten years he has been in Houston he has made a comfortable life for himself and his family. The monthly check he sends his sister covers the rent for shelter, but it is not enough to feed them. Jesus's mother is a domestic worker so her income is meager—the bare minimum. The food pantry at the church helps, but even with that, they still run out of food, and Jesus and his sisters are no strangers to hunger.

He occasionally gets odd jobs, but they are difficult to come by in this city of emptiness. Government support is nonexistent, and Jesus has privately vowed to make life better for his mother and sisters. His uncle has promised him work in construction if he can find his way to Houston. Once there and employed, he would also send money to his mother.

Jesus has been planning the trip for two years, and he wonders if he might also find his father in Houston. He also dreams about possibly setting enough aside to get an education for himself and his sisters. Maybe. Dreams are made of many maybes.

Jesus has talked with others who returned after making the crossings to Guatemala, Mexico, and then the United States. He has learned to use the computers at the library, and he has searched for information on how best to travel and to cross.

He has also read about the criminals who prey on the refugees, who house them and then rape them, rob them, and kidnap them and extort large sums of money for their release, then leave them for dead in the desert. Jesus is under no illusions that the journey will be easy—though he does believe that if he prepares well and plans carefully, he can outwit these dangerous criminals. Part of his planning has been learning the safest passages and the location of shelters where he can get support. His Catholic faith also keeps him mentally and spiritually strong.

He has heard that another caravan is leaving from San Pedro Sula in the morning. The caravan originated in El Salvador and grew to a thousand people by the time it reached Honduras. It is mostly comprised of young males, but families of multiple generations are not unusual.

Jesus would prefer not to travel in a large group, but he understands the advantage it provides in safety and company. He has decided it is time to go and that he will join this caravan. His plan is to break from this group at some point, but for now, there are advantages in their numbers, and the initial shield of safety that they provide will propel him forward. He is also curious to meet others who have committed themselves to making this journey. He is surprised by the number of families, some with young children or older grandparents. He once asked his mother about all of them leaving together, but it was not something she would consider.

• • •

Jesus has told his mother about his sudden plans, and they are trying to figure out how to say goodbye to each other. This kind of farewell is as old as the centuries and never gets less wrenching. Sending a child off to school, or a soldier off to war, or a family member to a hospital operating room has a tinge of the sorrow present when families separate from each other and travel thousands of miles across, oceans, deserts, and continents—many realizing they may never see each other again.

On the night before Jesus's departure, Rose Aguilar cooks her son a hearty and tasty dinner. She has packed him food that will last for several days—tortillas, bananas, mangos, nuts, and a large hunk of cheese. Rose wrestles in her dreams each night with a ghost of a husband and wakes each morning angry with him for leaving them. Now she worries that her son may succumb to whatever happened to his father in the north. Will she ever hear his voice again or gaze upon his handsome and caring face?

In the early morning, as the sun is almost up, Jesus hugs his sisters and mother. Tears streak their cheeks, and the lumps that have formed in their throats make words difficult. They are a close family, and their hugs and squeezes speak for the feelings they have for each other.

Jesus insists on saying goodbye to his mother and sisters at their apartment. He does not want them to follow him to the central square where he will meet up with the caravan at 7:00 a.m. Jesus is carrying his few belongings in an old backpack. Inside are a family photo, a Sunday missal, and a rubber ball gnawed on by a neighborhood dog. The ball is meant to squeeze the stress out of life, and it will also be pitched against the walls that appear along the way.

Tearing himself away from these women who make up his whole life, Jesus ambles through the familiar streets of San Pedro Sula. He passes all the familiar shops and wonders if he will ever return to his hometown again. As he nears the central square, he can hear the sound of the thousand people gathered together in one place.

Jesus can see the Cathedral of Saint Peter the Apostle towering over the central square where the migrants gather for their 1,425-mile trek to the U.S. border. They stay together by region and nationality. Most are Hondurans, who have joined the caravan just recently, but others are from El Salvador and Nicaragua. Once they cross the Guatemalan border, just thirty miles away, they will be joined by citizens of that country as well. Jesus can now see the families who have brought toddlers and small children with them. Some parents will be pushing strollers as each young child takes their turn riding through the long, hot day.

At 7:15 a.m., the cathedral bells ring, and a priest on the steps spreads his arms, reaching for the heavens, and beseeches the Holy Spirit and Saint Peter to grant the migrants safe passage. Everyone seems to know that this is the sign for them to start slowly marching off toward the border. At first, Jesus hangs back and trails the crowd. He knows he has decided to be one of them, but he also feels separate. He trusts no one. For him, this will be a long and lonely trip.

From the rear, the movement of the caravan starts slowly. At 7:00 a.m. air is fresh, but it does not take long for the higher sun and its heat to wear down the pilgrimage. The paved road has a dirt shoulder that the migrants use as they move forward. The traffic is very light, so some migrants bleed onto the paved road where the even pavement makes the walk easier, especially if a cart or stroller is used. Plenty of water is available early in the day, but all know the need to ration it. There may be one or, if they are lucky, two water stops today. Large sun hats with brims are a signature look of the caravan.

As the day goes on and the march continues, Jesus keeps to himself, but he finds he cannot completely remain back from the pack. He is too strong, and he is driven by a fierce determination that moves him past virtually all the migrants to the front of the caravan. Observing each one, each family and each individual member, Jesus is calculating their chances for reaching the U.S. border. The front of the caravan is led by young men and leaders of the expedition. They march with élan and confidence, even at the day's end.

When they get near the border of Guatemala, some twenty-five miles from the central plaza in San Pedro Sula, the caravan stops for the evening in a park in a small village. The exhausted walkers in small groups straggle into the park. Jesus is one of the first to arrive, and he heads for the park's water pipe, where he refills his water bottles and bathes his face and neck in the cold water. He then finds a spot to settle near a large banyan tree by a stream at the park's perimeter.

The shade of the tree and the coolness of the stream are a welcome relief from the drudge of the march. Jesus breaks off a chunk of cheese, and it reminds him of his mother. With his water, cheese and tortilla, he slides down the short slope to the stream. There he sets his food and drink aside and removes his shoes, massages his bare feet and then leans back on the slope resting his head on his backpack while his swollen red feet dangle in the running stream.

Jesus watches for the next two hours as groups of families and individuals traveling solo arrive at the park. Some children, incredibly, still have enough energy to chase each other in a game of tag, but most are off their feet and in the shade.

The twenty-five-mile walk on this day was too far. Some teenagers and young men help families and older migrants set up their camp. The caravan includes three nuns who are nurses, and they are applying ointment and bandages to blistered feet. The lone priest on the pilgrimage leads a prayer service before dark that serves as inspiration and solace for some walkers, but not all.

Those who started at the beginning in El Salvador have

already walked hundreds of miles. Jesus overhears some families discussing how difficult the trek has been. They are exhausted and are considering turning back. As the group continues north, some migrants who become discouraged will end their journey, while new migrants will be picked up along the way.

Early in the morning, they are on the move again, and, as part of the caravan, Jesus crosses into Guatemala, the first time he has left his home country. They are all immediately aware that they are being followed by news reporters and cameras, as well as members of human rights organizations such as Oxfam, Amnesty International, Doctors Without Borders, and Human Rights Watch. They are watchdogs for the migrants' safety and their international right to seek asylum and safety. The border authorities know this and now seemingly respect the oversight of these organizations.

Back in San Pedro Sula, Jesus had tried to prepare himself for this journey by reading the U.S. State Department bulletin, "Safe Roads and Regions in Guatemala." His talks with others in his neighborhood who travelled this route told him that the best way to manage the arduousness of the journey in his mind was to set limited goals each day. He would combine that with a vision of what awaits him when he succeeds in getting to where he is going.

Jesus makes each day's goal a pre-selected destination point. For this day, his goal is the Guatemalan town of Morales on the Motagua River, which will mean leaving the caravan behind. It will be another twenty-five-mile walk, but at the end is another park by the water and a church where he plans to spend the night.

A more distant goal for Jesus—one that is more significant— is the Guatemalan city of Flores, the island capital of the Department of Petén. He has been told that there is a cathedral in the city with a statue of a Black Jesus.

Jesus is Afro-Honduran, and this statue reminds him of his family's ancestry. To see Jesus Christ, his savior, looking like him is incredibly powerful. This image draws him in a religious way similarly to the millions of Muslims who journey to Mecca each year, or to the Sikhs who pilgrimage to Amritsar, or to the Catholics who walk hundreds of miles along the trail to Santiago de Compostela in Spain. For Jesus, Flores lies 225 miles away near the Mayan ruins of Tikal. That is many days of walking unless he's able to somehow find a ride.

The day's walk is again long, and again Jesus keeps himself preoccupied by looking for any signs of human activity as he hikes on his own down the long roads that bisect national parks. Few cars and even fewer humans pass through these remote regions of Guatemala. He knows he would be an easy prey for kidnappers here, and he looks out for ambushers, while checking the notes he made in the library back home to make sure this road has a safe travel designation.

Once in the town of Morales, Jesus settles for the night on the river property of the church of Our Lord the Prophet, which means he no longer has the safety of the caravan. He rests under a mahogany tree in an isolated area between the church and the river. He needs more water and walks two blocks to a town plaza and refills his bottles before retracing his steps to the area between the church and the river.

After eating more of the cheese and tortillas his mother packed for him, he lies down for a rest, slips the straw hat with its wide brim down over his face, closes his eyes, and soon is asleep.

Thirty minutes later, Jesus is startled by a kick to his leg. He is jolted awake and sees two men in their twenties towering over him and staring down at him menacingly. One holds a knife, and the other has a handgun.

Jesus thinks instantly of the money, the Honduran lempira, he has tucked in the vinyl cover of his Catholic missal—between the actual cover which slips over the front and back cover. He has the equivalent of $250, which he has painstakingly saved over the past two years while working odd jobs.

"Stay where you are!" commands the one with the gun.

The other robber bends down and begins going through Jesus's backpack. After tossing things out onto the ground, he yells, "Just old clothes and a prayer book and a photo. No money. Nothing of any value."

The robber with the gun waves it at Jesus. "Give me that ring on your finger."

Jesus removes it, hands it to him, and then pleads, "My father gave me this ring before he died. It is a simple ring not worth much, but it is the only possession of his that I have to remember."

The robbers look at each other and the one with the gun tells his partner, "Throw me his prayer book."

He opens it and feels the Lempiras through the cover. Now he is holding both the money and the ring. Looking down at Jesus, he sneers. "You pick. The ring or the money."

Jesus knows the sentimental value resides with the ring while his ability to survive is dependent on the money.

"Take the money but please leave me the memory of my father," Jesus begs.

The robber flips the ring down to where Jesus is sitting on the ground—and in a flash, he and his partner disappear into the woods along the river.

Jesus puts the ring back on his finger and is comforted by it. But he is also devastated and does not know what he will do when he needs money.

• • •

The walk the next morning to Chocon runs along a two-lane highway and has little traffic. Now that Jesus has been away from San Pedro Sula for three days, he begins to miss his mother and sisters, and, especially after the robbery, he begins to doubt whether it was smart of him to do this solo. Jesus has just a little bit of the cheese left and a bag of nuts. He brought with him a list of wild fruits and nuts that are edible, so he is always on the lookout for the bushes and trees where he might find something extra to eat.

According to his library reading, this road is not listed as dangerous, and Jesus reasons that perhaps it will be safe enough to get into a car with a stranger. He tries thumbing a ride with the few cars and trucks that pass, but none of them stop for him. The cool drafts of wind as the vehicles zoom past him are small consolation prizes that ease his disappointments.

At 5:00 p.m., he spots an open area in the woods where coconuts have fallen to the ground. He gathers them and on a nearby boulder labors hard to crack them open without losing the precious milk he needs to drink. The energy expended pounding the coconuts is balanced by the coconut meat and liquid he consumes for his dinner. After his dinner, he clears away the cracked nut shells so they won't attract animals to the area while he is asleep in the woods.

Jesus gets on his way the next morning at sunrise to take advantage of the cooler weather and the sun hiding low on the horizon behind the tree lines. As he walks, he eats the remaining nuts his mother packed for him. He guesses that he is a two-day walk away from Chocon. Gold finches in pairs become his companions as they feed on the seeds of the thistle weeds along the road. Their undulating flight and their musical whistles are entertaining, but the pairs of birds also remind Jesus of his lone-liness. As much as he misses companionship, he prefers to stay anonymous. Jesus trusts himself but is not sure about others. The low sun occasionally can be seen in the streaks of light it casts through openings in the woods. These observations take some of the boredom out of his walk.

Four hours into his walk along the narrow, tree-lined high-way, the tropical sun swings over the tree canopy, beaming onto the road. The heat from the asphalt plus the now oppressive sun beating down upon him makes the walk more difficult. Occa-sional clouds provide temporary relief, but these interludes are short and at the discretion of winds too high for him to feel.

When the sun is directly overhead, Jesus takes shelter in the shade of the woods near the road. He leans against the trunk of a large pine tree, sips his water, and opens his missal to a psalm:

Yes, my soul, find rest in God;
my hope comes from him
Truly he is my rock and salvation;
He is my fortress, I will not be shaken.

When the sun dips below the trees on the other side of the road, Jesus resumes his walk. After three more hours of walking, he refills his water bottles at a national park research station on the Rio Dulce. The ranger there suggests he camp near the sta-tion, and in the morning he will give Jesus a ride into Chocon.

These words are heaven to Jesus, who has been walking for so many miles. Among large trees he lays out his meager belong-ings and eats the last of his cheese and nuts. Before the sun sets, he reads once again the list of edible fruits and nuts that he can scavenge.

In the morning, the ranger keeps his promise and drives

Jesus into Chocon. The trip takes an hour. The ranger tells Jesus that Chocon has one gas station that also fixes tractors and cars. The shop's owner is good about helping people on the road and might give him work if he asks. Jesus goes there, and the man tells Jesus he will pay him to weed a small plot of land off the main road near the village. He also promises to arrange a ride in the morning that will take Jesus to Flores.

Jesus needs this money badly, and he is grateful for the work, but an afternoon of weeding the field under the tropical sun wipes him out completely. That evening he goes to bed hungry but sleeps soundly on the garage floor surrounded by tools and parts from transmissions and engines. In the morning, his promised ride is waiting to take him to Flores. The driver is a quiet man who is traveling there to pick up parts for a tractor.

After a two-hour drive, the driver leaves Jesus at a causeway leading to the island that is situated in Lake Petén Itzá. He walks the mile-long causeway on a narrow road that rests above the lake to the island entrance, all the while accompanied by shore birds.

Anhinga, large birds with very long slim necks and long sharp pointed bills, dive from on high into the water, their bills ready to spear a fish. When the Anhinga catch the fish, they are careful to flip it in the air and then catch it whole as it slides down their long gullet. Jesus has never seen such a bird before, and for a long while he is entertained by watching their antics.

He also spots another beautiful large bird, the Great Blue Heron, with a dagger-shaped bill, long neck, and long overhanging head feathers, looking like a skinny teen who won't get his hair cut. They somehow pull off a quiet beauty and grace. When these birds rise to fly, their two long skeletal legs dangle from their bodies like an afterthought.

Jesus is excited about reaching the small city. The town of

Flores has an inviting colonial arch that spans the road before the causeway meets the island. Sitting on top of the arch, at its center, is a small replica of a colonial house that symbolizes one of the prides of Flores, its colorful painted buildings.

The island's circular streets all converge at the top of the hill where the small cathedral is located. Jesus is stunned by the explosion of bright colors on the houses and quaint commercial establishments. Aqua blues, lime greens, lemon yellows, fading orange, and soft purples all mingle with many shades of red—from a delicate rose color on the buildings to a stronger rust on their tin roofs. These multiple colors remind him of the happiness he felt as a child gazing into a box of crayons.

Jesus winds his way through a commercial street of small restaurants. He checks the alley behind the restaurants to see where their refuse might be disposed and finds a single dumpster. He will come back here later in the day to salvage any discarded food.

He continues upward on the cobblestone roads to the central plaza at the top of the island. In the corner of the plaza is the whitewashed cathedral, Nuestro Señora de Los Remedios—a church dedicated to Our Lady of Remedies. The cathedral stands about six feet above the plaza in an enclosure bordered by a stone wall with iron pickets resting on top, guarding this sacred place of worship. A break in the wall opens to a ten-step staircase leading to the church's large red wooden doors.

Thirty stained-glass windows grace the perimeter of the church. They have importance as an educational tool, describing in pictures the stories of the Bible. The cathedral has double-fronted bell towers with domes over each tower. The towers are only three stories high; one houses a single bell and the other a string of bells. All the bells can be seen from the plaza below.

Jesus walks up the stairs through the opened red doors and

into the church where a priest is just beginning a short tour for a group of tourists.

"Why is the wood depiction of Christ on the cross in black?" someone asks. "Why is he Black?"

"This church has been used for many years by different cultures," explains the priest. "And those cultures have different ways of worshiping. The Mayans and Ladinos have mixed their own rituals with traditional Catholic rituals. Our congregation is dark-skinned. When the church many years ago caught fire and was destroyed, its crucifix above the altar was not destroyed but only charred black. The people took it as a sign and kept the charred crucifix when we rebuilt the church.

"Some of you may know that there is a Black Jesus in the Cathedral in Esquipulas. And I have been told in the United States, there is a Black Jesus at the seminary in Detroit. The people of the neighborhood in Detroit painted the statue black when there was a rebellion, I think, in 1967. So our crucifix is unusual but not completely unique. The skin color is important for many to be able to relate to Jesus Christ. And indeed, he may have had a much darker skin than that which is typically shown. But also, what is truly important is what is in his heart and what can be in our hearts as well."

Jesus follows the tourists to the altar where the Black Jesus is hanging and listens as the priest continues with his story.

"Once a year, we celebrate this crucifix and what it symbolizes. Our Cathedral is filled with Ladinos, Mayans, and others, but mostly dark-skinned people. We take down the crucifix and lay it flat by the altar and all the parishioners line up in procession to pass by. Some bend to kiss the knees of Christ. It is a very intimate and special time for our church."

Jesus listens to every word of the priest's story, and he wishes he could kiss the knees of Christ. Even so, this moment profoundly touches his heart. He slowly walks back to the center of town, wishing he could have shared this religious experience with his pastor, Father Ramirez.

Later in the early evening, Jesus returns to the dumpster where he is so happy to find discarded beans and rice. This is dinner for him, and he gathers it into a container and walks back to the plaza where he finds a tree to lean against and eat before falling asleep.

Just after dark, the priest who gave the tour in the cathedral is making his nightly rosary walk around the plaza and sees Jesus sleeping under the tree. They are strangers, but the priest recalls seeing the teenager earlier in the day in the church. He stops and gently shakes Jesus's shoulder.

Startled, Jesus thinks he is about to be robbed once again, but he looks up and sees in the half moonlight, a priest with a collar and a rosary in his hands, instead of a knife or handgun. With another blink, he realizes this is the priest who told the story about the black Jesus.

"I am Father Rodriguez," the priest says. "Come. You may stay in the cathedral for this night. I have a place where you will be safer and cooler. But you must be awake by 6:00 a.m. because that is when the bells ring."

• • •

Tenosique is less than an hour away. It has been a long second day of travel for the Gonzalez family. The bus carrying Maria Elena and the others will stop there so they can spend the night in a migrant shelter. In the morning, after Mass, they will board a new bus for the ride up the east side of Mexico.

They arrive in Tenosique early in the evening on Saturday and the temperature hovers around eighty degrees in this small city of about 30,000. Miguel has been here before, and he begins to tell Maria Elena a little about its history.

"The town is very old, founded in 1,000 B.C. The name means 'The house of weavers.' Maria, you are a weaver of sorts," he teases with a wink.

If this town was ever a place of weavers, that was 3,000 years ago, and it's no longer true today. The town's main business today is the facilitation of transportation for tourists crossing the border into Guatemala to visit the Mayan ruins. Its geographic location also positions it as the route for migrants, coming primarily from Honduras with hopes of catching a ride on what they call La Bestia or "The Train of Death."

This part of the route has been taken over by the criminal narco traders and their gangs. The people who live in these towns are conflicted in their views of the migrants. They empathize with the misery of their lives and understand why they are making this journey. But it is frustrating for the locals when some of the migrants get to Tenosique, abandon the trip, can't afford to return home, and then become a drain on the economy.

Tenosique has about 150 migrants pass through each day, and a number of them end up staying. A special problem for the town is the number of migrants who come there to catch one of the humongous freight trains that go to the Mexican/U.S. border. When the United States government began to pressure Mexico to curtail the train schedule as a way of easing the pressure on the U.S. border, many migrants arrived in Tenosique expecting to board one of the trains and instead ended up stranded there. Many of them were on the streets, begging for food and shelter. The only place they might expect to find help was a migrant shelter, known as La 72.

"The shelter was opened in 2011," Miguel tells Maria Elena, "by the saintly Franciscan brother, Friar Tomás Gonzalez Castillo.

The shelter can house up to 250 people at one time. And Friar Tomás has an open-door policy. He and his Franciscan brothers do not care if the people seeking shelter are single mothers with children, minors traveling on their own, families like yours, Maria, or members of the gay community. They are all treated with dignity and respect."

The shelter became known as "La 72" in 2010 to honor seventy-two immigrants who were massacred by criminals dealing in drugs and extortion in San Fernando, in the state of Tamaulipas in Northern Mexico. Friar Tomás maintains high ethical standards of dignity and support, and that is felt throughout the shelter where his clients are provided a bed, meals, counseling, and legal assistance. For the migrants, these kindnesses are a godsend.

At the bus depot, some of the passengers are met by family or friends and leave with them. Others are trying to get a room at the town's hotels, while the rest join Maria and her family at La 72.

Rocia has been in contact with Friar Tomás to interview him as well as others at the shelter who might want to share their experiences.

Friar Tomás wears his brown robe, cinctured at the waist. A simple cross hangs at his sternum. He has a broad smile as he greets his guests at the front door of La 72. He hugs the children who are part of the group.

"Welcome!! Please, please come in. We have been expecting you. We have a meal prepared, and you are fortunate because it is Saturday night, and every Saturday evening there is a party here at the shelter with music and dancing."

Maria Elena is taken aback by the Friar's joyful welcome and his elation over their presence. "Thank you, Father," Maria manages to say, mirroring Friar Tomás's open smile.

"I am not a priest," laughs Friar Tomás, "but a mere humble brother of the Franciscan Order. So, you may call me brother or friar or just Tomás if you like. Now let's get you settled."

Maria Elena and her girls share a small, clean room with two bunk beds. A communal bathroom with showers is just down the hall. They are weary from the long ride but eternally grateful that they have avoided the long hot walk they saw others struggling to make. Now they are anxious for a shower and a hot meal.

Miguel convinces Maria and Rocia to join in the festivities that evening. He argues that it is good for their legs and spirits to dance a little. A radio is tuned into Latin music resembling the sound of the Gypsy Kings.

"If the Gypsy Kings don't get you moving," Miguel says, "nothing will. In fact, we have a little gypsy in us by making this journey."

Jose and the girls enjoy dancing as a group, their young supple bodies gyrating to the rhythms of Latin music. They try to coax their mother onto the dance floor, but she continues to say no. She is just enjoying this moment watching her children dance and clown around. Maria wonders how they have stayed so strong while their lives are being upended.

Jose and Teresa leave their sisters and walk over to where their mother, Miguel, and Rocia are sitting.

Rocia is writing in her reporter's notebook. When Maria Elena sees them approaching she puts a big smile on her face. She knows this time they are not asking and will take her to the dance floor. They each gently grab an arm and get their mother to her feet. Camilla and Dio see what is happening and run over to join their siblings in escorting their mother to the floor.

Maria Elena does not want to reject this moment of joy, and she gives in to them. They deserve to see their mother happy.

And as the music begins again, to an upbeat song, Mama's moves are pretty good for a "weaver."

After several up-tempo songs, a slow tune follows, and Maria Elena takes this as a chance to return her seat. Before she is able to leave the dance floor, Miguel intercepts her and asks, "May I have the pleasure of this dance?"

• • •

Donald Trump is furious about the growing caravans of several thousand migrants making their way north to seek asylum or cross the Mexican/U.S. border without papers. He has threatened to close the border to keep these "illegal aliens" out of the United States.

Migrants were a key focus of Trump's 2016 campaign and building a wall to keep them out was a major promise. He has made the migrants his political scapegoats and built his right-wing coalition around closing the border to them. In the first two years of his presidency, he is no closer to building a wall or closing the border.

To fight back against the reasonable and sensible immigration reforms proposed by his rivals, President Trump fires up his base at rallies by claiming, "They are marching their own army against us at the border." Ramping this up even further, he bellows, "MS13 gang members and 'Middle Easterners' can be found in the caravans."

Trump trades on fear, and he knows that the more he stokes that fear, the more his voters will react. But what he says is not true. There is no army. The people in the caravans are mostly women and children and young men looking for work and a future. Most are escaping violence in their homelands. They carry no weapons, nor do they seek a confrontation. They are seeking a justice that is promised to them under international law—the right to asylum. In addition, the U.S. economy does not survive without these workers.

In the midst of Trump's harangues against migrants, an assassin chooses the Sabbath to enter the Tree of Life Synagogue in Pittsburgh's Jewish community of Squirrel Hill and kills eleven worshipping Jews. It is the deadliest anti-Semitic attack in American history. The assassin is an anti-Semite who wrote that "HIAS likes to bring invaders that kill our children." HIAS, a Jewish refugee organization whose work is similar to that of Catholic Charities, is one of nine organizations the U.S. government contracts to resettle and integrate migrants.

HIAS (Hebrew Immigrant Aid Society) began its work in the 1970s assimilating Soviet Jews in the United States. Now it has expanded its works to others, including Central American migrants. HIAS's president, Mark Hetfield, says that the climate of political rancor over immigration inspires their refugee relief efforts. "At a time when the United States is doing less and less for refugees," he says, "we feel we must demonstrate as a refugee people, that it is more important than ever to continue to welcome refugees as a community."

After the killings at the Tree of Life Synagogue, Hetfield defended his organization and its work by noting that, on more than thirty-five occasions, the Torah mentions that we should, "Love the stranger as yourself."

The Jewish community understands and recognizes the heart of the stranger because they have so often been refugees themselves. They understand the anguish and pain of leaving their home in search of another because their origin story is Moses leading his caravan in another desert in search of the Promised Land. The theme of the "wandering Jew" is replete throughout history—a history of being uprooted, chased, and murdered.

Soon after the murders at the Tree of Life Synagogue, rabbis around the country came together and raised their voices in support of the migrants and to denounce President Trump's policies regarding immigration.

Hasidic rabbis from New York's Crown Heights neighborhood joined with other rabbis to make pilgrimages to the Mexican/U.S. border. They called these witnesses' pilgrimages, "Let Our Families Go." In November 2018, they streamed to the border from Cincinnati, Ann Arbor, and all parts of California. They were a part of the larger religious/peace organizations that have been reactivated in response to the policies of the Trump Administration.

Rabbi Mariam Terlinchamp from Cincinnati said, "Increased militarization of our borders and zero-tolerance policies have created the conditions for a humanitarian disaster affecting migrants and asylum seekers. These policies violate every principle of decency, justice, and compassion that we hold as Jews. We are making this sacred journey to call on our government to stop the unacceptable practice of imprisoning immigrant minors and to ensure protection for those seeking refuge within our borders."

Rabbi Josh Whinston, of Ann Arbor, underscored that and said, "We as a people of faith, stand for reunification of children with parents or guardians regardless of immigration status. The time has come to bring an end to the outrageous practices that keep asylum seekers and immigrant teens in desperate poverty or locked in prison camps."

Aid for Central Americans in need began in the 1980s in opposition to President Ronald Reagan's policies in the region. He sent huge financial support to the Contras fighting to overthrow the government of Nicaragua and to support the right-wing repressive regimes in El Salvador and Guatemala. U.S.

religious and peace groups raised money and resources to counter Reagan and his CIA wars and to help individuals and communities harmed by the president's policies.

More than 600 U.S.-based organizations offered assistance with money, but also through educational and medical supplies, clothes, agricultural tools, and material for building hospitals. Organizations like Quest for Peace helped to raise millions of dollars in humanitarian aid. U.S. cities adopted cities in Central America, in an effort at people-to-people contact, forming bonds and ties in the 1980s that have been recently renewed. People of conscience are making pilgrimages to the border to bring visibility and voice to the crisis.

In addition to the pilgrimage by rabbis, retired nuns from the order Sisters of the Immaculate Heart of Mary, have literally stepped or wheeled themselves forward as prayer warriors. They walk the long hallway at their convent of Camilla Hall in Malvern, Pennsylvania. It measures 338 feet from end to end. It is their route of solidarity.

"Our pilgrimage took on a different shape than the traditional pilgrimage, but the miles walked and the prayers offered are very real," said Sister Mary Lyndon.

The sisters may be old and gray, but they are filled with the Holy Spirit. One hundred thirty of them covered 1,170 miles walking and rolling in their wheelchairs at their convent home and health care center. They answered Pope Francis's call for Catholics to stand with migrants by undertaking a spiritual pilgrimage on their behalf.

Other religious denominations and peace and justice groups are also undertaking their own border pilgrimages, marching relentlessly against President Trump and his inhumane policies at the border. Their witness for justice is spreading throughout the United States.

Today more than 68,000,000 persons in the world have been forcibly displaced, and 25,000,000 more are refugees. An underground network of sanctuary has emerged to ensure the personal safety and safe passage of these migrants. Like earlier sanctuaries, houses of worship are critical to this infrastructure of compassion. And the Catholic churches and shelters are in the forefront of this movement.

Each stream of Samaritans—whether they are rabbis, nuns in retirement homes, nuns on a bus, or doctors on Lampedusa—raises a voice for justice, emptying their pockets for the dispossessed and elevating their prayers in hopes of making a difference in the lives of "the stranger."

CHAPTER FOUR

La Bestia—Train of Death

The bus passes north through the state of Veracruz on a highway that runs parallel to railroad tracks. Rocia has now made friends with Maria Elena's daughters, and she is sitting with them when a large freight train pulls even with the bus. The train and the bus are both traveling about forty mph, and suddenly Camilla points out her window.

"Look!" she exclaims in surprise and horror. "People are on top of the train while it's moving."

That prompts her sisters to jump up from their seats and lean on the window to get a better look. The train is only twenty yards away on the other side of the shoulder of the road. The girls are in awe of what they see, their breath fogging the window.

Dio spontaneously starts waving and shouting, "Hola" to the migrants who are sitting precariously next to each other, covering every inch of the tops of these railroad cars. Mothers are cradling their toddlers and small children. Other cars behind them, are all carrying migrants searching for safety and a better life. Yet anyone seeing them crowded atop these moving railroad cars can tell this is anything but safe.

Teresa turns to Rocia and asks, "Why are they on top? Isn't it dangerous?"

"Yes," Rocia says, nodding to Teresa and Camilla and the others. "Unfortunately. I have seen this all too often. Sadly." She pauses a moment before telling them, "These trains are called 'La Bestia' after the dangerous look of the locomotive engine that pulls the railroad cars."

"Why are they up there?" Dio asks?

Without waiting for Rocia to answer, Camilla jumps in and says, "They have no money."

"Yeah" Teresa says. "No money to buy bus tickets."

"That is right, Teresa," Rocia says, sounding like their teacher back in Tegucigalpa.

Even though the girls are homeless themselves, they can easily grasp how fortunate they are inside the safety of the bus, compared to what they see outside with the people on top of the moving train cars.

Highway 101 and the Women of La Patrona

When the seacoast route up Mexican Federal Highway 101 became too dangerous to travel, the bus company mandated that its drivers go a different way. Since 2010, there have been so many cases of violence, including abductions, rapes, and death, that it has been stamped the "Highway of Death." In 2010, in nearby Fernando, seventy-two passengers were abducted and then murdered by members of a narcotics syndicate. The United States and other nations have issued high-level travel warnings against traveling in the state of Tamaulipas along Highway 101. If there is traffic on this road, it is in the daylight, and this is why the buses avoid 101 and instead head northwest.

The bus carrying Maria Elena and her family has been on the road today from Tenosique to Veracruz and now on to Córdoba, which is also known as "The City of the Thirty Knights." They have been on the bus for so long now that it feels like it's been thirty "nights."

Parts of Córdoba are still in disrepair from an earthquake that struck here in 1973. A half century of neglect has left the old colonial town of Córdoba without the charms of other Mexican colonial towns. The city sits some 3,000 feet above sea level, giving it wonderfully scenic views. One of the villages in the distance is La Patrona.

La Patrona is where La Bestia passes on its journey north, now angling to the northwest away from the dangers along the coastal road. The town has become famous because of the women who cook and feed the migrants who pass through it.

Twenty years ago, two sisters were sent by their mother to buy bread and milk. As they were walking along the tracks with their groceries, Bernarda and Rosa could feel La Bestia coming up behind them and getting ready to pass by them. They looked over at the train and saw men hanging from its sides, with one hand on the iron ladder leading to the top of the railroad cars and the other hand open and begging the sisters to give them something to eat.

Instinctively, Bernarda and Rosa threw their bread and milk to the migrants on the train.

They expected their mother to scold them for giving away their groceries to the hungry migrants, but instead, Dona Leonidas praised her daughters' kindness. Together they formed a migrant organization that would feed the migrants riding the trains. The women who do this noble act of charity are known as Las Patronas, a name taken from their village.

Each day the sisters, mothers, cousins, other family members, and friends cook some twenty kilos of beans and rice, which are wrapped in tortillas and tied together with a refilled water bottle. Some of the food and drink is placed in white plastic bags and knotted tightly so they can be easily handed to the migrants who lean and reach from the swift-moving train.

The women have also become affectionately known as *abuelitas*, or grandmothers. One of the cooks, Julia Ramirez, says with sympathy, "Who are we to judge people who just want a better life? I just want to make sure that for that one instant, they feel the generosity of a people who pray for them, because their journey is fraught with so much danger and malice."

The people on the caravans have experienced this generous spirit throughout most of Mexico. When they reach the end of a day that has included a twenty-mile walk, they are welcomed in the town square where they stop for the night.

Sometimes an army of foot massagers emerges in the squares to wash and rub their swollen and red feet, just as Jesus did for Peter after the last supper, and Pope Francis did when he washed the feet of twelve migrant Muslims.

• • •

After a long day on winding roads, the bus approaches Saltillo, Mexico, a large automobile-manufacturing city near Monterrey. Saltillo has several migrant shelters, part of a network of fourteen shelters in cities across Northern Mexico that have been recognized for their outstanding contributions to defending the rights of migrant persons.

Tomorrow the drive from Saltillo to Reynosa will take five hours. The last segment of the journey will cross into Tamaulipas, the deadliest state in Northern Mexico. This is where organized criminal groups are strongest and, in some parts of the state, they rule with impunity.

As the bus nears the terminal in Saltillo, Miguel calls churches in search of beds for his group of six. Rocia asks to join them if there is room. She finds that shelters are excellent places to hear personal stories, and people open up more when they feel a sense of security.

Miguel finds room for all seven of them at the shelter founded by Father Pedro Pantoa. Outside the terminal they see a bus stop and wait for the last local bus to take them five miles across town to their shelter. This adds another hour of travel through this gritty industrial city.

Upon arrival Sister Vivian greets them warmly and ushers them to a corner in a large community room where cots are set up. The corner with its two adjoining walls provides some modicum of privacy even though they are in a room filled with 200 migrants. Many are teenage boys and young men. Some are mothers with young children. Maria Elena and her children each settle on a cot, close to each other. They are also hungry because they have not eaten since breakfast in Tenosique.

Sister Vivian says, "The hot food line is closed, but there are sandwiches, apples, and water for those who have arrived late."

There are separate community showers for men and women. During their showers, the Gonzalez family washes the clothes they have been wearing for the last several days. They put on the one other set of clothes they brought and then enter the enclosed courtyard where they hang up their wet laundry.

Inside the community room next to his cot Jose sees a boy about his age who looks tired and lonely. Jose was given an apple with his sandwich which he is saving for tomorrow.

"I'm never able to sleep after eating an apple," says Jose. "Would you like it?"

The boy stares at the apple. "Gracias," he says, reaching out to take it.

"De nada," Jose responds. "I'm Jose Gonzalez. What's your name?"

"Jesus Aguilar."

"Who are you with, Jesus?"

"Solo."

Jose immediately feels his new friend's loneliness, and he thinks carefully before responding. Then he points to his family, to Miguel and Rocia, and says, "I am with my family and we are traveling from Tegucigalpa, Honduras."

"I am also from Honduras," Jesus replies. "I have been one week on the journey north. I started from my home in San Pedro Sula."

"What's that been like?" Jose asks. "Has anything happened to you?"

Maria Elena, Miguel, and Rocia are listening to the two boys talk, and Jose sees that they are interested, and he points to each and introduces them. "My mother, Maria Elena, our friend Miguel Cabrera, and Rocia, who is a reporter for an American newspaper. This is Jesus who has been traveling for a week by himself from San Pedro Sula."

Everyone nods and says "Hola" during the introductions.

Rocia asks, "Do you mind if we join your conversation?"

The boys welcome them to join in, and Jesus realizes how great it is to talk to other people after keeping to himself for a week. He is a handsome 15-year-old boy, but he is also a little shy. He knows he needs to communicate and make friends if he hopes to make it to the United States.

"Did you get this far by bus, like we have?" Jose asks him.

"No," Jesus says. "In Tenosique I hopped the freight train—they call it La Bestia—and I travelled on it to here."

Teresa is overcome by visions of the train and the people on top, and she shudders. "Weren't you scared on top?"

"Yes, but I was desperate," Jesus says. "I had been walking much of the way from Honduras through Guatemala. Once a truck picked me up, and we drove for two hours. I slept in fields and forests. The nights were dark, and the ground was cold. If I found a church, I slept there. At least the churches were often light and warm—even when the church was dark inside, I felt warm and saw light. I was always dodging the police and military who were looking for migrants or eluding gangs who wanted to rob me or use me for ransom.

"Soon after I crossed into Guatemala, I was robbed of the little money I had. Two guys. They let me keep my backpack because I have just a few old clothes in it, a prayer book and an old rubber ball that the dogs back home had chewed. They saw the ring on my finger that my father gave me before he disappeared, and said I had to give it to them. I told them that it is the only possession I have, and it reminds me of him. They took pity on me and let me keep it. It is a simple ring of little worth to them but very special to me. But my money, they took it all—hundreds of dollars that I saved over the years for this journey.

"In Flores, a priest saw me and let me sleep in the cathedral. The dinner I had that evening was rice and beans I found in a dumpster in the alley behind a restaurant.

"I had no food, only what I had eaten the day before in Flores. At the border of Guatemala and Mexico I saw people on rafts going across the river into Mexico. There was not enough room on the raft, so I asked if I could hold onto the side while they poled across the river. They said "OK." On the other side they gave me bottled water. On the road to Tenosique a small bus gave me a ride, and the driver told me about La Bestia. When we got there, I went down to the tracks."

Rocia is quickly taking notes as Jesus unveils his story.

"I walked there and saw many migrants camped by the tracks huddled around small fires to keep warm or to cook food. They were waiting for the train.

"When it came, I ran alongside it and reached for the bottom of the ladder, then pulled myself up. I don't even think I knew how dangerous it was until I did it. Many of the people trying to swing onto the train lost their grip and fell under the wheels. A lot of them died like that. I was lucky and was able to pull myself up on the ladder. I climbed to the top and soon found a railroad car that had a hole in the top. I like to travel alone. From the top, I lowered myself through the hole and into the car. I had no food and had not eaten since the day before in Flores."

At this moment in Jesus's story, both Miguel and Rocia shoot each other a quick look: they both believe Jesus is a very decent kid, and they each begin to think how they can help this determined and lonely boy who clearly could use some friendship.

"The railroad car was dark and smelly," Jesus continues. "Soon after the train left, I fell asleep to its sounds and movements. I was very tired. In the park near the cathedral in Flores, a kind man had given me this light blanket. I also found some plastic in the dumpster and made myself a poncho for when it rains. I slept there, in that black railroad car, until I heard excited voices from the other railroad cars that are filled on top with migrants like me.

"I climbed a rusty ladder back up through the hole, and the bright sun blinded me. It took me a few seconds to adjust my sight. That's when I saw we were in the small village of La Patrona. The grandmothers and other women were throwing food bags to us. There was rice, beans, tortillas and water. It was like a gift from heaven. It was my only meal that day."

"When I got the food from the *abuelitas*, I climbed back on top of the railroad car to where my hole was. Instead of going back in like a turtle into his shell, I stayed on top, leaned back on my backpack, and let the sun embrace my face. I closed my eyes and made the sign of the cross to give thanks for this gift. I stayed up there and felt the train under me as it ran north toward my destination. I had to give thanks again."

Jesus is looking at Jose and his family while telling his story, and he realizes that he is hoping they will ask him to join their group. They are all headed to Reynosa and the Catholic shelter there.

For Jesus and so many others traveling by themselves, loneliness is an almost overwhelming hunger for company and conversation. Jesus thinks of asking Jose about traveling with them. But Jesus is also aware that the buses are often stopped and searched for migrants, and he has no papers like the others. He has come so far on his own and concludes that he cannot risk the bus. Instead, he will risk apprehension from the police authorities or the criminal gangs in the state of Tamaulipas. He has turned out to be tough, elusive, and wily. His confidence is high.

This past week on the road has been arduous and mentally difficult. Jesus needs someone to share his grief as well as his hope.

Jose spots a photo Jesus has of his family. It is lying on his cot. "Who is that?" Jose inquires. "Is that your family?"

"Yes," Jesus says, proudly reaching for the photo to show his new friend.

"I have one also to share with you," Jose says. "Let's take them and go sit outside in the fresh air."

With each boy cradling his prized possession, they walk into the courtyard, ducking their heads under the multi-colored wet clothes hanging there to dry. They find a stoop where they sit and feel a refreshing light breeze wash over them.

Jose removes his photo from the plastic bag. "This is my family before my sister Dio was born and before the narco gangs murdered my father." Jose hands the photo to Jesus who studies it. This makes Jesus think about his own father who had been gone since Jesus was 10 years old. He also knows he must say something now about the death of Jose's dad.

Clumsily, Jesus says, "He was a tall man." And adds quickly, "I am sorry he is dead. Was he a good father?"

"Yes, I have good memories of him even though I was small. He was kind to my mother and sisters. He was always teaching me how to do different things like making little animal wood carvings, how to play his harmonica. Almost every day we kicked the soccer ball to each other. In the market, he lifted me up on his shoulders. And then with my small legs wrapped around his neck, he took his large hands and pressed my thighs against his shoulders. We walked through the entire market, and I could see everything. He was going to teach me to ride a bicycle before he was killed. I miss him very much."

Jesus could see that Jose was not crying but he almost was. "I am sorry for you and your family," Jesus said. "Were the killers caught and punished?"

"No. The police did not even try. Two weeks ago, the same gang came for me and beat me. They said if I did not join them, they would kill me and my family. I could never dishonor my father's memory by joining that murderous bunch. After the beating, my mother decided that we had no other choice than to leave our home. It is very sad."

Jose needs a moment before he figures out what to say next. Switching away from his family's story, he asks "Jesus, this is a nice photo of you, your mother and sisters. And your father?"

"He just disappeared when I was 10," Jesus said. "One day he was not there. I was told that he was going to the United States, but we never heard from him. He didn't even say good-bye or leave me a letter. Nothing. He just vanished from our life. I was, like you, close to him. So, I have these mixed feelings. Of love, yes. But also bitterness. He was supposed to protect and look after us. That was his job. He did not do his job.

"Sometimes I think he went to the United States to get a better job and to send money back to us like my uncle now does. But we never heard that he showed up in Houston where my uncle lives and works. So did he die trying to cross—maybe somewhere in the desert without water or companionship? Or did he just give up on us?

"Sometimes I have dreams of him. I have found him, and I am so happy. Then it is just a dream. But when I get to Houston, I am going to look for him. When I cross the border, I will start looking at every man's face I see."

Jose takes off his scapular and hands it to Jesus. "To protect you on your journey."

"Gracias, mi amigo," Jesus says and then kisses the image of the father of Jesus, and he makes the sign of the cross.

They are two fatherless, homeless Catholic boys, looking for hope and salvation. They are now fighting to stay alive and feeling the weight of responsibility for others—a heavy burden to carry at any age, but most heavy for boys barely out of childhood.

At 9:00 p.m. a bell tolls—signaling that it is time for the last prayer of the day after vespers and before the lights go out. A priest or nun usually leads the prayer. Tonight, Sister Vivian, who oversees night duty, will handle these duties. She chose Vivian because that is the name of the patron saint of tortured victims.

She asks for their attention for reflection. Some bow their heads, while some kneel next to their cots, and others rise out of respect. Sister Vivian begins:

The Prayer.
God, no one is a stranger to you
And no one is ever far from your loving care.
In Your kindness watch over migrants, refugees, and asylum seekers,
Those separated from their loved ones,
Those who are lost,
And those who have been exiled from their homes.
Bring them safely to the place where they long to be,

And help us always to show your kindness to strangers
And those in need.
We ask this through Christ our Lord,
Who too was a refugee and migrant
Who travelled to another land
Searching for a home.
Amen.

Sleep comes easily after this prayer. The new day awaits them.

• • •

Mexico's president, Andres Manuel Lopez Obrador, known by the letters AMLO, was handily elected in 2018 and began serving his term as a reform president on December 1 of that year. This occurred on the same day when Maria Elena and her family arrived in Saltillo.

One of AMLO's first acts as president was to propose a Marshall Plan for Central America—$30 billion over five years for economic development assistance and to bolster the rule of law. Obrador had the opportunity to talk to President Trump about his idea and his determination to attack the migrant issue at its source in Central America. The Central American Marshall Plan could possibly close the massive opportunity deficit throughout the region, helping people to stay in their home countries. AMLO's and Trump's positions are far apart because the American president has no interest in helping the people of the region.

The Mexican president's plan addresses the poverty issue there, but not the threats of violence or personal safety that drive people like Maria Elena and her family to flee their homeland. The breakdown in the rule of law is rampant, and those who chose to leave are expressing their lack of confidence in their governments to protect them—walking en masse out of their countries. Hundreds of thousands from Northern Triangle countries have left. The corrupt governments in those countries offer little hope of change.

Now Andres Manuel Lopez Obrador has proposed an idea to break that cycle of despair. Like former Costa Rican President Oscar Arias, Obrador is thinking big and acting boldly.

The people of Guatemala, Honduras, and El Salvador have come to expect that their presidential elections will be stolen. AMLO still believes the presidency was stolen from him in 2006. Twenty-five years ago, in 1984, Oscar Arias ran and was elected the new president of Costa Rica on a platform to end the wars in Central America. He won his election and united the other Central American presidents around his Peace Plan, which became known as the Esquipulas Plan, named after the city of Esquipulas in Guatemala where the presidents met. The plan worked, and it ended decades of civil wars and earned Arias the Nobel Peace Prize.

Poverty and violence morphed into another cycle after the peace process was initiated in the early 1990s. In Mexico tens of thousands of people have gone missing since 2007. It is impossible to know the actual number because so many families are scared of retribution if they report their loved ones as missing.

In 2017–2018, Mexico recorded its highest murder rate in modern history. Coupled with these staggering statistics was the lack of resources the previous Mexican governments had devoted to their law enforcement agencies. Mexico has only half the police officers it needs. And of those, only an estimated 40 percent meet basic competency standards. Only 10 percent have been trained in criminal investigations, and their average salary is barely $500 a month.

These deficits lead to only 4 percent of crimes in Mexico resulting in official punishment. The country faces a crisis over the lack of investment in police, prosecutors, and judges, and the result is a system that has become untenable.

This is why so many Mexicans feel there is no reason to call 911 when a crime occurs. Other observers suggested that this explains why most crimes go unreported.

During the night, Jose and Jesus quietly get up from their cots, leave the community room, and go out to the courtyard. Jose is worried his family's clothes may be taken. They gather the clothes that have dried and fold them with the same care Jose took when he folded Father Melo's vestments after Mass was served. Jose and Jesus pile the clothes neatly and place them under the cots where Jose's family is sleeping.

Continuing to stay as quiet as possible, he and Jesus slip back onto their cots for a couple of more hours of sleep.

At 5:00 a.m., people begin to wake. It is not the sound of roosters crowing that so many of them are used to hearing at this time of day, but the whispers of those awake floating over those sleeping in the large room. Everyone is trying to muffle themselves, even with intermittent coughs, but a crying child does not know to silence herself and pierces the quiet of the morning.

At 6:00 a.m., Sister Clare prepares the crowd for the morning prayer. In a soothing, hushed voice over the speaker system, she greets them: "*Buenos dias.* In a minute we will begin our day with a short prayer." She waits for two minutes to let people gather themselves, and then she begins.

"Dear Lord, you have brought me to the beginning of a new day. Help me to walk closer in your way today. Shine through me so that everyone I meet will feel your presence in me. I pray that you give me strength today. You know that there are struggles that I will go through. I pray that you will be with me. Take my hand, precious Lord, and carry me when I am too weak. Amen."

At breakfast, Miguel sits next to Jesus and gives him an envelope. Jesus opens it and sees that it contains money and a small piece of paper.

"Jesus," Miguel says. "I hope we will meet again. Perhaps at the Casa del Migrante in Reynosa. Also, inside this envelope is some money from Rocia and me to help you. I have also given you my cell number and the address for the shelter in Reynosa and a church in Matamoros."

"*Signor, muchas gracias!*" Jesus exclaims, almost overcome by this gesture.

Miguel continues: "Be cautious on your journey. I know you know that it is dangerous out there, especially once you leave the state of Nuevo León and enter Tamaulipas. If you get to the Reynosa shelter, I will work to get you legal counseling so you can make the best decisions. If you go on to Matamoros, there is a church there and a priest who may help you. I have also written down the names of the church and of the priest."

"You are very kind," Jesus says. "I hope to see you again. I will begin my travel soon. Today I will rest, think, and plan how best to arrive safely."

Maria Elena, her children, and Miguel and Rocia return to the terminal in Saltillo and board a bus that is headed to Reynosa. Their route is through a mountain pass and into Monterrey. The first part of their travel is through the state of Nuevo León. This takes up most of the five-hour trip. The law, and its enforcement, is better and safer than in neighboring Tamaulipas state. The part of the journey where their exposure to danger increases occurs during the last ninety minutes when they travel into the state of Tamaulipas.

Their destination in Reynosa is the Catholic shelter, Casa del

Migrante, that is run by the Daughters of Charity of Saint Vincent de Paul. They have only 120 beds but serve 1,100 migrants a month. When the beds are full, they pull out mattresses. They once had 400 people in the shelter. Catholic parishes help to fund this enterprise with money and volunteers, and they are subsidized with aid from Catholic Charities.

The ride to Reynosa from Saltillo climbs through a fog-filled mountain pass. On the other side of the pass are the Sierra Madre Oriental mountains, a gorgeous range that rises over Monterrey, creating a stunning backdrop, especially when the light is low on the mountains. As they ride through the fog, Miguel feels nervous. He can't stop himself from thinking that this is a place where a bus could be hijacked, and its passengers kidnapped and held for ransom.

The bus rambles through Monterrey, and Miguel once again assumes the role of tour guide. He has made this trip numerous times and is familiar with the Monterrey region. Many major multinational corporations have located here, and the employment numbers are much higher than the average in Mexico. The per capita income is double the Mexican average. Monterrey is the industrial capital of Mexico and one of the country's wealthiest cities.

Looking out her window, Maria Elena can see the difference in prosperity. The streets are paved and lined with trees and the people move purposefully as if their business depends upon their resourcefulness. The city has a formidable police presence on the streets. Their public transportation system looks new and efficient. Miguel says, "Monterrey has a rich history and culture and is often thought of as being the most Americanized of the cities in Mexico."

Maria Elena thinks to herself that this might be a good place to live and raise children.

. . .

Maria and Miguel sit next to each other talking about their children and making comparisons between their personalities. But Miguel is wary of what could possibly lie ahead. Across the aisle from them, Rocia is sitting with Teresa, who is asking Rocia many questions about her work as a journalist, a conversation Rocia is happy to have with this inquisitive young girl. In the row behind them sit the two youngest daughters, Camilla and Dio, who are playing a game to pass the time as the bus nears the border of the state of Tamaulipas. Across the aisle from Camilla, Jose is reading the sports pages from an old newspaper he picked up at the bus terminal in Saltillo. The bus is now ninety minutes from the town center in Reynosa.

Suddenly, in broad daylight, two bandits emerge from the back of the bus wearing bandannas covering two-thirds of their faces below their eyes. With guns in their hands, they walk to the front where one of them sticks his pistol into the bus driver's ribs.

"Mr. bus driver, I have a gun in your ribs," he says firmly. "Get off the highway at the next exit and follow the road to the right if you want to live!"

The other bandit, waving his pistol high into the air for all to see, commands, "Everybody put both hands on the top of your head! Now! Do what I say!"

Miguel remembers these two when they boarded the bus at the terminal in Monterey. He recalls how both looked at all the passengers as they made their way up the aisle to the back of the bus. He should have been more suspicious.

Rocia is showing a frightened Teresa how to put her hands on her head. Maria Elena turns to the seat behind her and is saying the same thing to her youngest daughters, who are also terrified and confused. Dio cries, "Mama, what is happening?"

Maria in a forced calming voice says, "Please Dio, just do what Miguel and I are doing. Put your hands on the top of your head." Both girls do as they are told.

Unbeknownst to the bandits and the other passengers, two bus marshals in civilian attire are also on the bus. President Obrador, on his first day in office, ordered that marshals be placed on these heavily traveled routes within Mexico. This was similar to air marshals placed on planes after the 9-11 airplane hijackings in the United States. The explosion of kidnappings on Mexican highways has dramatically crippled Mexico's once thriving and growing tourist industry.

One officer sits near the front of the bus and the other marshal is in the rear. Both are armed.

After the 2014 abduction of forty-three Mexican students from their bus—in one of Mexico's most notorious human rights atrocities (their bodies were never recovered)—immense national and international pressure was applied to the Mexican government to take actions against the narco gangs operating with privilege in many Mexican states. When former President Calderon, who was in office from 2006 to 2012, escalated the war on the drug cartels, many of the gangs branched out from drug selling to the lucrative crime of kidnapping and ransom.

The bus driver is clearly frightened and does what the bandits tell him to do. He exits the highway and turns the bus down an isolated back country road. About a mile down the road, he is instructed by the bandit to pull the bus up to a van.

When the bus stops, the bandit who has been giving orders to the passengers slowly walks up the aisle looking over each passenger. When he reaches the row where Miguel is sitting, he motions for Rocia and Teresa to get up and go to the front of the bus.

Maria Elena screams, "No, no, no!"

The bandit turns and points his pistol at her, his arms extending over Miguel's head and across his forehead. This causes more passengers to scream and duck down in their seats. Before the bandit can fire a shot at Maria, Miguel reaches up and grabs the bandit's shooting arm and shoves it skyward.

Surprised, the bandit pulls the trigger, and the bullet pierces the roof of the bus. Miguel pushes the shooter to the floor in the bus aisle, pinning the bandit down—though he still has the pistol in his hand. Jose is right across the aisle and is now next to the struggle on the floor. He stands and stomps his foot down on the assaulter's hand, forcing the gun free.

The other bandit yanks his pistol from the driver's ribs and spins to shoot Miguel and Jose. But before he can get off a shot, the marshal in the back of the bus rushes forward, drawing his gun and shooting over the three bodies on the floor and hitting the bandit in the chest.

The marshal in the front fires through the window of the bus at the van that is speeding away from the scene of the hijacking. Then he turns to take the pulse of the bandit who was shot and determines that he is dead. The other marshal handcuffs the bandit that Miguel and Jose took down. He is subdued, and his ankles are tied with Miguel's belt. He is then dragged to the front of the bus where the marshal turns the bandit face down.

The marshal then takes his own pistol and presses it against the back of the bandit's head. "You struggle and I will pull the trigger," he forcefully says. "Do you hear me?"

"Si."

"Do you understand me?"

Again, "Si."

The other marshal takes out his cell phone and calls his military command post to report the crimes and ask for aid and assistance. There is no reason to call the local or state authorities in Tamaulipas because there is basically no rule of law in this state. The authorities could very well be in cahoots with the drug cartel and notifying them could cause more troubles.

Everyone on the bus is shaken. The passengers are sobbing and trying to comfort each other. Maria Elena moves to the seat with her youngest daughters and sits between Camilla and Dio, drawing them close to her. Camilla is crying on her mother's shoulder, and Dio is trembling with fear. Maria Elena can feel her youngest daughter's body shake as she embraces her.

Soothingly, Maria Elena whispers to her daughter, "it is over, it will be all right." Of course, Maria Elena fears that this kind of nightmare may continue when they reach the border, perhaps even being separated from her children.

Rocia comforts Teresa. The 11-year-old is struggling to breathe as she watches Jose and Miguel helping one of the marshals tie up the bandit who tried to abduct her and Rocia. Rocia tries to turn Teresa's face away from the struggle in the aisle, even though it is happening only five feet from her. Finally, Rocia puts herself between the men in the aisle and shields Teresa from looking at the bandit, who is now subdued on the floor of the aisle.

Rocia thinks to herself that, after three decades of covering the violence in El Salvador, it is in Mexico where I barely escape death.

Finally, the bus driver takes the bus back on the highway and continues toward Reynosa with one dead bandit and another prostrate on the floor with a gun to his head. When they are twenty minutes from Reynosa, they see members of the military on the road ahead and pull over to the side of the road.

Two armed and official men come onboard the bus and, with the marshals, first remove the dead body and then come back to take the tied-up bandit with them.

When the marshals return to the bus, the passengers greet them with cheers of gratitude. Both marshals remain on the bus until it arrives at the terminal in Reynosa.

Rocia, who is still reeling from what has happened, somehow pulls herself together enough to furiously write a story she hopes will get to her editors before today's deadline.

With any luck, it could appear on the front page of the *New York Times*.

BOOK TWO

LAMPEDUSA

CHAPTER FIVE

Call Me Padre Joe—Going to Lampedusa

Joe Tobin is a large man—at six feet, three inches, he weighs 240 pounds. He is large enough that a *New York Times* article entitled, "A Different Kind of Cardinal" included a photo of Joe Tobin in an Indianapolis weight room, wearing a skull-printed do-rag around his head. When Joe is wearing gym shorts and a sweatshirt with sleeves cut off at the shoulder, he could be mistaken for someone who once played in the NFL or was perhaps a professional wrestler. He is a priest who, at age 65, can still contemplate bench pressing 225 pounds of weight. Few other archbishops can make such an impressive claim. He has been associated with "large" throughout his life, coming as he did from a large family and a growing parish. He also has a big heart that has opened to so many.

Even with that physical appearance, he has no swagger in him, just a quiet confidence of understanding who he is and the role he plays as a leader. Padre Joe, as he is affectionately known by school children, has a contented, peaceful face to go with his massive torso.

When people first see him, they don't know quite what to make of this gentle giant. His voice is thoughtful and generous, with none of the flamboyance of the caped TV evangelist, Bishop Fulton J. Sheen, or the outgoing Irish joviality of his fellow Cardinal, Timothy Dolan of New York.

Once, when Padre Joe was on a panel with lay men and women, some of whom were migrants, he demonstrated these qualities. He did not dominate the conversation. He knew their stories were more important than his views. In that way, he displayed the sense and instinct of a wise leader. He waited with patience, listening and thinking before engaging.

Joe Tobin comes from a large Irish Catholic family, the eldest of thirteen children. His father attended Mass every morning at 6:00 a.m. Nine of his cousins and three aunts on his mother's side of the family were nuns. When Vatican II opened-up long needed reforms in the Church, such as allowing altar girls, many the of Tobin family females took this opportunity to serve Mass.

He grew up in Detroit in the 1950s, in the city's Most Holy Redeemer parish, once the largest Catholic parish in North America, with 20,000 worshippers and fourteen masses each Sunday in a church that held 1,400. Holy Redeemer School was packed with kids of Irish, German, Polish, and Mexican ancestry. When the families of Irish, German, and Polish families moved to the suburbs and to other parishes, they were replaced at Holy Redeemer by Hispanic families, most of them from Mexico, making up 70 percent of the parish.

Most large Catholic families have one of their children enter the sacrament of Holy Orders, and many in the Church view this as a higher service than Matrimony, the other sacrament of service. In Holy Orders, an extensive period of education is followed by a man being made a deacon, priest, or bishop, their service dedicated to following the path of Christ in His image. Joe entered the Redemptorist seminary, and in 1978 he was ordained a priest and then was assigned to Holy Redeemer, his boyhood parish. In 1984, he was named pastor and served in that capacity until 1990.

As a seminarian, Joe went on numerous missionary trips to Latin America, and along the way learned to speak Spanish. That helped him to become the leader of his congregation, which became increasingly Hispanic. His goal was to blend together his constituencies. The Hispanic parishioners had always attended a Mass in the church basement, but Joe insisted on bringing them into the main body of Holy Redeemer to celebrate with others in the parish.

Joe took seriously his vow of poverty. Over the years he got himself assigned to missionary work and travelled the world serving the poor. In his late 20s, he worked in Guatemala and later in his early 30s, he was in the impoverished country of Honduras. In time, he caught the attention of the Vatican hierarchy, and as he rose to the highest level of his order, the Redemptorist, he was called to serve as their Superior General in Rome. In many ways, Joe travelled similar paths to the one followed by Jorge Bergoglio, the Jesuit who became the leader of his order in Argentina.

School children may have seen him as Padre Joe, but the Vatican hierarchy had new titles for him. With Pope Benedict's blessing, in 2010, he was given the title of Bishop of Obba. He was given a job he did not want, to investigate and report on the religious orders of nuns in the United States who some thought had strayed from Catholic orthodoxy. But how could he say "no" to a pope?

Together with Brazilian Cardinal João Braz de Aviz, Joe turned a most threatening inquisition of all U.S. Catholic nuns into a praise fest that honored the sisters' amazing work in education, health, refugee relief, and other missions of mercy for those among us who have the least.

After two years of changing the inquiry's direction, he was shipped to Indianapolis to serve as an archbishop. Some conservative Curia leaders wanted him gone because, in their eyes, he had failed his assignment to reach a conclusion they had already decided on. But the women in the Church heaped deserved praise on Joe for his sensitivity to their work and the skill he demonstrated in achieving a positive outcome. The nuns saw in Joe Tobin what many see in Francis—a direct connection between the parishes and the people in the neighborhoods, a pastoral ministry that matches their own religious ministry.

By 2012, Indianapolis had become a landing spot in the United States for refugees from the crisis in Syria. The city and its Catholic community had a long history of settling refugees from the Middle East, especially Lebanese immigrants with Syrian ancestry. This brought the issue of immigration right to Joe's doorstep. The recently elected Pope Francis had declared his support for the Syrian refugees worldwide, and Archbishop Tobin followed him in this, putting him at odds with Indiana's Governor Mike Pence, who had publicly declared the refugees a security risk.

The archbishop saw a family of four battered by years of war, and to Padre Joe they represented the thousands of other Syrian refugees who were seeking asylum from the horrors of their homeland. As he made his way through this quickly forming community of migrants, he saw in them the stranger who needed help in Jesus's parable of the good Samaritan.

The more active Joe became in the Syrian refugee community, the more he found himself in direct opposition to Governor Pence. He knew that, in opposing the governor's attempts to be unaccommodating to the refugees, he was following Jesus and Francis. He told the governor he respectfully disagreed with his position, and that the Syrian family in question would be supported by the Church, through the local Catholic Charities, which had a long history of settling 20,000 refugees who needed homes. In this way, Joe was speaking truth to power. On another occasion, he personally accompanied a refugee to his immigration hearing. His pastoral instinct, tending to his flock, is one of his leadership strengths.

Pope Francis was looking for leaders like Tobin and looking to elevate them within the Church. In 2016, Francis appointed him a cardinal—one of eighteen total U.S. cardinals. Tobin and Pope Francis share a devotion to the poor, the shunned, and those society terms the underdogs. Each man is a pastor at heart, who, in a modest style, wants to be with and serve "God's holy people." Their own lives demonstrate a moral force to their followers. When Francis was a cardinal in Buenos Aires, he rode the subway, and, when Padre Joe finishes a meal, he joins everyone to clean the dishes. Francis is a lifetime fan of the San Lorenzo football team, and Padre Joe listens to Bob Seger. They both believe that understanding popular culture is important for leading their flock.

Tobin was a natural choice for the pope.

In March 2018, at a forum at the Jesuit Georgetown University in Washington, D.C., Cardinal Tobin shared the altar of Dahlgren Chapel with moderator John Carr and two immigrants who had powerful stories to tell. The house of God was packed that winter afternoon to hear Joe and the other panelists.

Padre Joe told a story about the new pope contacting his Secretary of State, Cardinal Tarcisio Bertone, with a request, "I want to go to Lampedusa." The cardinal tried to talk Francis out of going and said, "Your Holiness, this would be your first trip and going may not be the message you want to send. You just got elected. Maybe it is not the time to travel."

A week passed, and the pope again told the cardinal, "I want to go to Lampedusa." The cardinal refused again, saying, "A trip like this is not just a 'one day to the next' kind of thing. There are logistics, media, and security concerns. These trips can take between six months to a year to plan."

Still another week later, Cardinal Bertone received a call from the vice president of Air Italia, the Italian national airline, informing him that they had just received a list of passengers for next week's flight from Rome to Lampedusa. One of the passengers was named Jorge Bergoglio!

Cardinal Bertone got the message and knew he had been bested. This pope would act based on his instincts about what he saw as the right thing to do. The next week Pope Francis made his historic flight to the island south of Sicily in the Mediterranean.

"Thus," wrote Austen Ivereigh, Francis's biographer, "the first Pope born of immigrants in the new world chose for his debut journey outside of Rome a small Italian island on whose stunning beaches thousands of bloated bodies over the years had turned up with the tide. There on July 8 he wept for the dead and made immigration a pro-life issue."

• • •

Others too would find their way to Lampedusa.

Mary recalled her first patient at the medical clinic outside of Port-au-Prince, Haiti. Mary still wasn't a doctor, and she was there with her mother, Phyllis, and her older sister, Nan, both of whom were nurses. Mary remembered gently touching the child's tongue with a wooden tongue depressor and softly instructed this girl, who was not much younger than she was, "Now open wide and say, 'ahhh . . .'"

Mary's foreordained journey into medicine began as she watched her mother and sister leave their home each day to work at Mercy Hospital in Port Huron, Michigan. This was about a fifteen-minute drive north along the St. Clair River, the natural boundary that separates Michigan from Ontario, Canada. The region on both sides of the river is known as the Blue Water area.

When her mother entered the house after her shift at the hospital, she would call out, "Hi, Mary. Homework done?" Phyllis knew she didn't really need to check up on her daughter because Mary loved her studies, especially her science courses, and she never considered her homework work at all.

During Mary's high school years, she went with her mother and sister each summer to Haiti to work at a Catholic medical mission near Port-au-Prince. That first summer, Mary came in contact with a level of poverty she could not have even imagined. She cradled toddlers with bloated stomachs, and she learned about medicine when she helped administer polio injections. Her other lesson that summer was the quality of mercy, when she spontaneously gave her allowance to a mother in desperate need to feed her family.

Her Catholic faith was also strengthened when she witnessed the care and love the providers at the clinic gave to their patients, while still honoring their dignity. In return was the gift of thanks received. Whether it was good karma, the Holy Spirit, or whatever you labeled it, Mary fell in love with the atmosphere of charity and mercy that blossomed inside that clinic.

Phyllis and Nan were also impressed with Mary's dedication and noticed how at ease she was with the patients. They began to encourage her to study medicine. Mary attended Wayne State University in Detroit and continued working at the clinic in Haiti during her summer breaks.

She received a degree in pre-medicine and sciences in June 2005, and her MCAT scores were high enough for her to enroll at some of the finest medical schools in the country. Mary became intrigued by a program offered by the Religious Sisters of Mercy, located in Alma, Michigan. She had always marveled at the dedication and happiness of the religious nurses she worked beside in Haiti. Mary had been contemplating a religious vocation for herself. By enrolling in the programs with the Religious Sisters of Mercy, Mary would join a religious order, combining that with going to medical school.

Mary entered the convent, and after finishing her novitiate and taking the vows of poverty, chastity, and obedience, she was sent by her order to the University of Michigan for medical school. Ironically, this was the same medical school where "Papa Doc" Duvalier, the infamous president of Haiti, had studied public health in the 1930s. In Ann Arbor, she also continued to study languages, mastering both Spanish and French, preparing her with a combination of skills she could use for service in many parts of the world. It was incredibly satisfying that, after becoming a medical doctor, her first assignment was to return to Haiti, where her interest in medicine had begun.

Over the years Mary became intrigued with the medical human rights organization Doctors Without Borders. She followed their work closely, reading about their charitable medical services around the world in war-ravaged countries and with refugees in border regions. She found herself regularly contributing to them from her modest salary. It was the kind of medicine she wanted to devote her life to.

One day, while she was working at the mission outside of Port-au-Prince, she read an article in the *New York Times* about North African migrants being rescued at sea and taken to the small Italian island of Lampedusa, which is closer to the Libyan coast than it is to Italy. The article said that thousands of migrants had lost their lives at sea, and many others arrived on the island in terrible medical condition. Lampedusa was being overwhelmed with migrants, and the clinic needed doctors and nurses. Mary was known now as Sister Mary Vernard, and she immediately petitioned her order for a transfer from Haiti to the small island off the North African coast, arriving there in late 2012.

The migrant crisis on Lampedusa was not new. Refugees had begun arriving from Africa and the Middle East in large numbers, starting in 1991. Lampedusa is a Mediterranean island of eight square miles that is seventy miles from the North African coast of Libya. It is also a section of the Sicilian province of Agrigento and part of the Pelagic Islands that thousands of years ago broke off from the North African coast during a tectonic shift. Its six thousand islanders had never experienced anything like this influx of people seeking asylum.

The island's rocky coast makes landing a watercraft difficult and dangerous. Still, migrants come on barges, rafts, or dilapidated wooden boats that are overcrowded and teeming with humanity. The dispossessed, originally from war-torn countries of Africa and the Middle East, are desperate to flee the violence and economic deprivation of their homelands, to seek a safer and better life in Europe.

Hundreds of thousands of them have come—fleeing murder and rape in Nigeria at the hands of Boko Haram, breaking away from the Arab Spring revolutions in Libya and Tunisia, escaping the Dantesque horrors of Syria and the Sudan, and leaving the confined indignities of their restrictive lives in Gaza. They come with virtually no possessions other than their children, who are their only hope. Since 1991, more than 400,000 migrants have sought the sanctuary of Lampedusa, and thousands have died at sea trying to get there.

Sister Mary Vernard arrived on the island at the height of the migration influx, a year before Francis was made pope. In 2012, about 60,000 migrants landed in Lampedusa; that number spiked dramatically in 2013 to 175,000. As Mary tirelessly worked in twelve-hour shifts to administer to those arrivals, she couldn't help being reminded of her own escape at sea as a young girl.

She was 12 years old and was trying to secure her family boat to a cleat when she lost her footing at the end of their pier. This was on the St. Clair River, a powerful body of water that runs for forty miles and is the connecting waterway with Lake St. Clair to the south. It drains the whole of Lake Huron, the second largest of the Great Lakes. The river's width is on average a half mile, and the flow on that day was racing at a treacherous nine miles an hour.

The instant Mary hit the water she was immediately swept away by the raging current. With no life jacket, it was a struggle for her to swim out from the water's grip, and it kept pulling her farther away. Soon she was a quarter of a mile down river and becoming increasingly frantic, thinking, *I am 12 years old, and I am going to die.* All she knew to do was keep fighting the current and praying that someone would rescue her.

Luckily, she came upon an enormous lake freighter carrying iron ore, and its large wake pushed her out from the current and closer to shore. Now she was able to float on her back and kick her way to shore. With the little energy she had left, she rolled over and made it to a swim ladder in front of a cottage. She crawled up the last step and collapsed on the lawn between the river and the cottage. She had traveled almost a mile down river from her home.

Mary never forgot that helpless feeling of being caught in the fast-rushing waters. It was foremost in her mind in Lampedusa when she saw migrants at the docks who were exhausted and often distraught because they had lost a friend or family member during their journey. It was a painful connection for her, but her experience also gave her an extra feeling of empathy for what had become reality for these migrants.

"I need more IVs. Anybody! Please!" she was used to yelling out. "We need to get them hydrated." Migrants rescued at sea are usually dehydrated or suffering from hypothermia, and this is the first step in their recovery.

Dr. Mary, as she had become affectionately known, was never surprised by the condition of the migrants when they arrived for care. It wasn't unusual for her to discover knife or even gunshot wounds they received before leaving their homeland or during their long and often dangerous journeys. Mary could also tell from the scars on their bodies that some of them had sold a kidney to pay for their fare and that of their families.

• • •

During the second year of her work in Lampedusa Dr. Mary had one of her most agonizing experiences at the clinic. She was making her usual rounds, trying to focus her mind on the patients she didn't recognize because there were always so many who were new.

In a corner she noticed that a father, his baby daughter, and his young son were huddled together. They had recently been pulled out of the sea and brought to the clinic. They had boarded an already-overcrowded boat in Libya, which sailed for a day and a half until it sank just a mile off the Lampedusa coast with 200 people on board. Instantly, there was a catastrophic loss of life. But this man, Mohamed, had survived with his two children.

Dr. Mary checked each of them for infectious diseases and dehydration while the man told her more of what happened.

When the boat tipped over, expelling most of the migrants, Mohamed's whole family was cast into the sea. His wife, his two sons and their baby daughter were with him on the boat, but he could not find his wife in the water. His two sons and the baby clung to him, and, floating on his back, he was able to keep his infant daughter on his chest while holding the hands of his two young sons.

Mohamed finally lost control of himself as he spoke, and yet through his sobs, he was able to describe his strength as waning. He knew he would not be able to save everyone and if he didn't make a choice, all of them would perish. He knew his older son was physically better able to hold his own in the water.

"I took one last look at my 7-year-old middle child, Omar," Mohamed whispered, gasping through tears. "I told him I loved him and then shook loose his grip. His last word was 'Papa!' as he floated away and was then swallowed by the sea."

The father told Mary he was able to hold onto his other two children until a short while later when they were rescued by a fishing boat."

There was a devastating silence between them. Mary knew to respect that. It lasted a while until Mary noticed that she too was crying as the father comforted his daughter on his shoulder.

• • •

(Father Soto's Voice)

For the new pope's inaugural trip outside Rome, the Secretary of State, Cardinal Bertone, and I together created something we hoped would be memorable for Francis and for those involved with the crisis in the Mediterranean and in particular on the island of Lampedusa.

After a short flight from Rome to Lampedusa, Francis and his papal entourage boarded an Italian Coast Guard cutter for a tour of the harbor and a brief commemorative ceremony. Cardinal Bertone had called upon his close Italian connections to secure the cutter to ferry Francis, our religious entourage, and a large press corps to the island's docks. I had requested that papal flags be distributed and hung on the fleet of boats that accompanied the Coast Guard cutter into the harbor. With Bertone, we chose the prelates who would accompany the pope for this historic commemorative event.

I also arranged for Francis to celebrate Mass on the island, which would include a procession from the dock to the boat graveyard. Acres of dilapidated vessels were piled in heaps, one upon another—rafts, barges, dinghies, sailboats, dories, old battered yachts, and even vessels resembling not much more than tubs or buckets. They were all mangled together, evoking an almost dystopian image of death and destruction that would soon be seared into the minds of all who saw it.

The high clerics accompanying the pope were dressed in black cassocks with red trim and red zucchettos, the small hats that resemble a beanie. The pope was in his traditional modest white garb that included his soutane (cassock), a white zucchetto, and a small white cape called a mozzetta. Francis wore unfashionable black shoes instead of the red shoes traditionally worn by the popes who preceded him. A modest iron cross hung from his neck. A spot was arranged for Francis to sit on the cutter that gave him an unobstructed view of the island.

As the Coast Guard cutter approached the harbor, it was followed by a flotilla of boats that included fishermen in trawlers and some pleasure crafts and tourist vessels. The fleet of boats on this bright and clear July day displayed banners hailing their "Francesco," while also flying the yellow and white papal flag. All appeared festive, as if they were ready for the pontiff to bless their fleet. Instead, the theme of the day was more solemn and penitential. The Coast Guard vessel cut its engine at sea, and that was the moment I presented the pope with a wreath of flowers that he then dropped into the water from the upper deck, commemorating the thousands of migrants who had drowned in these waters.

On this day the trawlers and their captains were not fishing for hake, red mullet, sardines, or the fast vanishing bluefin tuna. Instead, the workers on these boats were going to participate in an open-air Mass celebrated by Francis. Once the cutter docked and the pope was on shore, he greeted the thousands who had come to see him and hear his message. He smiled and waved to the crowds and when he came upon a mother and her baby he stopped and kissed the baby.

I knew from my many years with my friend, now the pope, how significant this visit was for him. We had spoken many times about the current migrant crisis. I could feel the anguish the pope was experiencing and understood the responsibility he feels to speak out and make the world aware of these horrors at sea and along these borders.

Francis was driven from the dock in an open-top automobile to the large gathering assembled beyond the harbor near the graveyard of dilapidated boats. Many of the migrants who perished during the crossing had paid traffickers to help them to embark from the lawless country of Libya. These vessels should never have been permitted to take to the sea. Their owners knew the conditions aboard were deplorable—they were death traps—yet the boats shamefully left from Libyan shores with their human cargo. The pope mentioned these traffickers in his homily, saying, "They exploit the poverty of others, and they are people who live off the misery of others."

The altar for this Mass was a small reconstructed wooden boat painted the red, white, and green colors of the Italian flag. I insisted that, along with an altar boy, an altar girl assist the pope, who now wore the purple vestments that represent penance.

At the homily, Francis preached to the expansive congregation. "Today no one in our world feels responsible for our brothers and sisters," he said. "We have fallen into the hypocrisy of the priest and the Levite whom Jesus described in the parable of the Good Samaritan: we see our brother half dead at the side of the road and perhaps we say to ourselves, 'poor soul,' and then go our own way. It's not our responsibility, and with that we feel reassured, assuaged. The culture of comfort makes us live in soap bubbles, which, however lovely, are insubstantial: they offer a fleeting and empty illusion which results in indifference to others—indeed, it even leads to the globalization of indifference. . . .We have become used to the suffering of others: it doesn't affect me; it doesn't concern me, it's none of my business!"

Francis continued speaking for another fifteen minutes or so, until he came to what he wanted say about forgiveness: "Lord, in this liturgy, a penitential liturgy, we beg forgiveness for our indifference to so many of our brothers and sisters. Father, we ask your pardon for those who are complacent and closed amid comforts which have deadened their hearts; we beg your forgiveness for those who by their decisions on the global level have created situations that led to these tragedies. Forgive us, Lord."

When the Mass was completed, Francis was taken on a tour of the clinic by its heroic director, Dr. Pietro Bartolo, and his wife, Rita, who was also a medical doctor, specializing in hematology. Many of the recently arrived migrants from Africa were in the clinic, and I expected Francis to engage with them. Instead of something rehearsed, I knew that it was best to let this unfold as naturally as it could.

As Francis made his way through the clinic, his pastoral instincts took over, and he talked animatedly with medical personnel and the migrants being treated. A teenage African boy wearing an Arsenal soccer T-shirt fell into the pope's embrace while he told the story of his family's death at sea. The boy was one of 7,000 orphaned children in Italy who lost their families on their deadly journeys for refuge. A pregnant woman from Syria cried openly, telling the pope about her husband's death, and the destruction of their home by ISIS fighters. Francis's face reflected the pain she was suffering.

CHAPTER SIX

Sister Mary Vernard on the Island and at the Vatican

When Francis finished his tour of Lampedusa, and after his meeting with Dr. Bartolo, followed by time spent thanking the entire medical staff, he then asked if he might have a word with Dr. Mary Vernard. He and Father Soto entered the doctor's small office and closed the door behind them.

Sister Mary leaned forward in her chair as she might in a confessional and asked the pope's permission to tell a story. Francis nod his assent., "Please tell me."

"Holy Father," Mary began, "as a young girl of 12, growing up on the water in Michigan, I almost lost my life in a fast-moving river current. I know how treacherous water can be. When I read about the humanitarian crisis in the Mediterranean, I knew I wanted to be there and provide care.

"For many years, I travelled to Haiti with my mother and sister, both nurses, to work with the impoverished Haitian population. It became my second home. Now this island and clinic are my home.

"Holy Father, help us. Keep us from seeing dead bodies in Lampedusa. Every single body I encounter carries the marks of its long and tragic journey. When despondency threatens to get the best of me, my colleagues, and the people of Lampedusa, help us find the strength to keep going. But this must change."

Suddenly, Dr. Mary was overwhelmed, and she started to weep quietly. Slowly gaining her composure, she begged, "Please, let us organize a way to bring the migrants here ourselves. There must be a better way."

A long silence followed while Pope Francis breathed deeply and looked into Mary's wet eyes with his own, which were now moist as well.

In a hushed and tender voice, he responded, "Sister, I want to share a story with you about St. Francis of Assisi. Riding one day on the plains of Assisi, Francis met a leper whose sores were so loathsome the very sight of them struck Francis with horror. But he dismounted his horse, and as the leper stuck out his hand to receive alms, Francis bestowed him with alms and then kissed the man. After that, Francis often visited hospitals, and served the sick, and sometimes gave his clothes and sometimes his money to the poor.

"Sister Mary, the spiritual battle for Christ begins with mortification and a victory over oneself. You, my daughter, have achieved that. You have provided the lessons of holiness to the migrants, and you have shown the people of Lampedusa how we should treat our neighbor and the stranger. And, like a ripple on the water, the message of your charity and mercy flows now to all corners of the earth. We will win this battle for justice as love will triumph over fear."

Mary cast her eyes down in appreciation for the pope's kind words.

Then Francis changed the tone of their meeting and smiled warmly.

"Doctor, I want to tell you a secret," he said, brightening his smile even more. "I have spies in the Vatican. Yes! And my spies tell me that your tireless work has negatively affected your health. They also tell me they are concerned about the stress you and others are under. I know firsthand how stress can overwhelm us, as I have at different times been overwhelmed with grief and difficult situations. You know, Sister, in the Bible, we are taught to rest one of every seven days. I want you to rest. For the moment this is how I will answer your plea. I will be helpful to you by sending some medical professionals to assist in the noble and important work being done here. I also want you to consider another idea I have.

"There is a vacancy in the Vatican Physician's office. I am not asking you to surrender your work with the migrants, but perhaps for just one month, a change of pace would serve you well and allow you to recoup some of your health. Would you be willing to consider coming to the Vatican for just a little while to work with me and others? No need to answer now. We want you to come back to your work on the island. But we want you rested, refreshed, and filled with the Holy Spirit. We also want you as a witness to tell the world what you are seeing and doing in Lampedusa."

Sister Mary could hardly believe what she had just heard.

The Holy Father then bowed his head in prayer and reached out for the hands of Father Soto and Sister Mary.

"Dear Jesus,

Our journey through life is long and hard. We cannot make this trip alone; we must walk together on the journey.

You promised to send us a helper, your Spirit.

Help us to see your Spirit in those you send to journey with us.

In the refugee family seeking safety from violence,

Let us see your Spirit.

In the migrant worker bringing food to our tables,

Let us see your Spirit."

Dr. Mary and Father Soto knew to join in with the chorus.

"In the asylum-seeker, seeking justice for himself and his family,
Let us see your Spirit.
In the unaccompanied child, traveling in a dangerous world,
Let us see your Spirit.
Teach us to recognize as we walk with each other, You are present.
Teach us to not only welcome the stranger in our midst but the gifts they bring as well: the invitation to conversion, communion, and solidarity.
This is the help you have sent: we are not alone.
We are together on the journey, and for this we give you thanks. Amen."

Throughout the prayer, Dr. Mary couldn't stop herself from pondering the extraordinary offer the Holy Father had made for her to work in the Vatican.

In any case, she thought to herself, *I cannot say no to the pope.*

• • •

Francis did as he promised and sent help to Lampedusa. Father Soto, having heard this, took the initiative, did an assessment of what the clinic needed, and recommended to the pope that first they have medical supplies shipped to the island. Soto also recommended that three medical doctors, with experience working with immigrants through their work with Catholic

Charities, be sent to join the staff of the six doctors who were already a part of the clinic.

Sister Mary was also impressed when the other part of the pope's promise was acted upon, and she found herself at the Vatican, where her responsibilities were two-fold. First, she was part of a team of doctors who looked after the pope's health needs and attended to others in the Vatican community. The second part was for her to meet with print and TV reporters and tell them her stories about the immigrants she had met and treated on Lampedusa.

Soon after Sister Mary arrived at the Vatican, she was shown to a simple yet charming apartment on Via Candia near the pope's residence and the Vatican museum. This was her first time in Italy, and she was excited to be there. She was looking forward to walking through the city's many neighborhoods and to exploring the renowned Vatican museum, Saint Peter's Basilica, the Sistine Chapel, and the remnants of ancient Rome. Used to twelve-hour shifts on the island, Dr. Mary was thrilled when her workday ended after eight hours so she could see the city.

Yet for all her excitement about this new experience, in this new place, Mary was also nervous about her new job. She was in awe of the Holy Father, and she worried she was not up to what the pope was asking of her.

Dr. Mary had read about a previous physician to popes, Renato Buzzonetti. He began in the Vatican medical service in 1974 and worked closely with four popes—Pope Paul IV, Pope John Paul I, Pope John Paul II, and Pope Benedict XVI. He was the first doctor to examine John Paul II after he was shot by Ali Ağca in May 1981. And one year later, in Fatima, Dr. Buzzonetti administered the initial first aid after John Paul II was stabbed by the ultra-conservative Spanish priest Juan Fernandez Krohn.

Popes under Buzzonetti's charge were said to have received

excellent care. Dr. Mary knew she has a high standard to meet. This job had always entailed a heavy responsibility. She hoped that, once she became more engaged in her practice, the tension of her new position would lessen. Dr. Mary reasoned that, like an actor on stage or a soccer player on the pitch, the focus of doing her job would overcome the stress of being in the limelight.

Not long after Sister Mary began her work at the Vatican, Father Soto gently encouraged her to write a short book about her work with the migrants who had come to the island. He told her it would be good therapy for her to put her experiences on paper and then to speak about them. This book would also help fulfill the part of her job that involved spreading the stories of the migrant crisis.

Dr. Mary eventually came to enjoy talking about her medical care on Lampedusa on Catholic radio and television broadcasts and to writers at the highly regarded newspaper the *National Catholic Reporter*. The more she told her story on air and in the press, the more she warmed to the idea of a book. She welcomed the guidance of the Vatican communication center and of Father Soto, who had extensive writing and editing experience.

Mary opened her book by writing about her near loss of life in the river at the age of 12. From there, she wrote about her experiences in Haiti. She spent three hours each day reaching out to Spanish radio and TV in Latin America. Reporters and TV commentators in the United States were also receptive to what she had to say and were eager to elevate her voice. President Trump's poisonous rhetoric and bigoted policies on the U.S. border have created space for alternative views.

In Europe, the election of anti-migrant leaders in Hungry, Austria, Italy, and Poland strongly suggests that a growing movement on the continent's right is threatening democracies in other countries too. Dr. Mary's voice is becoming increasingly important.

She devoted the rest of the book to the stories of migrant families she has met in her three years on Lampedusa. When she finished the last page, she was confident she had done what Pope Francis and the others at the Vatican asked her to do.

Her timely book, *When Mercy Seasons Justice*, became an international success. She captured the desperation, pain, and sometimes even joy of the migrants and their families. In addition, she documented the shame of those who turned their backs on them. The book is so compelling and heartrending, it is hard to imagine anyone not reading it entirely in one sitting. *When Mercy Seasons Justice* speaks to mercy and justice—and the world community can use more of each.

• • •

In April of 2018, at a small neighborhood café on the via Ronaldo, Father Juan Soto and Dr. Mary meet for dinner. For the past four years, during the month each year that Mary spends at the Vatican on a break from her work in Lampedusa, they have worked closely to craft a message that can reach the Catholic world and beyond.

They each have a glass of Brunello on this lovely evening, where a shaft of moonlight falls across a corner of their table in the courtyard. Over a seafood salad and a pasta dish, they talk about their wonder at living and working at the Vatican.

"I thought I lived in the smallest place in the world, but the Vatican tops it all," says Mary.

With less than a thousand residents, the Vatican is the smallest country in the world. A walled fortification, the Vatican is roughly a hundred acres—the size of a small Iowa farm.

Mary jokes, "It would take about an hour to walk the circumference of my new nation."

The Vatican may be small, but inside this city-state are significant holy places and stunning works of art, such as Michelangelo's magnificent paintings on the ceiling of the Sistine Chapel, which includes the powerful panel entitled "God Creating the Sun and the Moon."

The Vatican is also the residence of the leader of more than a billion Catholics. Incomparable ecclesiastical art adorns these ancient walls and ceilings. The movement of prelates and other men of the cloth is a reminder of the holiness and power that mingle among the greatest works of art—St. Peter's Basilica, the Sistine Chapel, works by Michelangelo, Botticelli, and Perugino.

All this shines a light on the gross inequality of women still being treated as second-class citizens in Christ's church. The Vatican Museum and the Vatican Library, depositories of histories and artifacts, also contain the stories of how the history of women has been twisted and falsified. A stained-glass ceiling was even created to keep women "in their place."

During dinner, Mary and Juan Soto slip cautiously into a discussion of women's issues and the unaccountable ways bishops have shielded themselves from responsibility in the sexual abuse crisis. The evening's joy is tempered by a sadness brought on by these present calamities.

Father Soto says he has spent a good part of this day briefing Francis on the Study Commission on the Women's Diaconate. "I am afraid that they will not be able to agree," he says referring to the commission that Francis created to study the question of whether women could become deacons in the Catholic Church.

"Why not?" Mary asks, before answering her own next question. "Were the appointments to the commission made with this outcome in mind?"

Mary raises her eyebrows and widens her eyes to let Father Soto know she understands that this is likely what is going on. Nuns as well as activist Catholic women are watching this issue very closely and are skeptical about the impartiality of those who have been appointed to the commission. The women are fed up with their church keeping women "in their place."

Soto is taken aback by Mary's Machiavellian assertion. He thinks of Dr. Mary as a smart and compassionate woman, with the toughness to do very emotionally difficult work. This is the first time he has seen this side of her. He was expecting to have a dinner conversation about medicine, but her inquiries make it clear to him that she wants to dissect and diagnose the politics of this issue.

"Sister, there is some truth to what I think you are alleging," he says. "The commission was not assembled in order to deadlock on a resolution of the question. But the pope does believe that, in order to make women eligible to become deacons under the sacrament of Holy Orders, it is important to hear the voices of traditional conservatives on the commission."

"Well," Mary says, in a slightly annoyed tone. "Was that strategy a mistake? It looks to many of us as if the commission is hopelessly at a stalemate." She pauses a moment before continuing. "Look, as a woman I have experienced the sexist ways of male physicians, of predatory professors, and of verbal assaults in the form of sexual comments, teases, and insults my entire adult life. I do not live in a bubble! I am tired of patriarchal old men telling me and my fellow sisters where our place is. Why aren't there more Cardinal Tobins to speak out on this injustice and fairness issue? If the Church lacks moral authority on the issue of gender, how in God's name does it expect its followers to believe its work on the sexual abuse issues that it has made a mess of?"

Soto is more than surprised by the boldness of her speech. In response, he asks a simple question. "How do we make this work?"

He should not have been surprised that Mary has an answer. "Have two members retire from the commission," she says. "Then have Francis fill those vacancies, while at the same time expanding the number of slots on the commission. Fill them with allies, not foes. And then have a vote to recommend to Francis the answer to the question.

"Even on the grounds of the conservative traditionalist, the arguments are moving in favor of women being included. Relatively newer documents like the Dead Sea scrolls speak to this issue. After all, it was Saint Paul in Romans 16 who mentions Phoebe, 'a deacon of the church at Cenchrea.' There have been many eloquent theologians who have spoken on this, including Sister Joan Chittister. And what in heaven's name is wrong with the Church trying something new and different? Do you think for one moment that, if the Church had women priests and bishops, the sexual abuse crisis would not have been handled differently? There is no question in my mind that it would not have been tolerated."

Mary sees that Father Soto is straining under her interrogation, but she has more to say. "There is an old Nike ad with a tagline, 'Just do it!' Father, I would strategically promote people who share our view. Give them the opportunity to express themselves to Francis, particularly those whom the pope quietly admires. Has the pope read the letter from the late Cardinal Carlo Martini, that was released after his death in 2012? That letter provides a path for Francis to follow. Do you know of this letter, Father?"

"Yes, I know of it," he says, well aware that it is better for him not to reply to anything else she says.

They each see that the evening has become more contentious than they wanted. They turn back to more mundane issues.

This evening is not for wallowing in contention or sadness, even though the heaviness of the issues is buried within each of them and quietly understood by the other. They refuse to be smothered by it and seek instead to wring out the joys of life that are within their reach.

A good place on this moonlit evening is with the glass of Brunello and each other's company.

• • •

Pope Francis and Dr. Mary enjoy each other's company. Francis had studied chemistry earlier in his life and has always been interested in the healing sciences, even though he has taken the route of a practitioner of healing souls.

The more Mary gets to know the pope as a person, the more fascinated she is by him. Each sees the goodness in the other. Over the years, as their relationship developed, Francis offered Mary a sabbatical to return for two months instead of one month so she could broaden her outreach to the media about the growing immigration crisis. Her time away from the island has also been good for her mental health.

In January 2018, Francis invited Dr. Mary and the other Vatican doctors to his "papal apartment" to talk about the results of the physical examination and tests they had performed a week earlier. Walking from her own apartment on via Candia, Mary is preoccupied with how she and the others will break this news to the pope. Her mind is entirely focused on this one important task.

She is oblivious to the hawkers pitching St. John Paul II mini statues, a favorite of tourists. A motorbike swerves to avoid hitting her as she enters the busy street. Her mind is preoccupied, and she is unaware that at this moment the motor traffic has the right of way. It's almost a minor miracle that she survives the short walk to the pope's apostolic apartment.

As Mary enters the main gate, she nods to the Swiss Guards, with whom she has developed a casual familiarity. The guards play a ceremonial role, but they are also a security detail, and they are one of the oldest military units in the world. At the Vatican, they are responsible for the pope's safety, the safety of those working in Vatican City, and the security of the artwork and the Apostolic Palace.

The Swiss Guards are dressed in uniforms that go back many centuries. Broad stripes of red, blue, and yellow run north and south on their waist shirts, pantaloons, and knee stockings. The sleeves are puffed, as are the baggy pantaloons. Mary can't help but think that their outfits look "puffy." They remind Mary of the costumes she has seen at Italian Renaissance festivals. But today not even that simple association interrupts her absolute focus on delivering her message to Francis.

Over the last six months, the physicians have been watching the pope's health steadily decline. A recent exam shows that Francis has put on weight, and that has led the medical staff to tell Francis he needs to change his diet. They were kind yet firm with him, limiting the number of times he could eat his favorites, pasta or pizza, to just twice a week, rather than his daily helping. That may have been a good step toward controlling the pope's weight, but recently he has become fatigued more easily.

Dr. Mary remembers watching the television news and seeing the new pope on the balcony overlooking the plaza filled with 200,000 rain-soaked onlookers who were also curious about the man who would take the name Francis. She recalls even then that Francis looked exhausted, with his mouth agape as if he were laboring for his next breath. Mary later learned that when

Francis was 19 years of age, a lung problem had required that doctors remove part of one lung, and that was followed by a painful thirty days of hospitalization.

The pope keeps a hectic schedule at the Vatican and in his international travels. His days are filled by meeting with his councils, greeting dignitaries, visiting the poor and working-class neighborhoods in Rome, spending a good deal of time writing, and devoting many hours to prayer and meditation. At home in the Vatican, he wakes up at 4:00 a.m. and is in bed between 9:00 and 10:00 p.m. When he is travelling, his days are different.

For the first five years of his papacy, Francis travelled to forty-three countries on five continents, and he made twenty-two separate trips within Italy. His work intervening in conflicts between countries had led to a rapprochement between the United States and Cuba, and between North and South Korea. He also helped to end the war in Colombia, and he had held talks on the situation in Sudan.

Now, at age 81, he has slowed down his schedule considerably. But to stay connected, he has adapted to some new technologies. One of Francis's gifts has always been his curiosity about communication tools. He was introduced to Twitter around 2013, soon after becoming pope, and his posts have a following in the millions. He also is on Instagram, and he texts and uses email. Of course, with an audience of that size, Frances is aided in his social media outreach by his staff of media experts. All this enables him to stay engaged and accessible to his followers.

When Dr. Mary is just outside the papal apartments, she presents her credentials and then is greeted by Cardinal Georg Ganswein, Prefect of the Papal Household, who ushers her upstairs to the apartment where two other doctors are seated and waiting for Francis.

At the same time, Father Soto and Francis walk slowly from the pope's more modest living quarters at the guesthouse, Santa Marta, to the traditional residence in the Apostolic Palace that he now uses only for meetings and gatherings. Father Soto recalls the look of horror on Francis's face when they first toured the apartment in the Apostolic Palace. It was one room leading to another and all stuffed with heavy furniture. Francis was overwhelmed with its opulence and materialism. He knew then that he could not live there and decided instead to use it only for meetings.

The pope enters with a warm smile on his face. Francis knows the news from his doctors is not going to be good. He knows his own body, and after 80-plus years, he can feel it is breaking down. He also knows his energy level has plummeted, alarmingly so, recently. He needs their medical information and opinions so he can plan for the end of his temporal life.

Francis sets them all at ease. "Thank you for coming. It is always good to see my friends. Let us have a frank conversation about the test results." He pauses, then softly adds, "I know that I am dying."

With humor he looks skyward while pointing his index finger toward heaven and says while laughing, "But not today, inshallah."

This eases the tension in the room and signals to the doctors that Francis is ready for the news.

Each doctor takes a turn summarizing the symptoms Francis is experiencing, such as shortness of breath, fatigue, dizziness, chest pains, rapid or irregular heartbeat.

As Father Soto listens to this recitation, he recalls the words of the renowned writer and theologian Frederick Buechner, who wrote that aging is like "living in a house that is in need of increasing repairs . . . , cracked and dusty, the windows are hard to see through, and there is a lot of creaking and groaning in bad weather."

Soto senses the beginning of the end. He knows that the pope's declining health and probable death are not too far off. He also understands that conservatives in the Church are out to damage the pope's papacy by making his remaining time stressful. But even at this dark moment, Soto also loves and admires the strength in Francis that allows him to make light of his mortality with his "inshallah" comment.

While the discussion between Francis and the doctors continues, Soto's attention drifts into a fond memory of an event that had occurred decades ago on a very cold winter July day on the street above a subway stop in Buenos Aires. Father Soto and Bishop Bergoglio were returning from a visit to one of the city's working-class parishes. As they ascended by staircase to the street level, they were greeted by a beggar. Bishop Bergoglio stopped in his tracks to behold this middle-aged man, slight of build, without a coat and in bare feet.

The Bishop removed his coat, approached the beggar and draped the coat over his shoulders. Then looking down at the beggar's soiled and red bare feet, he asked, "Where are your shoes?"

"I have no shoes, Padre."

The Bishop looked down at his own shoes and then at Father Soto's, sizing up the situation. Soto knew what his Bishop was signaling and could see that he was a better fit. He bent down, removed his shoes and socks and gave them to the beggar. The Bishop smiled at his aide and dear friend, nodding his approval and joy at the exchange. Then Bergoglio embraced the beggar and whispered something in his ear before handing him a few pesos.

Next, Bergoglio hailed a cab. Inside the cab, Father Soto asked, "Bishop, where are we going?"

His friend turned and with a smile, said, "Where else? The shoe store!"

After Francis hears all the doctors' diagnoses, he asks them,

"Could my irregular heartbeat be caused by my drinking maté? And might my heart be weakened by the lung problems of my youth?"

Mary answers the pope. "Your Holiness, your tests indicate that you may have suffered one or a series of silent heart attacks that have damaged your heart and affected its ability to pump blood. Your abnormal heart rhythms, called arrhythmia, may be accentuated by the drinking of maté, but that may not be the only reason for their irregularity. When did you start drinking maté?"

Francis tells her he had been introduced to it decades ago, and he was told it contained properties that are healthy and promote good health. It is a smoky green tea with a high caffeine rating, and he drinks it every morning from a gourd, through a straw.

"The Jesuits, going back centuries, encouraged the native Guarani people to drink their maté to combat the destructiveness of alcoholism," Francis explains. "The Jesuits were the protectors of the Guarani who were often abused and taken advantage of by the colonists."

Mary absorbs this information and remembers that he had also asked if there were consequences from the partial removal of his lung some sixty years ago.

"Pope Francis," she says compassionately, "though we cannot rule out the possibility that your lung condition has weakened your heart, we rather doubt it, given that you have functioned within a very good range of health in the decades since its removal. What has more likely happened is that your heart chambers have over your life started to harden. Your heart muscles are struggling to pump the blood that is necessary for your body to work."

Mary hands Frances a written report that summarizes his test results, as well as the conclusions that she and the other doctors have reached.

Francis has congestive heart failure that will limit his life, particularly his ability to travel and work the long days he has become accustomed to as pope.

Francis scans the report and asks, "And my mind, my ability to think and reason and speak?" All three doctors agree that those functions should remain stable and not be affected.

The pope nods with relief. He knows he is entering the final chapter of his life. He inwardly prays that he will be given the strength to use his remaining time well.

Dr. Mary's demeanor remains professional in her discussion with Francis, but deep down she feels sorrow and pain for the pope. Francis is courageous, and he will need that courage to confront those in the Church who want to destroy him and his legacy.

Mary loves Francis's humanity. She sees Christ in him, as mercy is at the pope's core. It is the quality of his mercy that bonds them together.

• • •

By early April 2018, stories about the separation of migrant family members were dominating the world press, and Pope Francis was troubled by what he was reading and hearing.

"Juan," he said to Father Soto, "tell me what you know about migrant children being separated from their parents or guardian at the Mexican/U.S. border facilities."

Soto exhaled, his face overcome with concern and pain. Ever present in his mind are the *desaparecidos,* those who had been "disappeared" during the Dirty War that raged through Argentina from 1976 to 1983.

"The media is reporting that the Trump Administration policies have led to thousands of migrant family members being separated from one other. The Trump government, unbelievably, has not been keeping records of either the whereabouts of the children or their families. And this bungled process has turned into a humanitarian crisis that has captured the world's attention. The nightmare of losing your child is universal and heart-wrenching, and the thought that the U.S. government would instigate this is devastating. Our cardinals and bishops in the region are contacting their elected representatives and demanding investigations and accountability."

Father Soto found himself unable to continue for a moment, until he finally said, "It's outrageous for them to split families."

With a puzzled look Francis asked Soto to walk him through how these separations occur."

Soto paused to organize his thoughts. "After the migrants have walked the thousand-plus miles to the U.S. border—a trip that sometimes takes them a month—they either surrender at the border and ask for asylum or are apprehended and brought to the central detention and processing center. President Trump's new immigration policy is called 'Zero Tolerance,' and it is void of mercy."

Soto continued: "The adults are held in federal jails and then prosecuted. Their children are then put under the supervision of the Department of Health and Human Services. But what is happening to the children is neither healthy nor humane. Making matters worse, many children are separated again, this time from their siblings, and sent to foster homes and institutions located in the United States.

"There are rumors that these separations have been going on for the past year and that now upwards of 5,000 children, many very young, ages 5 through 9, have been taken from their families. A large number of teens are also placed in group homes without their parents' knowledge of their whereabouts.

"The courts in the United States have ordered the separations stopped, and they're demanding the reuniting of families."

"Juan," Francis said. "I have heard these children are crammed together in large caged enclosures. Is that so?"

"According to photos and testimony by staff in the facilities, I'm afraid so."

Francis pondered what he had just heard. "These injustices are counter to not only international law but also the core of our Catholic faith. Juan, I want you to make a visit to the border and tell me what you see. Ask Bishop Mark Seitz to help you plan your trip. You may also want to call upon my friend Cardinal Retes in Mexico City. Get his take on the situation. Maybe the nun from McAllen, Texas, who runs the Humanitarian Respite Center can help you enter the detention center there. What is her name?"

"Sister Norma." Soto said.

"Yes, beautiful heart and warm smile. Maybe she can accompany you on your visit."

Father Soto responded carefully. "My guess is that she is overwhelmed with the flood of refugees at the border. Even so, I will definitely visit with her at the center and get her thoughts on the crisis. But perhaps Sister Mary, with her refugee experience and medical knowledge, can accompany me. We could then report our findings to you and, with your approval, to the media. Sister Mary's work with refugees in Lampedusa over the years has caused her to have quite a list of inquisitive and helpful journalists."

"That is an excellent idea," Pope Francis said. "I know I will benefit from Sister Mary's observations along with yours."

• • •

(Father Soto's voice)

After a long day in the air, we grab a cab at the McAllen airport and go directly to the hotel located near the Humanitarian Respite Center and Sacred Heart parish. In the morning, Sister Mary and I meet for breakfast at the hotel with Sister Norma and Delores Becerra, a clinical psychiatrist and professor at Stanford University.

Entering the hotel coffee shop, Sister Norma, upon recognizing us, breaks into a wide-open smile and with her arms extended exclaims joyfully, "*Hola! Buenos dias!* You have come at a very busy and demanding time, but we are excited to receive you and have prepared two days of visits and meetings."

Turning to Dr. Becerra, Sister Norma introduces her to us and then adds, "Today after our talk at breakfast we will visit the Border Patrol Processing and Detention Center and afterwards the Respite Center at Sacred Heart Parish. Then tomorrow you will go to Brownsville, about an hour's drive south, to visit Casa Padre, the boys' migrant facility that has 1,500 boys, ages 10 to 17.

"We are fortunate to have Dr. Becerra with us," a smiling Sister Norma says. "Let's take advantage of her presence and talk about these facilities and the effects on children who are separated from their caregivers."

After we order from the menu, I ask Dr. Becerra what she thinks about the separation of children from their caregivers.

"Father Soto and Sister Mary, it is an honor to meet both of you. Sister, I have read your inspiring book and know from your work in both Haiti and Lampedusa that you have personally experienced the pain of those separated from their loved ones and family members. I thank you for your devotion to those you serve. And Father Soto, I am an admirer of Pope Francis—so it is truly an honor to speak to you both about the crisis at our border.

"First, trauma has negative effects on children's neurological and emotional development. The trauma has serious repercussions on the brain. Being taken from their caregivers is the most stressful thing a young child can experience. It works like this.

"A young and vulnerable brain that is still developing and is exposed to traumatic stress will in response secrete hormones that will alter brain structure and brain function. The hormones are called cortisol and can be toxic to the developing brain cells in the area of the brain where you store memory and memory is retrieved. These brain changes due to high cortisol are responsible for anxiety, depression, and post-traumatic stress disorder (PTSD) that are seen in survivors of abuse and trauma. Sister Mary, you have written about this in your book regarding the African and Mideastern migrants that you have treated on Lampedusa, so you know of the irretrievable damage that is done."

I listen carefully as these accomplished and caring women engage in a back and forth about their experiences with children who have been separated from their family members, and I take notes for our report to the pope.

The four of us drive directly from the hotel coffee shop to the nearby Border Patrol Processing and Detention Center. As we approach the center, hundreds of women are demonstrating with signs that read, *Where are my Children!* and *Trump Has Stolen My Child!* They carry large photos of their children. The women wear white wrap around head coverings with their children's names written on them, emulating the Mothers of the Plaza De Mayo in Buenos Aires.

My thoughts flash back to the 1990s and my office in the Curia Building on the Plaza de Mayo. Each Thursday I went to my window and watched the mothers of the *desaparecidos,* the disappeared, congregate with their signs and photos and march to the other side of the Plaza to the presidential palace demanding an accountability and release of their children. Thirty thousand disappeared and were tortured and murdered by the military junta in power. These *desaparecidos* were labeled subversives. They were social activists, student organizers, union workers, religious leaders, academics—the kind of people that today Trump has demonized in the United States.

Bishop Bergoglio's office was adjacent to mine, and sometimes together we would stand at the window with sorrow in our hearts watching these brave *madras et las abuelas.* Half of our working day was spent inquiring, rescuing, or hiding those who were pursued by the generals and their minions in their Dirty War. Now as we prepare to enter the center at the Mexican/U.S. border, I can feel their pain.

The center and detention areas are now a mass of humanity, as those seeking asylum and refuge are physically overwhelming the U.S. facilities. Under the *Flores* court decision, clinicians like Dr. Becerra and Dr. Mary are allowed inside, and Sister Norma has secured entry for herself and me.

All of us are taken aback by how freezing cold it is inside the building. Some of the migrants who have worked in meat processing plants call the center the *hielera,* the ice box.

Large fenced cages are erected throughout the open areas housing the refugees. The gray of the fencing and cement floor match the mood of the incarcerated. The migrants are packed into the cages like prisoners. The staff and migrants have labeled the caged area "the dog pound." Mats cover the cement floor and there is no hint of joy or redemption within these walls.

Most migrants are still in their filthy, sweaty clothes and wear dazed and repressed expressions on their faces. Having come so far, they look as if every ounce of hope has been stolen from them. Many of the guards and staff seem indifferent to the migrants' plight, infected by a similar despair.

I am wearing my Roman collar. As I walk among those who are caged, a 12-year-old boy draws my attention by pleading, "Pray for me, Father. Can you help me find parents and little brother?" I stop and we talk through the steel fencing as if he is still in Mexico and I am in the United States, a kind of Trump wall within these walls.

"Father, I am here for three days, I want my family. Please help!"

His name is Roberto Guzman, and he and his family walked with a small caravan from San Salvador. I promise that I will try to find his other family members. Roberto and I lace our fingers through the openings in the fence, and we recite the Hail Mary asking Our Lady for help. "Roberto, I will go and check and get back to you before I leave today." At this welcome news he forces a smile as tears fall gently from his weary yet beautiful eyes.

I spot Sister Mary. I can tell right off that she is saddened but not surprised by the state of depression that pervades the center. The stress level is very high. How could it not be? Families are dispossessed, homeless, and now separated. Add exhaustion and fright about their futures, and the result is a poisonous atmosphere of doom.

"Father, I just spoke with a Guatemalan mother who walked here with her 5-year-old daughter. While we were talking the girl clung to her mother, wrapping herself securely around her mother's body as though at any minute now they could be separated. The mother confided to me that, on their journey, she was abducted by gangs who sexually violated her and ransomed her back to her relatives. Her daughter witnessed the abduction and the assault. Of course, now the mother hears all the stories of separation and is fearful they will be victims once again. She has also lost a son to Guatemalan gang violence."

Sister Mary and I walk with Sister Norma to the administrative office inside the processing center, and Sister Norma introduces us to the deputy administrator whom she has worked with over the years. Sister Mary and I plead the cases for Roberto Guzman and the Guatemalan mother. The administrator checks to see if Roberto Guzman's family are somewhere in the building.

They are, and they are scheduled to leave to a family center near Dilley, Texas, tomorrow. She assures us that she will make sure that Roberto is with them and that the Guatemalan woman and her daughter will remain together and also taken to Dilley. She explains to us that Dilley is the immigration service's best-run family center.

We thank the deputy administrator, and as we leave the center we return to the mother and daughter and then Roberto to share with them the good news. Sister Mary and I take some solace in these individual unifications because we both know from our years of work that many more families will be separated and their lives irreparably damaged.

We arrive at the Humanitarian Respite Center on the grounds of Sacred Heart Parish. The contrast from where we just were could not be more stark. The detention center was gray and devoid of color, but the respite center is filled with the gay colors of the children's rooms and the red, blues, greens, and yellows of the toys that are scattered about. The children's rooms are walled with bookcases holding colorful books and toys. Light pours in from windows and skylights and also from lighting fixtures in the shape of a dancing ballerina and a soccer player kicking a ball.

When the exhausted migrants first enter the respite center, those working there pause and turn to greet the weary travelers and cheer their arrival. No one is left to wonder, "What is next?"

or "How long will I be here?" Each migrant or family unit is assigned a chaperone, who answers their questions and guides them through the transition process while they are here.

We are taken to the used clothing department inside the center and watch as the new arrivals are issued clean and serviceable clothing. Unlike the detention center, each person is given a bag of toiletries—soap, toothbrush, and toothpaste. A doctor or nurse is always available for those with health needs. The migrants are fed from the refectory, a name taken from the Latin for *refiners,* "to remake or restore," via the Late Latin *refectorium,* which means "a place one goes to be restored." Those serving the food are upbeat parishioners who have come to cook and serve—many of whom have once been migrants themselves. Intermittently, festive music plays throughout the center to lighten the mood.

The city of McAllen has constructed long communal tents with air-conditioning next to the center where the families sleep. Private outdoor shower and bathroom facilities are located next to the tented area. Adjacent to the Center is Sacred Heart Church, a place for meditation and prayer.

• • •

Father Soto's Notes of His Tour of Casa Padre
In the morning, Sister Mary, Dr. Becerra, and I are driven to Casa Padre, an old Walmart that was converted into a massive shelter/detention center a year ago in March 2017. It was built to hold a thousand boys between the ages 10 and 17, but it is bulging with 1,500 mostly unaccompanied boys who have made their way here from the Northern Triangle countries. The facility is privately owned and operated by a nonprofit company,

although the family that owns it pays themselves a handsome compensation.

Casa Padre employs hundreds of trained staff, including cooks, teachers, counselors, attendants, guards, maintenance workers, and medical professionals. The cost for detaining a single migrant in a facility like Casa Padre is an astounding $273,000 per year.

The facility is clean, and each child has a bed with proper bedding. A school, a library, and recreation facilities keep the children occupied. Medical personnel work onsite in a sanitized environment. The children get three meals a day, although they complain about the quality and blandness of the food.

Even though the infrastructure is well-groomed, a sense of loneliness permeates the building. Internment at Casa Padre can range from weeks to months, and reconnecting the boys with their families or guardians can take that same amount of time. As Drs. Mary and Becerra have outlined for us, these separations for the children are stressful, leading to serious mental health problems that will follow them for the length of their lives. Casa Padre has strict institutional rules, including not allowing the children off the property, which makes their confinement feel like a detention. There is no freedom and family at Casa Padre.

BOOK THREE

THE VATICAN

CHAPTER SEVEN

Scandal—Catholics Abused—Church Besieged

Not long after Francis is given his medical prognosis, two major scandals—one in Chile and the other in Pennsylvania—threaten to further damage the Church. These two follow in the wake of a prominent scandal in Australia, in which government authorities charged the country's cardinal, George Pell, with a history of "sexual offenses." In addition, Ireland has recently been racked by massive sexual abuse scandals involving priests and other religious members of the Church. Particularly disgusting is the systematic sexual abuse in Ireland's Roman Catholic–run childcare system in the Reformatory and Industrial Schools.

The reforms of Vatican II, followed up more recently by ones Francis has already put in place, will now be lost unless the pope is seen as acting decisively. The scandals involve predator priests and their cover-ups by bishops, cardinals, and yes, even popes. The Catholic Church is in a crisis of its own making. The distinguished American Jesuit Tom Reese used the words "awful, disgusting, horrifying, sickening" to describe how Catholics are feeling as they try to make sense of what is happening in their church.

Chile is one of Latin America's most staunchly Catholic countries. The Church's establishment failed for years to act on the sexual abuse charges against Father Fernando Karadima, a prominent priest who catered to Santiago's wealthy conservative classes. On a trip to Chile in January 2018, Pope Francis refused to meet with Karadima's victims and dismissed allegations of inaction by the bishops as "slander," even though as early as 2011, the Vatican had found Karadima guilty of these offenses. It was a dark mark on the papacy of Francis.

A justified uproar followed the pope's apparent indifference to accountability for these crimes as well as his public insensitivity to the victims. To his credit, Francis reassessed and acted. After long discussions with Father Soto, Francis asked two Vatican investigators to seek the truth, and they produced a damning report that demonstrated the systematic concealment of Father Karadima's sexual abuse by the Catholic hierarchy in Chile.

Francis's response was strong. He apologized for his "grave error," and he summoned all thirty-four Chilean bishops to the Vatican for meetings. Even before that, he met in April with Juan Carlos Cruz, a victim of Father Karadima. Francis spent a good part of his week with Juan Carlos Cruz and offered a deep personal apology.

In Francis's meetings with the Chilean bishops, they all offered letters of resignation, and he accepted some of them. The Chilean hierarchy of the Church had been caught red-handed, hiding their sins from the pope and then fabricating Karadima's innocence. Francis's quick turnaround demonstrated his commitment to righteousness and now put him squarely in the lead of reformation within the Church's hierarchy.

As Francis seemed to settle the controversies in his native South America, the Church was rocked by a devastating report from a Pennsylvania grand jury. The report found that more than 1,000 children had been abused by hundreds of priests over many decades while bishops covered up the crimes. In response, Francis wrote, "The abuses described in the report are criminal and morally reprehensible. We acknowledge as an ecclesiastical community that we did not act in a timely manner realizing the magnitude and gravity of the damage done to so many lives. We showed no care for the little ones; we abandoned them."

Father Soto watches as this problem is unfolding for Francis and the Church—namely that neither the pope nor the Vatican offers any concrete measures to identify or punish the bishops involved in these abuses or their coverups. Soto keeps hearing and reading that the Church faithful are waiting for more. An expression of sorrow, as sincere as it may be, is not a real plan to deal with the massive cover-up of egregious abusive behavior. The U.S. Conference of Catholic Bishops expresses shame and remorse and acknowledges that much of the blame rests on the shoulders of the bishops. The bishops promise to bring about changes.

In Ireland, the Catholic Church is dying. Once the rock of Peter, a place where the Church had enormous support, where a vast majority of Catholics attended weekly Mass, it has, according to an article published around this time in the *Irish Times*, become a shell of itself. The article received a great deal of attention by showing that weekly Mass attendance levels in Dublin are currently at 20 to 22 percent of the population and are as low as 2 to 3 percent in some working-class parishes. Fewer seminarians are training to become priests. In 1990, more than 500 were in training at the national seminary, but that number is less than eighty today. The majority of priests currently in service are over the age of 60.

That is the situation Francis faced when he made a historic visit to Ireland in August 2018 for the World Meeting of Families. While the pope was in Dublin, former Vatican ambassador to Washington, D.C., Archbishop Carlo Maria Vigano dropped a bombshell by calling on Francis to resign. Vigano said he had told Francis about the allegations of sexual abuse against American Cardinal Theodore McCarrick five years earlier, but the pontiff had done nothing about it. Vigano released an eleven-page letter in which he wrote: "He (Pope Francis) knew from at least June 23, 2013, that McCarrick was a serial predator."

On the plane home from Ireland, the pope faced the press, but despite the uproar would not address the specifics of Cardinal Vigano's allegations.

In the United States, there were calls for an overhaul of Church leadership in the places where the abuses took place. Theologians and lay leaders also called for mass resignations of U.S. bishops. More than 3,000 theologians, lay leaders, and educators signed a letter calling for actions similar to what had been done in Chile. Their statement read, "We are brought to our knees in revulsion and shame by the abominations that these priests committed against innocent children. We are sickened in equal measure by the conspiracy of silence by bishops who exploited victims' wounds as collateral in self-protection and preservation of power. It was the complicity of the powerful that allowed this radical evil to flourish with impunity."

Other reformers in the Church are seeking to remedy not just the problem but the very structure within the Church that leads to it. Much of this discussion centers upon the subject of "clericalism."

Francis had spoken to this earlier in his papacy, and, when he did, the old boys' network within the Church was not happy with him. He was threatening the conspiracy of silence within the Curia and the hierarchy of the laity, where the mere mention of "reform" or "rocking the boat" is viewed with disdain. This is where the status quo is rigorously protected. The privileges that have been constructed and garnered by men within the Church have been sacrosanct for them for centuries, at the expense of others in the Church.

The Church structure is a pyramid with the clerics near the top, and the prelates at the very pinnacle. Then there is the male laity, below them women, and at the bottom gay and divorced Catholics. The pyramid structure is brutally unequal, and that is further reinforced when young Catholics are taught that the sacrament of Holy Orders is a higher calling than the sacrament of Matrimony.

• • •

Blase Cupich is the Archbishop of Chicago and was one of Francis's appointments to the rank of cardinal. Along with theologian Father Bryan Massingale, they wrote in 2018 that "clericalism assumes a sense of entitlement by some ordained men and could be conducive to exploitive behavior. It is not a question of gay or straight or beyond binary, but rather that they have, by reason of their clerical status, access to privilege and power within the ecclesial community that can insulate them from accountability."

Cupich and Massingale also wrote that the catechism of the Catholic Church teaches that "ordination confers an indelible spiritual character on a priest. A priest is seen differently than a lay person." And Mary Hunt, the respected and learned feminist theologian, wrote in the *National Catholic Reporter*, that a priest's "place in the hierarchical structure reflects this difference. His role as a sacramental presider and as a decision-maker are contingent on it."

The structure is a large part of the problem, and structures can be changed.

In a 2011 interview with an Argentine Catholic news agency, then-Cardinal Bergoglio said, "We priests tend to clericalize the laity. We do not realize it, but it is as if we infect them with our own disease. And the laity, not all, but many, ask us on their knees to clericalize them, because it is more comfortable to be an altar server than a protagonist of a lay path. We cannot fall into that trap—it is a sinful complicity."

In the summer of 2018, Thomas Rosica, a Canadian writer and priest, wrote in the *National Catholic Reporter*, "Clericalism means focusing fundamentally on the things of the clergy and, more specifically, the sanctuary rather than bringing the gospel to the world."

Father Rosica continued: "Clericalism infects the clergy when they become too self-referential rather than missionaries. But it affects lay people worse, when they begin to believe that the fundamental service God is asking of them is to become major donors, recipients of Papal honors, 'ministers of hospitality,' lectors or extraordinary ministers of the Eucharist at church rather than spreading the faith in their families, workplaces, schools, neighborhoods, and in places where we priests cannot enter."

Changing the pyramid structure will lead to a better Church and will allow women to become priests and priests to marry. The Church will be more open and totally accepting of gay and divorced Catholics as well as changing the doctrine on birth control, which most Catholics want. These are changes advocated by many of the liberation/reform wing of the Church.

Many Catholics agree that for the Church to survive and grow through evangelizing, it must reform itself. But it's hard to imagine any of the major reforms going forward until Catholics have faith and confidence in their church leadership—a confidence that has been poisoned by the sexual abuse scandal and the treatment of women. The only way the Church can grow is through strong and radical changes in how it faces up to these scandals and the cover-ups that now haunt them.

Father Soto and Pope Francis know they have major decisions to make, and the first entails the Church to come clean on its complicity in the abuses and their cover-up.

• • •

Not only the media but the faithful in the pews were justifiably harsh in their criticism of the Church while Pope Francis was figuring out how to react to the increase in abuses and the scandals that followed. During all this, Francis kept to his own schedule, and that included sustained periods of self-reflection and diagnosis.

Discernment has been an important part of Francis's Jesuit training. It traces its beginnings to its founder, Saint Ignatius of Loyola. Discernment is the ability to obtain sharp perceptions of something and make nuanced judgments about its properties or qualities. For Francis, discernment is what he needs now. But the public and the Church faithful want action on the crisis immediately. However, Francis knows that whatever actions he takes must be the right ones. His first step is to speak out forcefully against these evils.

When Juan Carlos Cruz and the other Chilean abuse victims visited the Vatican, Francis said, "I was part of the problem. I caused this, and I apologize to you." After the Pennsylvania grand jury report, Francis said, "We failed the little ones—we abandoned them." And during his 2018 Christmas message, Francis spoke directly to priests who abuse: "Turn yourselves in!"

These strong statements were filled with empathy for the victims, but still missing was any sign of a significant action plan going forward. Apologizes and sorrow by themselves are not actions, such as requiring all bishops to release the names of the abusers in their diocese.

Francis's opponents inside and outside the Church pummeled him, along with the rest of the Church leadership. Two of the nine cardinals in his leadership circle—Cardinal Francisco Javier Errazuriz from Chile and Cardinal Pell from Australia—

were abusers themselves, or were involved in covering up for others (although in 2020 Cardinal Pell was released from his confinement in Australia when the High Court of Australia overturned his 2018 conviction on charges of sexual offenses).

Soon after Francis returned from Ireland on September 6, 2018, he used his morning homily in the Domus Sanctae Martae, to say, "A sign that a person, that a Christian, does not know how to blame oneself, is when they are blaming others, to badmouth others, to stick their nose in other people's lives. It's a bad sign. Do I do this? It is a good question for getting at the heart of things."

Francis then went on to say, "Accusing oneself means feeling shame and misery deep down inside one's heart." He then added, "We must convert, we must do penance. Asking people to reflect on the temptation of accusing others."

Francis faced many questions. For example, are his words a reaction to his accusers, such as Archbishop Vigano? Or is Francis preparing a path to acknowledge that he knew early on about Cardinal McCarrick's sexual abuses? Is this leading to a completely transparent review of the decades of abuse within the Church and the subsequent cover-ups? Is it possible that involvement in these cover-ups may have extended to the highest reaches of the Church hierarchy?

• • •

After a period of discernment, Francis begins to grasp the urgency of undertaking significant reform. He and Father Soto engage in long discussions about the problems and how to address them. The first step beyond apologies is listening to others who were victims and to those in the pews who feel betrayed. Soto argues vigorously for more diversity in the Church's leadership.

Father Soto is aware that too much of the solution to the scandals rests with the cardinals, and he also knows the fatal flaw in the Church's structure is the absence of women and laity. When Soto was a young religious academic in Argentina, he loved to attend diocesan panel discussions. Right away, he was aware of the absence on those panels of lay Catholics and women. Early in Soto's Jesuit life, he saw that the Church's resistance to change, and especially to accepting women, undermined its credibility and efficacy as an institutional instrument for justice.

In preparation for his dinner meeting with Francis, Soto prepares a paper and sends it ahead to Francis. It lists the ten things. he believes the Church must do in order to grow and improve its access to the people. Second on the list, after listening and apologizing to the victims, is a change in the pope's cabinet of advisors to include women.

"Juan, I have read your paper," Francis says at dinner. "We have been discussing many of these points for years. A lot of what you are advocating would be new ground for the Church. By the way, I must commend you on your scholarship regarding the significant role of women in the Church in the first century. I know that the Benedictine Joan Chittister and the academic Phyllis Zagano have been leaders in this scholarship."

The pope and Soto had agreed some time ago that in private Soto could call him "Padre Francis." It is their way of recognizing Francis's elevated status while also acknowledging their almost forty years of working together closely. It allows them to discuss things as equals, although they both know the power to make decisions ultimately resides with Francis.

"Padre Francis," Soto begins—this appellation always brings an ever so subtle, playful smile to the pope's face. "While some of the nine cardinals in your cabinet of advisors have served you well, I think some of them have not. It is long past time for a fresh perspective from others in the Church. Father Reece and I were recently discussing the idea of having real shepherds of the Church on your council. All wisdom does not reside with red hats. And we are recommending two priests for your consideration. Also, three women and four cardinals."

The new team of advisors includes two activist priests who have demonstrated extraordinary courage. The Afro-Honduran priest Father Ismael Moreno Coto, better known as Padre Melo, has a sterling human rights record in Central America, championing migrants and the poor. Father Melo's work has become so widely recognized that he has been targeted for death by people associated with the corrupt Honduran government.

The other priest in the "shepherd mold" is Father Peter Daly, who has been a parish priest for more than 30 years. Father Daly's name had been brought to Francis's attention when Father Soto and Francis read Daly's account of the meeting when Daly stood up to Archbishop Theodore McCarrick almost twenty years ago in Washington, D.C. At that meeting, in front of 200 other priests from the Washington Diocese, Daly accused the bishops of covering up the sexual abuses. His confrontation with McCarrick was a bold and courageous attack on the prelates of the Church, but not out of character for the priest. Father Daly led his parish in Prince Frederick, Maryland, opening a large food bank that feeds 150 families a week, recruiting parishioners to build houses in Mississippi and Nicaragua, and establishing a prison ministry and a land conservation program. Retired now, Father Daly is also an immigration lawyer, and he writes a column for the *National Catholic Reporter* that Francis has read and admired for years.

These two priests are joined on the team of advisors by Carolyn Woo, a professor at Notre Dame University who is a former president of Catholic Relief Services. She has a reputation for being mission-driven and getting things done. Another new lay addition is Anita Vincent, a catechist from Bangladesh. At age 49, she is seen as one of the rising leaders in the Church. Joining them is French Sister Yvonne Reungoat, Superior General of the Salesian Sisters, whose order works with the poor in 89 countries.

In addition to these three highly regarded women, the pope has asked Cardinal Ouellet of Canada, Cardinals Cupich and Tobin of the United States, and Cardinal Turkson of Ghana to join his circle of advisors. All four have already developed a close relationship with Francis during his papacy.

By adding these new councilors, Francis is sending a powerful message of change to the governing body of the Church as well as to the international Catholic community. The essence of his message is that the laity will now be included in significant decisions, that priests like Father Daly and Moreno Coto have a place of respect and influence in the Church, and finally, and perhaps most significantly, that women will be given access to the highest levels of Church decision-making. These choices are a dramatic change from the past.

These changes also reflect Francis's acknowledgment that the sexual abuse scandal has driven the Church off a precipice and recovering requires the best leadership the Church has to offer. Francis believes his changes to the circle of advisors is an important step forward.

These changes are consistent with the pope's support for decentralization of power, which can be traced back to his long career in Argentina.

Francis gathers leaders about him who tell him his papacy is in grave danger of being consumed by these scandals, and they counsel him to lead with alacrity and strength. The pope asks his new leadership counselors to prepare a memo that would include the thoughts of individuals from a broad spectrum within the Church, including female and male laity, pastoral priests, leaders in religious orders, and bishops.

More than half of the appointed commission members come from the laity. Not only is this memorandum a statement on gender and clericalism, it is also a document that is critical of the bishops. The scope of the reforms is historic.

The memo begins by stating plainly that the Church is facing perhaps its greatest challenge since the Reformation, which occurred more than five hundred years ago. The Church must choose which path to follow—either evolve or die. It is that dire.

Parts of the memorandum, and its recommendations, read as follows:

A Truth and Reconciliation Commission shall be established with the task to investigate the sexual abuse scandals and the accountability structures that were in place to address the abuses.

Investigative hearings shall be conducted to arrive at the truth.

3) The commission shall be composed of lay and religious persons, but the majority of the commission shall come from the laity.

4) The commission shall report back to the pope, on a date certain, such recommendations as it deems necessary and that are fair and appropriate for the grave injustices that have occurred.

5) The commission recognizes the positive strides that were made in the Dallas Charter (For the Protection of Children and Young People) since 2002. However, the gaping hole in that Charter regarding accountability by bishops must be closed.

6) The laity on the commission shall come from the following designations:

Those who have been sexually abused or their representatives.

Representatives from academia with expert knowledge in psychology and theology.

Representatives from the legal communities, both canon and civil law.

Representatives from the divorced Catholic community.

Representatives from the gay community.

Representatives from a wide field of geographic areas and cultural concerns.

7) Regarding the appointment of religious members to the commission, we recommend to Pope Francis an article in the September 8, 2018, *National Catholic Reporter* by Melissa Musick Nussbaum entitled, "Bishops, be like parents—try to be better than you actually are."

In the article, Nussbaum writes, speaking of Ezekiel, "The word of the Lord came to me. . . . What came to Ezekiel was a cry against the shepherds, 'who have been posturing themselves.' The imagery is Psalm 23 violently upended: shepherds feasting in green pastures, shepherds resting beside the still waters. And the sheep they were supposed to lead there? They are abandoned."

Further on, Nussbaum writes, "I could almost hear Ezekiel's voice rise:

'You did not strengthen the weak nor heal the sick
nor bind up the injured.
You did not bring back the strayed nor seek the lost.
but you lorded it over them harshly and brutally.
So they were scattered for lack of a shepherd,
and became food for all the wild beasts.'

And then God warns through the prophet,

'Because my shepherd did not look after my sheep . . .
I swear I am coming against these shepherds.'

Continuing on, Nussbaum wrote that "most of the parents I know try each day to be better people than they actually are. And that is all I ask of our bishops and cardinals. Try to be better than you actually are. Try to act like a good shepherd. Feed my sheep. If you are feasting in the green pastures, make sure the sheep have eaten first. While the sheep are drinking from still waters, you be on the watch for wolves. And if you find that you are no longer a shepherd or, Jesus help us, even a sheep but one of the wolves on the prowl, take off your vestments. Remove your miter. Put down your staff. Return your pallium to Peter's grave. And go somewhere quiet, away from the donors and the scarlet cloth, and the bowing and the rings, and try to find your way back. You'll probably find it washing dishes or cleaning toilets. Shepherd's stuff.

"May God have mercy on your souls."

8) The religious members on the Truth and Reconciliation Commission shall be composed of priests, religious other than priests, from orders both female and male. Bishops may be added.

9) Members of the commission shall be appointed by the pope.

10) Women's voices on the commission shall not be muffled or buried in the report(s). Their voices should be commensurate with other commission members. It grieves us that we need to admonish on the gender issue, but it is long past time that the Church faces up to this glaring inequality.

It would behoove the Church to elevate the voices and

positions of women within the Church. Institutions that afford women dignity and equality will be institutions more steeped in justice for all. There should be no religious exemption by gender if the Church is serious about its recovery from this abominable stain.

The Church is filled with capable and righteous women—many of whom are excellent leaders.

Catholics should view this crisis as a time to accelerate reforms, not retreat from them. Pope Francis has chosen the right paths toward reform. As Michael Gerson wrote in *The Washington Post* on August 25, 2018, "the founder of the Catholic faith was a radical religious reformer. An opponent of complacent religious leaders, a tough critic of hypocrisy, and a defender of children. And he calls on his followers to restore a house in ruins."

Pope Francis takes the memorandum to heart and pays careful attention to its recommendation for a Truth and Reconciliation Commission. One of his first moves after reading it is to appoint Sister Joan Chittister as chair of the commission. This is especially significant because in the past Sister Joan, arguably the premier female theologian in the Catholic Church, has been known to buck the Vatican.

• • •

Father Soto has just reread the Nussbaum essay for the umpteenth time. When he first read it in the *National Catholic Reporter*, he was overwhelmed with the author's imagery and her ability to shape Ezekiel's poetic dialogue to fit the sinful cover-up by the bishops. Her admonitions to the prelates mirror what many in the pews have on their minds. Soto wants Francis to read Nussbaum's article, but he isn't sure how to present it to the pope. To help him, he calls a friend for guidance. He has learned recently that she is never too shy to have an opinion.

"Sister Mary, Juan Soto here. How are you?

"I am fine Father. And you?"

"Too busy."

"I can imagine. Many fires to deal with at one time."

"Indeed. I have just emailed you a piece by Melissa Musick Nussbaum in the *National Catholic Reporter*. I think it is powerful and that Pope Francis should read it. But I am not sure how to present it to him. My initial idea was to present it to him as a preface to the report from his new council of advisors. Would you please read it and tell me your thoughts?"

"Certainly Father. I will be back to you shortly."

Sister Mary reads the Nussbaum piece and is also impressed with the strength and creativeness of the writer. But she does share Father Soto's concern about attaching it to the report. She calls him back to discuss what to do.

"Father Soto, it is quite a scathing and powerful commentary on the bishops. However, my inclination would be for you to take it to the pope independently from the memo. Since I do not know the contents of the memo, I cannot fully comment, but I see no problem with sharing it with him separately. After all, the pope's new Council of Advisors has four cardinals who might not like the pairing of the memorandum with the Nussbaum piece."

"Sister Mary, those are my thoughts as well. Francis has his hands full trying to get the bishops to turn the corner on this scandal and embrace reforms. But I want him to see it and read it because I think it captures the anger and loss of confidence that many Catholics are feeling."

Even though their conversations have been all about their friend, the pope, and how to handle Church business, Father Soto and Dr. Mary always enjoy talking to each other.

• • •

In August, Pope Francis had faced serious charges from Archbishop Carlo Maria Vigano who released a statement claiming that Pope Francis had been told about sexual abuses committed by Cardinal Theodore McCarrick years ago. And further, Vigano had charged that, when he became Pope, Francis released McCarrick from sanctions that had been imposed by Pope Benedict. Vigano's charges were followed by a long six weeks of silence from the Vatican, which presented Francis's enemies and those with opposing views with a clear field to insinuate and accuse, to slander and cast doubts upon Francis as a person and as pope.

At the end of the silence, these charges were finally addressed by the high-ranking Vatican Cardinal Marc Ouellet of Canada, the Prefect of the Congregation of Bishops. Vigano had actually asked Ouellet to support him on the charges, but Ouellet responded with a firm "no," and he called the allegations against the pope, "monstrous and unsubstantiated."

When Pope Benedict stepped down in 2013, the conservative clerics of the Catholic Church, aided by a conservative Catholic laity, were stunned when a progressive in the mold of Jesus of Nazareth was elected pope. Conservative Catholic traditionalists watched disdainfully as Francis, through his personal actions and style, refashioned what the Church of Christ might become. That led some in conservative circles to set out to destroy his papacy and what it represented.

Cardinal Ouellet, who took it upon himself to defend Francis against the charge of complicity in the McCarrick cover-up, looked at the historical documents and said, "Unlike today, back then there was not sufficient proof of his alleged culpability." Ouellet also expressed his bafflement at how McCarrick had risen to become a cardinal and an archbishop of Washington, D.C., after he had been accused of abusing minors and seminarians. But, as Ouellet pointed out, Francis had had nothing to do with McCarrick's promotions in New York; Metuchen and Newark, N.J.; and Washington, D.C.—all of which had occurred during the papacy of John Paul II. To the contrary, he said, "Francis was the one who stripped him (McCarrick) of cardinal dignity when there was a credible accusation of an abuse of a minor."

Writing publicly and directly to Archbishop Vigano, Ouellet's words were stinging: "It is abhorrent for you to use the clamorous sexual abuse scandal in the United States to inflict an unmerited and unheard-of blow to the moral authority of your superior, the Supreme Pontiff."

Francis removed McCarrick from the College of Cardinals and had him isolated in prayer and penance in a Kansas monastery, waiting for the Vatican investigation to be completed. The verdict, when it came, was overwhelming in denouncing McCarrick. He was found guilty of soliciting sex during confessions and committing "sins" with minors and adults "with the aggravating factor of the abuse of power." Francis then defrocked McCarrick, stripping him of the rights of the priesthood.

During his weekly meetings with Francis to discuss appointments of bishops and their responsibilities within the diocese or administrative jurisdiction, Ouellet has witnessed Francis at work. Ouellet believes that "Francis treats persons and problems with great charity, mercy, attentiveness, and seriousness."

Ouellet further said that "the pope has demonstrated tireless energy to welcome all miseries and to address them through generous comfort of his words and actions, who seeks to announce and communicate the joy of the gospel to all, who lends a hand to the families, to the abandoned elderly, to the sick in body and soul, and above all to the youth in their search for happiness."

Ouellet's last words on the matter described Vigano's charges as "an unjust and unjustified attack . . . , a political plot that lacks any real basis that could incriminate the pope and that profoundly harms the communion of the Church."

• • •

Institutional politics, whether in a legislature, a university, or a church, has categories of actors—those who are part of the established order, those who challenge that order, and those who wait to just survive without either conviction or courage in acts of self-preservation.

Under both John Paul II and Benedict, the Church's refusal or inability to stem and punish the sexual abuse abominations created a moral as well as a competency vacuum. Some say that part of this period can be attributed to leaders in the Church "staying too long," past the time when one's physical, mental and spiritual health has diminished. For more than three and a half decades, the travesty of these cases of sexual abuse had been allowed to go on, not only in the United States but all over the globe.

In the chaos and uncertainty of this lack of leadership, lay members of the Church began to take on more active roles. One of the earliest conservative capitalists to fill this vacuum was the fast-food magnate, Thomas Monaghan, the founder of Domino's Pizza, the largest pizza seller worldwide, and owner of the Detroit Tigers baseball team. In 1983, he used his church philanthropy to establish the Ave Maria Foundation, and he created and funded the Ave Maria Law School and staffed it with professors such as Robert Bork and Antonin Scalia. In 1987 Monaghan helped to form Legatus, an organization for Catholic CEOs who earned more than $4 million a year. He was a member of Opus Dei and a Knight of the Sovereign Military Order of Malta.

In the 1980s, Monaghan was the face of the new wealth capitalist in the Church. In the new century, that role was assumed by Tim Busch, a new breed of Catholic tycoon with deep, conservative pockets. The *National Catholic Reporter,* in an October 2018 editorial, stated that "they have been monitoring this brash operator and founder of the Napa Institute because he is among the most aggressive of that cast of U.S. Catholics whose primary ambition, it seems, is to convince the rest of us that the Christian Gospel was actually promulgated to justify the most extreme expressions of American-style capitalism."

Busch has worked his way onto the campus of Catholic University in Washington. D.C., where, according to the editorial, "his name is affixed to the business school and where he conducts conferences on how to dress up libertarian economics in a Catholic costume."

This is the Busch world that houses the likes of the discredited and ambitious Archbishop Vigano as well as John Nienstedt, the Archbishop of St. Paul-Minneapolis, who in 2015 was charged with mishandling sexual abuse cases and was under investigation for his own personal misconduct.

Father Soto's day begins with prayer but not with the celebration of Mass. The stories of sexual abuse scandals are pursued by inquiries from the media that require a response from the Vatican. He has much to do this day. He is in his office by 6:30 a.m., and his assistant, Father Michael, enters with a large stack of clips. Father Michael had already sent the *National Catholic Reporter*'s lead editorial to Soto last night by email.

Father Soto saw the message from Father Michael but has decided to wait until the morning when his mind was fresh to read it. He is at his desk sipping tea and is reading the opening paragraphs when Michael walks in.

"Morning, Father. The pile of clips is getting taller. I will return in an hour with the new clips as stories are released online. I have a few early overnight clips from the United States on the top."

"Please stay here a minute," Soto says, "until I finish reading this editorial."

Father Michael knows his boss either wants to vent or to talk about how to approach the problem they are facing. Father Michael is almost always pleased to be included in these discussions even if Soto is doing most of the talking and strategizing.

Father Soto continues reading the editorial: "Busch's ecclesiology embraced a clericalism of the highest order. He was the kind of hierarchical toady who had the money to court the highly placed and treat them to his institute's summer gatherings in California wine country for bouts of what he called 'in-your-face Catholicism.'"

Finally, Soto reaches the end of the editorial and notes this admonition: "The work ahead is too serious and critical to be left to the charlatans and religious carnie barkers who have, all along, been part of the problem. . . . The work ahead will require more than bluster and misappropriated slogans. It will require accessing the deepest levels of our sacramental tradition. It will require the imposition of unprecedented accountability of bishops. It will require bishops with the will to confront the toughest questions about how the clerical culture arrived at this point."

As Soto finishes reading, he turns his gaze to his assistant. "Michael, those in the Church who are trying to bring Francis down are stoking these fires. This is the first strong editorial that addresses the clerical culture of the religious right within the Church, calling out its selfish 'me first' philosophy, one that is fronting for unfettered capitalism at the expense of virtually everyone else, including the workers who are often paid poverty wages and our environment, which is ravaged by those who run these industries."

Michael stares intently at his boss, trying to think of something to say, but nothing comes to him.

"The destruction of the Amazon and the workers who slash and burn at the direction of those who are defiling our earth," Father Soto continues "These carbon-addicted industries and their industrial leaders are destroying our planet. It is time that we counter them." Soto waves the editorial at Father Michael. "And this is the beginning of the counter-attack."

Michael is now excited. He knows the days ahead will be exhilarating as Soto and Francis plot to regain the high ground and move the Church into a new reformation.

• • •

Father Soto is working on a memo to Pope Francis about how he should respond to the latest round of scandal stories, when Father Michael bursts into his office with information that has been leaked to him about a story that will appear in major U.S. papers in the next couple of days.

Father Michael, his eyes wide with dread and excitement, tells Soto that Pennsylvania's Attorney General, Josh Shapiro, will soon be issuing a report based on the findings of a state grand jury, that includes more than 1,000 cases of abuse by 300 priests, dating back seven decades. This damaging and devastating report also includes accusations of lax accountability by the Pennsylvania bishops.

Soto feels like a boxer who has just taken two stinging left jabs to the head and then a powerful right to his solar plexus.

The news almost knocks the wind out of him. He hasn't felt this shaky since the accusation of cowardice against Francis in the early 1980s in Argentina. Father Soto knows those stories from decades ago were false, and he has a feeling that this story may be amiss as well. Nevertheless, Father Soto is reeling.

Soon after the grand jury report is made public, it dominates worldwide headlines, and yet the Church's reaction is virtually invisible and mute—and this comes just after its initial mishandling of the Chilean scandals by their bishops and priests, as well as the McCarrick scandal.

Most columnists and editorial writers seem to be using the convenient 12-page summary at the opening of the 1,356-page report to attack the Church. Their attacks are damning, and this paves the way for other states' attorneys general to pursue their own reports. Soon a dozen states are following a similar path.

Not everyone has that reaction. After the report is released, the Jesuit writer, commentator, and author of a book about the Vatican Thomas Reese—who is not known for his sympathies toward the Vatican—begins to raise questions about the report's accuracy. Then a full five months after its release, Peter Steinfels, the former religion writer for the *New York Times*, publishes a stinging critique of the report in the Catholic journal *Commonweal*.

Steinfels charges that the Pennsylvania report is "misleading, irresponsible, inaccurate, and unjust." He acknowledges the horror of clerical abuse and the terrible damage done to children, but he complains that "the grand jury report made no distinction from diocese to diocese, from one bishop's tenure to another. All are tarred with the same brush."

When the *New York Times* story did break later, Father Soto read Thomas Reese's report on Steinfels's *Commonweal* article and was relieved to discover that Steinfels found "that a major fault with the report was its failure to acknowledge the impact of the 2002 Dallas Charter, which changed dramatically how the Church responded to abuse. The charter required the reporting of credible accusations to police, the establishment of lay review boards, and the removal of any priest guilty of abuse."

Soto also knows that the Pennsylvania Report is simply a rehashing of many old cases. Since 2002 and the adoption of the Dallas Charter, these kinds of cases have become rare—only two cases of sexual abuse in the report occurred during the last decade. However, it is unfortunately true that the report had initial credibility because of the Church's failures.

All this activity prompts the U.S. Bishops' Conference to schedule a series of meetings, conferences, and a retreat that once again raises expectations.

CHAPTER EIGHT

The Bishops Fail Again

The four prelates representing the U.S. Conference of Catholic Bishops are ushered into the pope's office in the Sanctae Martae, near his apartment and close to Vatican medical services. They are Archbishop Jose H. Gomez of Los Angeles, Cardinal Daniel DiNardo of Galveston-Houston and president of the conference, Cardinal Sean O'Malley of Boston and president of the Pontifical Commission for the Protection of Minors, and Msgr. J. Brian Bransfield, general secretary of the conference.

They have all met Francis before, and they are immediately struck by how fatigued he appears. His breathing is labored and his handshake weak when he greets each of them.

"Welcome," Francis says. "Please have a seat. We have much to discuss."

"Your Holiness," Cardinal DiNardo begins. "We thank you for this meeting. We come to seek your assistance in pursuing a fair and just approach to addressing the sexual abuses that have ravaged so many lives and stained our church. While we have made some progress since the Dallas Charter in 2002, it is painfully clear that there are critical omissions in the charter. We come before you in a humble and penitential spirit so that we can admit our failures and move forward to reconcile with those we have so grievously failed."

Francis stares intently at Cardinal DiNardo, and there is a long pause in the room. The pope and Cardinal DiNardo have not always been on the same side. Yet Francis has to admit that DiNardo has struck the correct tone for this meeting. Slowly

Francis nods his head before moving his eyes from DiNardo to his ally and friend Sean O'Malley. Francis has worked with Cardinal O'Malley in his role as president of the Pontifical Commission for the Protection of Minors.

"Cardinal O'Malley knows well, perhaps more so than any of us, the progress we have made since the Dallas Charter," the pope begins. "And he is also aware of the charter's grave limitations."

Francis again pauses and catches his breath, and then takes a sip of water. O'Malley is confused as to whether Francis has invited him to comment or whether he should give the pope time to gather his strength before he continues. O'Malley decides to wait, and he watches Francis methodically swallow his water while he sadly thinks, *Like the water slowly flowing into Francis's body, the pope's days are slipping away.*

Turning now toward Cardinal DiNardo, Francis says, "I have been discussing the charter's shortcomings with Cardinal Cupich—as you may already know."

Francis has learned that very little can be kept confidential in church politics within the Curia. He now assumes that any meeting he has outside his close circle will become known to the media and will reach other decision-makers in his ecclesiastical orbit before he can tell them himself.

After a moment the pope begins again. "Our beloved church is under unprecedented attack as a result of our failures. We have been on the defensive against some of these attacks. It is now time for us to take the offense. It will take courage and leadership. We have no other choices.

"As you know, as a Jesuit, I have a strong belief and training in discernment. We like to take ideas apart and discuss them. This takes much time, and, in a more normal environment, it is worth taking the time. However, for thirty-four years the Church has wrestled with these evil acts by our clergy. It is long past time for strong and bold action. We cannot afford to flounder. We cannot afford to again fail those who have been so grievously harmed.

"Until this time I have been extra careful about rushing to judgment on the guilt of a priest or bishop. Now all accusations that are reported will be pursued. Bishops will be held accountable by a joint cleric and lay panel. Dioceses will no longer have the option on transparency for priests and bishops who have sexually abused others."

Francis is reaching the end of his statement, but he pauses again to catch his breath. With an ironic smile of recognition, the pope turns to Monsignor Bransfield and says, "I understand that in your country only fifty out of 190 dioceses publicly list priests and bishops credibly accused of abuse."

Monsignor Bransfield wordlessly acknowledges that those numbers are correct.

The pope continues. "I will be proposing these ideas and others at a synod of top-ranking bishops from around the globe . . . " Another long pause by Francis before he finishes his thought. "In February, the end of February. But before then, it is my hope that your conference of bishops will meet in November to discuss, in a frank encounter, some of these ideas. And that you help persuade the doubters of the importance of adopting these ideas. Full transparency, a code of conduct for bishops, the appointment by bishops of cleric, and lay boards to oversee accountability."

With a determined expression and in a most serious tone, Francis says firmly, "We must put our house in order." Then, in a caring voice, "I would also suggest that after your meeting in Baltimore all the bishops go away for a retreat to reflect on your role as shepherds."

• • •

The gathering of U.S. bishops takes place in Baltimore on November 12, 2018, a week after the U.S. midterm elections when the Republican Party, the party of President Trump, has taken a beating. Francis has designated Cardinal Blase Joseph Cupich, the Archbishop of Chicago, to serve as his apostolic representative to the Baltimore conference.

The Vatican and Cardinal Cupich hope the conference will have a vigorous discussion of issues facing the Church, but they are also nervous about how some of the voting could turn out. They know that they need a two-thirds vote to pass any resolution of substance that the pope and the cardinal want.

Many bishops at the conference were appointed by Pope John Paul II and Pope Benedict, and more often than not they reflect the conservative views held by those previous popes. The Baltimore conference is being held ahead of a February international confab at the Vatican. Francis and Cupich know that a defeat at this earlier conference in Baltimore would be another devastating blow for the victims and the Church. They seek the services of someone who knows something about bishops, counting votes, and implementing strategy.

John Carr sits in the back room of Agua 301, a restaurant on the Anacostia River in the Capitol Riverfront neighborhood of Washington, D.C. While waiting for an old Vatican friend, he quietly reads the *New York Times*. The sun pours in through the restaurant's large windows overlooking the boardwalk that leads to the baseball park five minutes away.

Looking up from his newspaper, his glasses perched on the tip of his nose, he looks out the window and sees Father Juan Soto walk in the front door of Agua heading to the back room towards him. Carr rises to greet his old friend. Over forty years ago, John Carr was a seminarian in Minnesota, beginning his career in the Catholic Church around the same time as Juan Soto in Argentina. They have collaborated on many social and economic justice campaigns over the decades.

Carr served for more than twenty years as the Director of the Department of Justice, Peace, and Development at the U.S. Conference of Catholic Bishops. He recently has become chairman of the board of Bread for the World, and he is also the director of the initiative on Catholic Thought and Public Life at Georgetown University, which seeks to share Catholic social thought more broadly and deeply while reaching out to a new generation of leaders. In 2012 Carr was a Residential Fellow on religion and politics at the Institute of Politics at Harvard University.

In Washington, D.C., he is highly regarded by the media, and his views are often solicited on the intersection of religion and politics. His well-honed skills for surviving and navigating the controversial arenas of religion and politics are supported by a thoughtful strategic mind and a wonderful sense of humor.

After some catching up on their personal lives since they last saw each other, Carr exclaims, "What in God's name is happening to our country and our church?"

This has become a routine question to ask in Washington, where life feels like one crisis on top of another. Yet neither man has a constructive answer.

Carr knew, when Father Soto requested this meeting, that they would be discussing their mutual concern for the victims of the sexual abuse scandals and how the Vatican's mishandling of it was affecting Pope Francis and the Church. Both men know there is no room left for additional blunders.

Another reason Father Soto is seeking Carr's help with the Bishops' Conference is Carr's years of counting votes in the United States House and Senate on issues important to the

Catholic Church. That had been one of his jobs when he worked for the Bishops' Conference. Soto and Francis need a clear picture of where the bishops stand if votes are called on questions of conduct, transparency, and accountability.

When the waiter comes to their table, they each order an Arnold Palmer and munch on tortilla chips and salsa while they wait for their lunch.

"John, thanks for taking the time to meet," Father Soto says. "Francis is very worried that the annual Bishops' Conference in Baltimore will get out of control and complicate our February Synod at the Vatican. We are regrettably finding too many bishops who don't understand or even care enough to prioritize this sexual abuse issue. We need your help. We need to wage a massive education campaign to enlighten them before the international Synod at the Vatican in February."

Carr recognizes the gravity of what his friend is saying, and hopes he can help. "Juan, ever since you called me about getting together, I have been busy trying to imagine a path that Francis might consider, one that fits his passion and goodness."

Soto nods in appreciation of his friend's thoughtfulness.

"I know that the pope's history has been built upon a decentralized collegial approach to issues and problems," Carr continues. "But at some point, after discernment, after conferences, after meetings and prayers, Francis must be required to act like the successor to Peter. He must act like the head of a church in crisis."

Carr looks into his friend's eyes to see if he has said the right thing—or right enough for him to continue. "It seems to me that many are ready to follow his leadership—a leadership that begins with listening to the victims and those representing them. Juan, when Francis meets with the bishops in February in Rome, he must make listening to the victims the first order of business. The pope must then require each bishop do the same exercise in their native lands before they journey to Rome."

Father Soto has anticipated that Carr's advice might run along these lines, but he is delighted to hear his friend articulate it so directly.

"Secondly," Carr says, "before the bishops arrive in Rome, I would have Francis call each of them on the phone to talk about what he wants them to support at the Vatican in February. The bishops must know exactly what the pope expects on the questions of a code of conduct, a third-party reporting mechanism, transparency, and accountability to a mixed board of lay and clerical members."

Yes. Soto nods in agreement with all of this. The phone calls would not have occurred to him, and this immediately confirms his decision to seek out Carr's advice.

"By having these conversations during advent and the celebration of Christmas," Carr continues, "Francis will be enjoining them during a positive time in the liturgical calendar. My experience has been that most bishops will be thrilled to talk with the pope. Forgive the political analogy here, but when a senator or congressman gets a call from the president, it is a big deal. It underscores their own importance, and irrespective of political party, it means a lot to them. I think that same principle would apply to a progressive Catholic bishop or a conservative traditionalist. They will be flattered and honored to be talking to the Vicar of Christ.

"Juan, you know that most U.S. senators at some point entertain the idea of being the president. Well, I suspect that many cardinals have thoughts about being pope."

The two men recognize the seriousness of what they are discussing, but to ease some tension, they chuckle lightly at human ambition.

Carr then returns to his strategy. "The phone conversations will also give bishops a chance to vent to the pope on whatever is on their minds. The pope may acquire some needed feedback and a few important ideas and suggestions from his bishops. These calls will be both cathartic and educational for all involved."

"I have a question for you," asks Soto. "How would you manage the votes on these questions at the Baltimore meeting?"

There is a pause while Carr thinks. "Well, it seems to me that, when the bishops meet, we have to be properly organized to assess how they feel collectively. Are they unified or close to it? Or are they all over the lot in their opinions? I think we need a 'whip' operation to find the answer to that. Are my numbers right, that if all 285 active bishops show up, which I doubt, the bishops will need roughly 190 votes to achieve the two-thirds necessary for passage?"

"Yes, that number is correct," Soto replies. "Let's hope Rome and Cardinal DiNardo are talking with each other prior to the conference in Baltimore. It would be another dark mark against the Church leadership if one of these reform resolutions were put up for a debate and failed to garner the two-thirds vote needed to pass. If that happens, then another round of charges of incompetence or deafness will be leveled against the Church in Rome as well as the Church in the United States. The goal should be to have them speak with a unified voice and to approve a strong common-sense reform package."

With this degree of a broad strategy in place, the two friends continue to enjoy their lunch while developing a memo that Father Soto will take back to Rome for Francis's review. Then the pope will send the memo to Cardinal Cupich, who will represent the Vatican at the Baltimore conference.

• • •

A prominent Catholic bishop declared that the year 2018 was a nightmare for the Catholic Church. This prompted an activist from BishopAccountability, an organization that documented the abuse crisis in the Catholic Church, to declare that the real nightmares were being lived every day by the victims who suffered these abuses. As the end of the calendar year approached, many in the Church and organizations representing the victims of abuse hoped that a series of high-level conferences and meetings would yield solutions to the question of accountability.

Catholic bishops gather every fall in the oldest diocese in the United States, in Baltimore. In 1632, before the Revolutionary War, when Maryland was a colony, Catholics came from Europe and settled in this area. Centuries later, the annual fall assembly of U.S. Catholic bishops has been meeting at the Marriott Hotel near the waterfront, where 300 or so prelates look forward to renewing old acquaintances over crab cakes, libations, and prayer.

This is not so in November 2018 because, as the bishops arrive in Baltimore for their three-day gathering, this year they know they face scandal, disgrace, and collapse of their church. All this is at the forefront of their minds.

Meanwhile, it is midday at the Vatican when Cardinal Ouellet enters the office of Pope Francis, where he is going over a speech with Father Soto.

"*Buenas tardes*, Pope Francis. Good to see you, Juan," the cardinal says.

Francis looks up and then rises to greet his friend and defender. It is their usual Tuesday meeting to review and discuss appointments to bishop and other high positions within the Church. There are 1.2 billion Catholics in the world, led by 5,000 bishops. The process of whom to appoint and where they will serve is an exhausting and important task that the pope and Cardinal Ouellet take very seriously. The cardinal in his capacity as the Prefect of the Congregation of Bishops is considered by many to be the most powerful cardinal in the Church.

"Marc. Good to see you, as always. Please come in. Juan and I are just finishing some remarks I will give this evening. Please take a seat. We will be with you in just a minute."

The cardinal finds his favorite wing-backed chair unoccupied. Before he takes out his notes for the meeting, he surveys the pope's modest office. A small crucifix is mounted on the wall above the credenza behind the pope's desk chair. On the credenza is a photo of the pope as a young priest with his mother and father as well as his two sisters and two brothers. Next to that is another photo of his beloved grandmother Rosa. On another wall hangs a painting of Mary holding the baby Jesus. On the third wall are two paintings. One is of Saint Ignatius. The second is of Saint Francis of Assisi painted in the El Greco style, resembling one of the twelve Apostles that the Greek painter is famous for having painted. The Saint Francis painting each week draws the attention of the cardinal. Once, Cardinal Ouellet even asked Francis about the painting of Saint Francis.

"Why in the El Greco style?" Ouellet asked, and Francis smilingly answered, "Perhaps I think of him as the thirteenth apostle."

Before the cardinal finishes scanning the room, the pope and Soto complete their editing and turn their attention to the business of the bishops. It is well understood that Father Soto is indispensable to Francis. He is given great deference at the Vatican. If you want to become a bishop, an archbishop, or a cardinal, it is best to put together a campaign to gain the support of all three people now assembled in the pope's office.

"The whip team is presently meeting at breakfast in Baltimore to determine if the votes are there to proceed," Soto reports. "Blase will call in an hour to give us the results."

. . .

Along Baltimore's Aliceanna Avenue near their hotel, a husband and wife are demonstrating, as they walk the streets, with a sign that reads, "Repent. Resign." Soon enough, they are joined by others who are equally outraged by the dereliction of the bishops. Members of the Survivors Network of those Abused by Priests (SNAP), and the Bishops Accountability Project join the demonstration, which is demanding action and accountability. Their presence underscores the shame that the clergy have brought to the Church, and to themselves.

A bevy of reporters, pens poised over small notepads, interview the demonstrators while keeping an eye on the cars pulling up with the bishops arriving to the confab.

Inside the conference hall, the bishops are similarly clad in black cassocks with red piping, matching silk-covered red buttons, and red sashes. A small black cape lined in red covers their shoulders and the pates of their balding heads are covered by zucchettos.

They sit at long rows of tables with their laptops open, a contrast of technology against their traditional garb. The scene is a bit eerie, as if choreographed for a North Korean parade. All men and no women—same dress. The room may have been arranged to suggest equality, but there is not even a token of it there. The saying "Men of quality don't fear equality" describes this room. There is fear here.

The bishops are also scared about the collapse of their dioceses. A May 2015 PEW survey found:

1) The percentage of Catholics in the United States declined from 25 to 20 percent from 2007 to 2015.

2) For each new Catholic convert, six current members left the Church.

3) More than a third of those born between 1981 and 1996 claimed no religious affiliation, and. of those who did, only 16 percent identified as Catholic.

4) Fifty-four percent of Catholic Church members were women, and Hispanic Catholics comprised 41 percent of the Church.

5) The number of men in the United States who became Catholic priests declined from 60,000 in 1965 to 37,500 in 2015.

The Pennsylvania Report and McCarrick scandal surely added to the decline by accelerating the retreat from the Church. Bishops at the conference reported significant declines in contributions at Mass—and the contributions that were made often were designated to specific needs, such as education or Catholic Charities, rather than going to sustain the parishes. And many parishioners had put their contributions on "hold," waiting to see if any "action" was forthcoming from the Church.

The bishops arrive in Baltimore hoping to find solutions to these problems by answering questions that deeply trouble their churchgoers about the Church's response to the sexual abuse scandals.

In the weeks leading up to Baltimore, John Carr has met with Cardinal Blase Cupich and Cardinal Daniel DiNardo to build an organization of twenty bishops who can survey their colleagues to ascertain their views on the questions surrounding bishop accountability. The first revolves around standards for the bishops' conduct. The second concerns an independent party reporting mechanism for the misconduct of priests or others within the Church. Third is the establishment of an oversight commission composed of six laity and three clergy to review the reporting. Additionally, Francis has already stressed his insistence that every diocese list those who have been known to have committed sexual abuses and those who have covered up these crimes.

At John Carr's first organizational gathering of the whip bishops, he proposes a teach-in at the Baltimore conference. When they are all together, he told them the origin of the term *whip*.

"In the parliament in Great Britain the political parties have internal organizations of members called whips. Their jobs are to educate and convince other members to support their parties' position. The name whip is derived from the fox hunt where men on horses follow a pack of dogs who are focused on their prey, usually a fox. The riders who are positioned near the front of the chase and on the outside of the pack are called the 'whippers in.' Their job is to keep the dogs together and focused on the fox."

The bishops chosen to whip are highly respected. Many hold geographical positions of power, such as archbishops who have bishops under their supervision. Some are retired and considered nonactive, though they retain influence as a result of long-standing relationships with other bishops. Some members of this whip team, like the saintly Bishop Thomas Gumbleton of Detroit, are admired for their holiness and their lives spent seeking justice that is seasoned by mercy. In addition to Gumbleton, cardinals Tobin and Cupich, as well as Archbishop Gomez, are part of the whip team who are assigned to talk with other bishops about supporting the pope's goals.

Some of the more conservative bishops who are at the conference are strict constructionists on the question of church-state issues and are troubled by the organizational lobbying effort that has commenced. They want their religion divorced from political applications such as whipping. But there is an old saying that nuns often use with their students, "God helps those who help themselves."

When the whip reports come in, Carr is troubled by them. The bishops are confused, not of one mind, and all over the map. Some want reform x but not y and z. Others support a different combination, while some want no reforms. A few incredulously blame the problem on the victims, while others scapegoat the homosexuals in the Church. A few blame the media.

There is no unanimity. When attendees are pressed to say how they will vote on the idea of total transparency, fewer than the two-thirds needed say they will. They also are short of the two-thirds on the question of an oversight committee of lay leaders and clerics.

Cardinal Cupich calls the Vatican and interrupts a meeting between the pope, Ouellet, and Soto. "I do not have good news," says Cupich. "The votes are not there for reform. They are divided and not close to the two-thirds vote necessary to pass anything."

Cupich shares the details of his reports with the Vatican leaders. While disappointed, the Church leaders are not surprised. Polarization in religion is following the fault lines in political polarization around the globe.

"Well then, we need more time to convince them," says Cardinal Ouellet. "Whatever we decide, it cannot jeopardize the February Synod of Bishops. While today the spotlight is on the meeting in Baltimore, the spotlight will shine even brighter at the Vatican in February."

Cupich interjects, "The chair of the conference, Cardinal DiNardo, and others want to proceed with votes on these questions."

Ouellet is firm in his view. "They cannot vote. It will jeopardize our chances of success at the February Synod." Turning to Francis, Ouellet says, "Pope Francis, we have a herculean task staring at us. If we are to turn the corner on the sexual abuse crisis, then we must act as one Church, and that requires a massive educational effort with our bishops. I had not realized how out of touch so many of the U.S. bishops are on an issue this visible and important. They desperately need leadership, and we must give it to them. Nothing right now is more important." The pope has been nodding his head in agreement.

"Marc, I agree. What do you suggest?"

"There is only one way to make up for the lost years," Ouellet answers, "and that is a real effort on your part, along with perhaps a few other bishops. Each bishop at the Synod needs to personally hear from you. And we will help you make that happen."

When the "do not vote" message reaches DiNardo and the rest of the conference on the opening day of November 12, there is great consternation among those gathered inside the hotel ballroom as well as among those protesting on the streets. The press writes another story of another failure of the Church to act, insinuating that the Church is in disarray.

Cardinal Cupich suggests that everyone attending the conference continue to debate the proposed reforms. He is right that they need to vent and discuss even though they are all aware of how negatively their inaction is being communicated to the world.

Cupich wisely sees that these proceedings have to be part of the process of dealing with a crisis that has now consumed the decision-makers. They are at the brink. The collapse is occurring around them, and they feel the urgency. The possibilities now are reform, more collapse, or perhaps even a schism within the centuries-old Church.

• • •

Advent and the joy of the Christmas season provide little comfort from the public beating the Church is receiving from the media and from the people in the pews after news of the stalemate in Baltimore becomes widely known.

Two questions are on people's minds: "How did the Church sink so low?" and "Is there a way out?" Most Catholics, and certainly the public at large, believe the sexual abuse scandal has exploded from just a few wayward priests to many. The Baltimore conference's failure to address these issues is a precursor to a systemic crisis throughout many cultures and religions in all parts of the globe.

Many of the U.S. Catholic bishops have been looking forward to reflection and prayer at an upcoming retreat at Mundelein, a seminary outside Chicago. Going to the Chicago area in January by a lake—brrr—sounds like penance. But it's an escape from the excessive materialism and celebrations that have supplanted the true meaning of the Christmas season. This will also be a chance for the participants to renew their spiritual core and to fortify themselves for the task of rebuilding a trust that has been lost in their parishes and dioceses.

Even in the bitter cold, when bishops might rather be on a beach in Florida or a golf course in California, the spirit of their vocations means that a retreat to Mundelein Seminary, on the ice-covered Lake Saint Mary, is an attractive alternative.

They also know they are there at Francis's suggestion and that the pope's close ally Cardinal Cupich is hosting them. The pope graciously volunteered the "papal preacher," 84-year-old Franciscan Father Raniero Cantalamessa, to lead the retreat. Perhaps this will help them individually and collectively find their footing after their failures in Baltimore as well as their collective neglect of the many victims of decades of abuse.

Freshly into the new year, the bishops arrive by car through ornate iron gates, which are supported on each side of the road by large red-brick pillars. The gate opens to the largest seminary in the United States, on 600 acres along Lake Saint Mary in Illinois about ten miles inland from Lake Michigan and close to Chicago.

The pastoral setting this winter day is blanketed in fresh white snow under a deep winter blue sky. The property is surrounded by woods, and white tail deer in their gray winter coats graze on the seminary grounds.

The dozen red-brick buildings are architecturally set in the pattern of a cross, the arms of the cross creating walkways along the lake. The bishops will stay at the Cardinal Stritch Retreat House near the conference center. The meals during this six-day retreat are taken in the refectory, a large white communal room.

A good deal of time at this retreat will be spent at the heart of the campus, the Immaculate Conception Chapel, the design of which is uncharacteristically not Catholic but instead resembles an old New England Protestant Church. Its very white interior is large enough to accommodate several hundred prelates.

These magnificent facilities were designed for the outdoors where swimming and kayaking on the lake and hiking in the woods were at the ready for contemplative seminarians—a perfect place to meditate or to walk the grounds saying the rosary.

The winter options outside of the Immaculate Conception Chapel include the grand library for the mind and the gym and weight room for the body. Still, the heart of the place is the Chapel that exercises the soul.

While the sexual abuse scandal is on the minds of most bishops, it is not the featured topic for the retreat. Yes, the preacher of the papal household alludes to the abuses on several occasions during his eight talks to the bishops, but his presentations dwell mostly on other topics that touch on clericalism, which is a significant part of the Church's problem. Getting to the heart of the Church's failure is not a quick or easy process, given the centuries of clerical deference within the Church. The abuse of power, sexual or otherwise, is wrapped in a millennium of ecclesiastical deference.

The press reviews of the retreat continue their scolding tone. Most suggest that the bishops once again are missing the mark. The consensus in the press is that there has been too little discussion of the sexual abuse crisis, and that Father Cantalamessa seems indifferent to the scandal. Some in the press see him as someone whose time has passed.

But many who were in the pews listening to Cantalamessa come away with a different, more appreciative view. Bishop Lawrence T. Persico, of Erie, Pennsylvania, describes the preacher's talks as "powerful and engaging." He tweets that he is glad the group had been given time to reflect and pray upon their role as shepherds, stressing: "We must start there to be able to offer healing. I am taking this very seriously but feeling positive."

Archbishop Gomez, who was with Francis when he proposed the retreat, believes that Cantalamessa focused "attention on our vocations and our responsibility as bishops in this moment in the Church. We are praying together as a visible sign of our unity as bishops and our communion with the Holy Father. There is a collegial spirit here and a firm commitment to address the causes of the abuse crisis we face and continue the work of renewing the Church."

Several other bishops comment on the preacher's ability to focus their attention on the Holy Spirit and the significance of His guidance in these troubled times. Priests and nuns in Central America are also turning to this theme as they counsel migrants and asylum seekers who are locked in their own crisis and their own journeys.

• • •

At a press conference that concludes the Catholic Leadership Roundtable meetings in Washington, D.C., John Carr intones in a memorable line, "The patience of the people of God is exhausted with the episcopal and clerical culture that puts itself first."

The purpose of the Leadership Roundtable meeting, just three weeks before the Synod of Bishops in Rome, is to focus on "best business and management practices," but the attendees are not able to stop themselves from talking about the sexual abuse scandals and the root causes of them. The frustration, disappointment, and agony at the gathering are palpable.

One participant is overheard saying to a bishop, "You're looking at your world dying," and another prominent Vatican spokesperson says, "This has been the summer from hell for the Catholic Church, and our sins are blatantly exposed for the world to see." Those left in the pews are asking, "What are you willing to do to fight for what you believe, and what matters to you and your family?"

The feeling among the 200 conference participants is that the clerical community as an institution has failed the Church. Everyone seems to agree the Church's salvation rests with women, the laity, and the religious community, and it desperately needs the voices of its reform priests and prelates (some of whom are at the conference).

The Church is about the sisters in Africa who minister to the sick and dying in the depths of poverty, who care for those suffering from Ebola, Guinea worm, and AIDS.

The Church is about the Maryknoll brothers and sisters in Latin America who risk their lives in war-torn countries to bring education, healthcare, and the word of God to others.

The Church is Maria Elena Gonzales, whose world revolves around the structures of the Church and her Catholicism as the instrument of faith and hope for herself and her children.

The Church is about all the women teaching in our Catholic institutions, or caring for the elderly, the sick, and the dying in Catholic hospitals and hospices.

In a discussion group at the Washington meeting, one member of the laity tells a bishop that even Houdini could not have escaped the shackles the Church has bound itself in. But it must find an escape, and it has to begin with spiritual grounding. It also has to include the best of what has worked in the United States since the 2002 Dallas Charter. The purpose of this Washington meeting is for the participants to determine what those best practices are.

The Leadership Roundtable draws quite a crowd, which includes lay leaders such as Dr. Kimberly Smolik, the CEO of the Roundtable, John Carr, canon lawyers, abuse survivors, child psychologists, experts in civil law, theologians, social workers, teachers, and nurses. They are joined by reform clerics, including Cardinals O'Malley, Tobin, and Cupich. In addition, another twelve bishops and Jesuit Father Hans Zollner, the head of the office of child protection at the Vatican, are there.

The three discussion points for the conference center on root causes for sexual abuse, leadership failures, and best practices for dealing with this abuse and bishop accountability.

Some of the best suggestions are collected into a report that is shared with the bishops who will be meeting in a few weeks for the Synod of Bishops at the Vatican. John Carr says about this historic meeting of bishops, "It should have happened a long time ago. And it is a miracle that it is happening. It never happened before."

• • •

Two things are clear in the weeks leading up to the Synod of Bishops. The first is that Pope Francis and his supporters are lowering the expectations for reform. The second is the pope's preference for autonomy and decentralization of power, which is ingrained in him from his ecclesiastical life in Argentina. So it is inevitable that the reformers and the victims of abuse are going to be disappointed by the results of the conference.

Behind the scenes, Father Soto is giving background briefings to a half dozen prominent Vatican journalists.

Father Soto says, "Francis is tolerant of other practices within Catholicism whether they are in the eastern rite in Ukraine, the African influence in northern Brazil, or the charismatic branch of the Church that sometimes 'talks in tongues.' He also has been very open to the Vatican II message of opening the Church to fellowship with worshipers of Judaism, Islam, Hinduism, and Buddhism.

"Francis does not advocate one size fits all dictates emanating from the Vatican that apply to everyone. Instead he sees a more generous and inclusive church. He recognizes the Church in the Congo may differ in some practices from the Church in Mumbai, which differs from the Church in Buenos Aires. Francis believes that local control is preferable to control from afar. The Vatican's consent for autonomy of bishops in their own dioceses has been the center of an ecclesiastical tug-of-war going back many centuries." Father Soto hopes to gain a more sympathetic ear in the press by helping them understand the context of how Francis views the papacy.

Francis asks the bishops to meet in their own communities

and listen to the victims. The pope, having talked to many bishops, understands that there are some who do not think this is a major church problem. They fail to grasp how broad and deep the sins and crimes of sexual abuse are throughout most cultures. But in Rome, listening to victims' testimony is to be the first order of business.

The bishops' summit features live presentations by the victims, as well as videos of them recounting how the abuse has damaged their lives. Some of the prelates weep openly over the pain for which they and the Church are responsible.

On the third day of the meeting, a Nigerian nun, Sister Veronica Openibo, scolds the male gathering as a mother would her disobedient children. "Why did the Church allow atrocities of sex abuse to remain secret? Now the Church is in a state of crisis and shame."

Sister Veronica urges church leaders to "acknowledge that our mediocracy, hypocrisy, and complacency have brought us to this disgraceful and scandalous place we find ourselves in as a Church. How could the clerical church have kept silent, covering these atrocities?"

Sister Veronica then added that she had heard of sexual abuses by clerics in Nigeria dating as far back as 1990. Also, sexual abuses are "exploding in some Asian and African countries the same way as elsewhere."

On the subject of clericalism, she observes, "It worries me when I see in Rome and elsewhere the youngest seminarians act as though they are more special than everyone else, thus encouraging them to assume, from the beginning of their training, exalted ideas about their status. What damage has that thinking done to the mission of the Church?"

Sister Veronica is seated a few feet away from Pope Francis. "I admire you, brother Francis, for taking the time as a true

Jesuit to discern and be humble enough to change your mind, to apologize, and take action." She encourages everyone assembled to follow that example. She thanks Francis for asking us all to check those moments when bishops have acted "strangely, ignorantly, secretly, and complacently."

It is astonishing for the Church hierarchy to hear an African woman who is a religious leader laying it all out as Sister Veronica does. She is strong, thoughtful and frank, and the prelates need to hear her. At the end of her talk, she asks that they "allow more light into the Church."

It is a simple plea—one on the minds of millions of Catholics around the world.

As the four-day conference is ending, one of the victims plays a violin solo with a melody that is so melancholy and tender that it sends another wave of shame and pain through the prelates, who once again weep openly.

BOOK FOUR

THE MEXICAN/U.S. BORDER

CHAPTER NINE

Sister Norma and Jesus

The violence on the bus has shaken the Gonzalez family. Once they reach the shelter in Reynosa, Rocia finds herself comforting Marie Elena in a corner of the common room, while Sister Carlotta shows the three girls the room that they will share with their mother.

"Maybe this journey is a mistake," Maria Elena tells Rocia. "We almost lost you and Teresa to those kidnappers. God knows what they may have done to both of you. You can see how scared the girls are now. I'm confused and don't know what to do. The gun battle just triggers memories of what those criminals did to my husband. They are capable of anything."

As Maria Elena finishes, Rocia sees that she has tears in her eyes.

"Maria. I am so sorry our trip is ending so violently," sighs Rocia in a comforting tone. "I share your fear and concern for your family, and this has been a difficult journey. But we are almost at the border. The military police have just come into the shelter, and they will want to talk with all of us."

Rocia looks around for them before continuing. "It is very important that you tell them in your own words how the kidnappers attempted to abduct Teresa and me and how they almost shot you for speaking out. Having your statement on the official record will help you and the children to obtain asylum. Yes, it was a terrifying experience, but now we can use it to show how your family has been tortured. First your husband Juan, then Jose, and now you and Teresa have been subjected to violence."

Maria Elena seems puzzled by this, confused by how something so horrifying could lead to any good. But she has learned that Rocia is someone she can trust.

"I am writing about all of this," Rocia adds, "and the newspaper story will be an additional piece of evidence for you to use. I know how difficult that experience was on the bus and how confusing all of this must be for you, but please try to stay strong and cooperate with the military police as they take your statement."

With heart-breaking emotion in her voice, Maria sobs, "Rocia, I am so afraid that I will be separated from my children and will lose them like so many other parents have lost their children at the border facilities."

"I understand," Rocia says. "I have heard these stories too, but we will not let that happen. You have Miguel and me, and we will do what we can to protect you and Jose and the girls."

"When I look at my girls, I see a fear they didn't carry before the shooting. They used to have hope, but no longer. This terrifies me."

The military police arrive with all their disciplined efficiency and begin getting statements from Maria, Miguel, Rocia, and the children, as well as others on the bus who witnessed the attempted abduction and the deadly gun battle.

Miguel finishes his interview and helps Maria calm her daughters, who have been scared by the interviews. Miguel's heroism on the bus cemented a relationship he was already building with the Gonzalez family. He has proven his ability to protect them, and his presence is reassuring and most welcome.

Rocia is under a tight deadline for her newspaper. She wants to be supportive of the family, but she also knows that filing her story will be even more helpful to them. She retreats with her laptop to a quiet space in the shelter and begins writing a story about the attack on the bus, and also a sidebar that spotlights the heroism of Miguel and Jose. She writes, "Others may have frozen in the presence of the gun wheeling bandits, but Mr. Cabrera and the 13-year-old Jose wrestled down and disarmed one of the kidnappers, preventing further bloodshed and harm to the passengers."

After the family finishes their interviews with the military police, Sister Carlotta takes them to the kitchen for soup and bread. Rocia has been writing for more than an hour, and she decides to take a break and join them.

Before they eat, Sister Carlotta asks Maria Elena if they would like to take a few minutes to pray. Maria Elena nods, and they all sit around a table and bow their heads. Rocia puts her arm around Teresa's shoulder, and Maria has her arms around Camilla and Dio, pulling them gently close to console herself.

Maria Elena is happy to have Miguel and Jose join them at the table just as Sister Carlotta begins to pray, "Dear Lord, our guests have suffered a most painful experience. Draw them close to your bosom and hold their hands as they cross the border and petition for mercy. Let Your own mercy manifest itself in the actions of others, the border guards, the immigration officers, the asylum judges, and others whose paths the Gonzalez family will cross."

Tomorrow is the day when the Gonzalez family, accompanied by Rocia, will cross at the border station between Mexico and the United States and ask for asylum. Miguel and Rocia are convinced they have a powerful case. Rocia believes it is important at this moment to share with them how she sees things and what their chances are.

"Upwards of 23,000 migrants have sought asylum across this border in recent years, and roughly 20 percent have been granted asylum," she begins.

Maria Elena is noticeably disturbed by this low percentage, and Miguel attempts to reassure her by saying, "I am going to call Father Daly, who has been following our journey and knows our case well."

Miguel is happy to reach Father Daly, who is now working as an immigration attorney. Father Daly elaborates on what they already know, some of it frightening, but his overall positive view bolsters everyone's spirits as they prepare themselves to enter the American legal process. Father Daly believes that the Gonzalez family has a strong case to make for asylum.

Maria Elena and Jose are confused about the word "asylum" and ask Father Daly to explain it.

"Asylum," he says, "is a protection granted to foreign nationals—that is, you, Maria, and your family—already in the United States or at the border, who meet the international law definition of a refugee. The United Nations convention and the 1967 Protocol define a refugee as a person who is unable or unwilling to return to his or her home country, and who cannot obtain protection in that country, due to past persecution or well-founded fear of being persecuted in the future 'on account of race, religion, nationality, membership in a particular social group, or political opinion.' The United States Congress incorporated this definition into U.S. immigration law in the Refugee Act of 1980."

Mother and son nod in agreement, even though they are not familiar with the language or the laws.

Father Daly then tries to be more personal with his explanation. "Once your family presents themselves to the border authorities, they will be taken together to a processing center to fill out papers. You most likely will be given a notice to appear at a much later date for the hearing. Often the hearing date will be many months or even years away. In the meantime, you and your children might be housed in detention together or in some cases separated from each other. If the detention facilities are filled—and they are now—you can be released into the community. That is most likely what will happen."

Father Daly was answering so many questions, but he was raising so many more. Already Maria Elena was wondering how she would find shelter for herself and her children while she waited for a hearing date.

"And by the way," Father Daly says, "about 95 percent of the refugees do return for their hearing date. That's important because how asylum is handled and adjudicated depends on the numbers of refugees seeking asylum, the capacity of the detention centers, the number of adjudicators handling the case loads, and the political dynamics at the moment." Maria Elena hardly knows how she can sleep with such uncertainty facing them all tomorrow.

• • •

"Until then, I didn't realize the seriousness of the problem," Sister Norma Pimentel said while speaking to a reporter from the popular *Texas Monthly* magazine in 2014. "Some of the cells were crammed with many children of all ages. One small cell had so many children they were all stacked up in there, with no real sleeping quarters because there was nowhere to lie down even. It's also suffocating—with no air-conditioning, and it's hot and there are no windows or anything. I was able to get inside where the kids are, inside that little cell, and that was where you experience what it feels like to be in a place so cramped and tight, day and night, with the lights on all day and night."

Sister Norma has been called an incident commander because she builds communities and gets things done. She recognizes the importance of people trying to understand each other, of imagining yourself walking in somebody else's shoes no matter what their citizenship or what their views. The Border Patrol respects her because they see her treat migrants humanely and generously. She approaches border agents the same way. She recognizes the unique role each person plays in the daily struggle for survival and for upholding the law and a semblance of order at the border.

As Sister Norma continues to speak with the reporter, she describes the condition of the families. "When the families arrive, they are exhausted from a grueling journey through Mexico. They are most often distraught and depressed. They have left another life behind and are entering a new and unknown life. Tired and hungry, they sometimes spend days getting processed at an overcrowded Border Patrol station."

The Rio Grande Valley has been Sister Norma's home for many years, and this is where she has served for the past twenty-three years as the executive director of Catholic Charities in the Rio Grande Valley. The area encompasses both McAllen and Brownsville, Texas. In 2014, when the number of immigrants began to overwhelm the facilities in those cities, Sister Norma organized community leaders and established respite centers in both places that were just blocks away from the main bus terminals. The centers were in the parishes of Sacred Heart in McAllen and Immaculate Conception in Brownsville. An outpouring of volunteers from both parishes opened their arms to the migrants.

"When migrants enter the respite centers, they are greeted by a roomful of applause," Sister Norma says. "The volunteers clap their hands and chant, 'Welcome! Come in!' Overwhelmed by the warm greeting, the migrants finally feel safe.

"We match the families quickly. They are assigned a volunteer who serves as their chaperone for their stay. The families take showers and get outfitted with new clothes. Some see a doctor. They get a meal from the Salvation Army or the Food Bank. Save the Children volunteers watch the kids as the mothers take care of getting necessities for their upcoming bus journey. If they stay the night, they sleep in an air-conditioned long tent provided by the city."

Sister Norma has been at the heart of the refugee struggle for more than two decades, and she has become well-known and well-regarded in the refugee relief and Catholic communities. Her leadership and compassion have been so heroic that she has drawn the attention of Pope Francis.

On a September evening in 2015, the church of the Sacred Heart in McAllen, Texas, is filled with regular parishioners along with many refugees. On a large nine-by-nine-foot screen placed in front of the church's altar, a surprising image is projected. From the Vatican, some 6,000 miles away, Pope Francis is beamed by satellite. The pope's larger-than-life image dwarfs those in the front pews who are just a few yards away. The church's stunning stained-glass windows, rich in azure, create a celestial ambience for the pope's presentation. This evening Francis is doing more listening and praising than presenting. He is incredibly pleased by the charitable work being done by those in the pews, and this is the kind of Church outreach Francis wants to spread.

Pope Francis is smiling broadly at his audience to show his appreciation for all the work being done by Sister Norma and her volunteers. The pope wants to recognize the work of Sister Norma and her co-workers and to praise the work of U.S. nuns. First Francis listens intently to the introduction of Sister Norma and then hears the stories of young mothers and children who share with the pope their plight and their dreams.

After the powerful personal accounts from the mothers and children are finished, the pope acknowledges their struggles and then says, "There was a sister there, from a religious order. I want to see her."

"Oh, that's me," Sister Norma exclaims. "He is actually speaking to me."

Francis then motions with his hand, as he often does, and says, "Come, come, come, come," waving Sister Norma forward from her pew and into the center aisle. "I want to thank you. And through you to thank all the sisters of religious orders in the United States for the work you have done and that you do in the United States. It's great. I congratulate you. Be courageous. Move forward."

These are encouraging words for Sister Norma, and generally for all U.S. nuns. Now these words from Francis represent a welcome reversal from the Vatican's prior views on their "unorthodox ways."

Francis is not finished, and in his own somewhat unorthodox way, he joyously says to Sister Norma and the others, "I'll tell you one other thing. Is it appropriate for the pope to say this? I love you all very much." Sister Norma returns to her seat, and her tears begin to flow.

"I was still in heaven, still experiencing his presence," she recalls. "He was telling me that he loves us very much. Oh, wow! I will cherish this moment forever. I am blessed."

• • •

Jesus Aguilar spends his next three days traveling from the shelter in Saltillo to Monterrey. Before he leaves the shelter, Miguel gives him a list of shelters and churches where he can find sanctuary and safety.

In Monterrey, Jesus arrives late after an exhausting day of walking twenty miles that includes trekking through a mountain pass. In the city he stops to rest and eat at a modest neighbor-hood restaurant and asks the waitress where he can find the Church of Christ the Worker.

Jesus orders a meal of tacos, beans, and rice with the money that Miguel and Rocia gave him in Saltillo. It is late, and the day-light is now growing short. With directions in hand, Jesus pays his bill and walks to the bus stop where he takes the crosstown bus two miles to the neighborhood of the parish. He walks a cou-ple of blocks to the church and in the darkness tries to open the church door, but it is locked. Exhausted by his long day, Jesus finds a covered church entryway. Here he removes his blanket from his backpack, lies down, and quickly falls asleep.

In the early morning darkness, Jesus is nudged awake. Star-tled he once again sees a Roman-collared priest staring down at him. Father Martinez is there to say Mass, and he smiles at Jesus as the boy wipes sleep from his eyes.

"I am Father Martinez. Come inside and get warm. After I celebrate Mass, we will get breakfast at the rectory. What is your name?"

"Jesus, Padre."

"Ah! Just like our Savior. You too are looking for a home. Where are you from?"

"Honduras, Padre."

"Come, Jesus, let us honor and praise your namesake. Then after Mass we can talk a little more."

After Mass, over eggs, tortillas, and coffee, Jesus tells Father Martinez about his life in San Pedro Sula, the family he left behind, and his journey to cross into the United States.

"Well, my young friend, this is your lucky day," Father Mar-tinez says. "You must have prayed intently in church. I am driv-ing with two nuns to a refugee conference in Matamoros at the parish of Our Lady of Refuge Church. It's just across the river from Brownsville, Texas. If you wish, you may join us."

Jesus's face brightens and of course he accepts this kind offer. It's a ninety-minute ride in the priest's car, as opposed to three dangerous days for him on foot. Later in the morning, he meets Father Martinez at his car, and is introduced to the two nuns. They talk some about the border crisis before Jesus nods off to sleep to the rhythms of the car's motions. Jesus is physically spent from yesterday's long walk and is grateful that Father Martinez and the sisters understand that he needs to rest.

"Jesus. We are here," announces Father Martinez, twisting in his driver's seat to look back at the boy. "It's three o'clock. Let's go and find our host, Father Anthony. I suspect he will know where you can rest tonight."

They walk several blocks to Our Lady of Refuge Church where Father Anthony is preparing to host sixty lay and religious conferees. The increased numbers of refugees in caravans and small groups have created a humanitarian crisis in all border towns along the Rio Grande River. But, despite being very busy, Father Anthony is always patient and accommodating—especially when he is with children or boys who are on the run.

Father Martinez and Jesus find Father Anthony in the parish hall directing volunteers who are setting up tables and chairs. Father Martinez introduces Jesus and his story to their host. Father Anthony immediately turns to Jesus and says, "You may sleep in the church for two days, but there is another boy there also." Father Anthony turns to look for another boy who is unfolding chairs. "Carlos, please come." He motions with his hand for Carlos to come over and meet Jesus.

Carlos is a 16-year-old who has made his way from San Salvador, El Salvador. His story is eerily similar to Jesus's. Carlos too has left a mother and siblings who are poverty stricken and who live in a similar gang-infested neighborhood that is overcome by fear and intimidation.

The two boys become instant friends and bond quickly into a team. Their goal is to cross the border together. They know they are safe for the next two nights when they can sleep in the church. The next two days can be used to plan their crossing of the Rio Grande near Brownsville, Texas. It is important to scout just the right spot to cross. In preparation the boys walk to the river to watch carefully to see how often the U.S. Border Patrol vehicles pass by the location they have chosen. They calculate that, after a vehicle passed, they had thirty minutes to get across the river from Mexico and into the United States before another patrol vehicle passed this spot.

The boys decide they will cross together two nights later.

Luckily, the sky is cloudy that night, somewhat covering the light of the moon. They crouch in some scrub and watch carefully as the border patrol SUV drove past their site. In the dark of the night, they are bent down like soldiers on a mission getting ready to attack. The boys believe they have thought of everything. But how could they have known that sophisticated cameras are pointing at the waters, filming any movement? Even on the darkest nights, the cameras sense the heat of bodies and create an image that is relayed to the border patrol vehicles policing the riverfront.

Jesus and Carlos, despite the confidence they have in their plan, are frightened as they dash down the embankment to the river's edge, where they have prepared a raft that will take them across. They quietly dog-paddle through the calm water. Carlos thinks of the young toughs in his old neighborhood who were constantly bullying him and his family. His paddle strokes in the river grow stronger as his anger increases remembering their intimidations. Jesus, on the other hand, is thinking of how much he misses his mother and sisters.

Both boys are also filled with adrenaline-fueled excitement about the new life awaiting them in America, and the possibility that they will be able to send money to their families back home.

Ahead, the shoreline is approaching, and they suddenly feel the jolt of the raft hitting the river bottom. They reach out in the muck of the river to pull themselves closer to shore. Feeling the earth and grass, they realize they have done it! Jesus is the first off the raft, and he pulls it out of the water enough for Carlos to jump off as well. They have little time to celebrate because they know their journey isn't finished yet.

As they crawl up the embankment, they are met by several vehicles that have suddenly turned on their searchlights. Blinded by the intensity of the lights, their hearts sink. Speaking in Spanish, a patrol agent orders them to halt and put both hands on top of their heads. They are searched, handcuffed, and pushed into the caged backseat of a border patrol SUV. They are both stunned and terrified. Now they feel like common criminals. How could they have come this far only to have it end this way?

Soon they are at the Detention Center in Brownsville.

• • •

Casa Padre is an old Walmart turned into a massive migrant detention center for boys. About 1,500 boys between the ages of 10 and 17, most of whom are unaccompanied, live in what some reporters have described as prison-like conditions. By the time Jesus and Carlos reach Casa Padre, the flow of migrants over the past year has become so heavy that this is now just one of a hundred such facilities in the United States.

This detention center employs around 1,000 trained staff members, including cooks, teachers, counselors, attendants, maintenance workers, and medical professionals. The cost for detaining a single migrant in a facility like Casa Padre is an astounding $273,000 per year.

Jesus and Carlos rise every day at 6:00 a.m., and the lights go out in the evening at 9:00 p.m. The facilities are so crowded that the children attend school in shifts, and their day is regimented very much like a prison. Each boy is allowed two phone calls a week.

For the first three weeks, Jesus does little other than go through the routine of the day, until he decides to reach Miguel and tell him what has happened.

Many of the younger boys have been separated from their families and have become withdrawn and depressed, some of them suffering from post-traumatic stress syndrome that may haunt them for the rest of their lives. They have no choice but to wait, longing for their families, with no sense of when their nightmare will be over.

Some of the older boys begin to act as big brothers, or surrogate fathers, to the younger ones. A few older boys befriend the visiting priest who comes on Sundays to say Mass. They ask the priest if he can bring something comforting for the "little ones who are always sad." That is when Catholic Charities sends over an assortment of stuffed animals, like teddy bears, that they leave resting on top of the blankets that cover the cots of the smaller boys.

• • •

Three months have passed since Jesus and Carlos were captured at the river. They are having breakfast in the dining hall.

"Hey, Carlos," Jesus whispers. "See that laundry truck parked at the dock? I have been watching it all week. The driver pulls up and into the dock by the kitchen, he opens the back doors of the truck and always wheels out a large laundry cart. And you know what else he does? He always leaves the doors open.

"The cargo bin of the truck is filled with sheets, pillowcases, cook uniforms, and other linens. He dumps the cart full of laundry into the truck after each stop on his route. Our detention center must be at the end of his route because he always needs to push the laundry deep inside the truck."

"Jesus," Carlos whispers back. "I understand what you are telling me. There is no guard by the door that opens to the dock."

"Right." Jesus says. "There is no guard. Let's talk about this more tonight."

Two weeks later, after having monitored the laundry truck every day, the two boys execute their escape. Once the driver enters the kitchen with his empty cart, the boys slip out of the cafeteria door next to the dock. They enter the truck's cargo bin and dive into the soiled laundry, tunneling to the back of the compartment.

Jesus takes one item with him. It's the photo of his family, which he hides under his shirt. Like two quiet mice invisible beneath the laundry, they wait breathlessly for the driver to return with his cart and more soiled laundry.

The doors are then shut to the cargo bin, and the boys listen for the sound of the truck's engine. They feel it slowly back up and then feel the turn of its wheels as the truck moves forward and out of the detention center. In about ten minutes, the truck arrives at another loading dock.

The engine stops, the driver jumps out of the cab and slams the door shut. In a few more seconds the doors to the cargo bin are opened wide to allow the cart to make its way out to the dock. Soon there are no sounds.

The boys feel like they are participants in a game of hide

and seek. In the eerie silence, they pop up together, climb over the linens, and enter the dock. They lower themselves the three feet to the parking lot below and run for daylight away from the unknown building where the truck has stopped.

Jesus looks back every so often as they run and is surprised that no one pursues them. Soon they are on the road to Houston and freedom.

CHAPTER TEN

Detention Center and Then Starting a New Life

The time has come for the Gonzalez family to cross the border. All their travel, often into danger, has been building to this moment. Maria Elena had been anticipating this and dreaming of it, and now she is also dreading it. She isn't clear what is waiting for her, and that scares her, and now she also has to part with new friends she's made on this journey.

The family gathers outside the shelter in Reynosa, with Miguel and Rocia. Miguel and Maria Elena have become very fond of each other, and they hug, wondering after meeting in these strange and extraordinary circumstances whether they will ever see each other again.

Maria pulls back, looks her protector in the eyes, and says, "You saved my life and Theresa's. And you became friends with Jose. We could not have come this far without you."

She embraces Miguel again, and Jose and Teresa see how happy their mother is despite the sadness of the parting. They think their mother and Miguel make a nice couple. The kids then join Maria in hugging Miguel. Overcome with gratitude and sadness, he says, "I will miss you all. We will stay in touch. I just know we will see each other again."

It is now Rocia's turn. As she hugs Miguel, tears are running down her cheeks, and she too thanks him for saving her. "Miguel, we have each other's phone numbers, so let us correspond by email, text, or better yet by phone," she says. "I still need to interview you for my stories."

"Yes, of course," he replies. "We will talk. Merry Christmas, Rocia." Everyone then remembers that Christmas is only two weeks away.

A bus from the shelter takes Rocia and the family to the border, where they will cross over a bridge into the United States. The McAllen-Hidalgo-Reynosa International Bridge crossing over the Rio Grande River is a one-kilometer walk on a pedestrian lane that is located next to nine lanes of traffic. It is noisy and smells of exhaust fumes.

Before they begin their bridge walk to the border station, Rocia and the family squeeze together into a bear hug. They have been through joy and pain on this journey. And like Miguel, Rocia has bonded with them and now holds on to their loving grips longer than anyone expects.

When Rocia gently frees herself, she turns to Jose. "Your family will need your strong support, and you will need to help each other," she says. "These next few weeks will not be easy. You will be confined until you have your 'credible fear interview.' If all goes well, and it should, you may be released due to the overcrowding at the detention facilities. You have my phone number and Miguel's. And I think that Miguel gave you Sister Norma's number for the respite center in McAllen."

Jose and Maria Elena nod an affirmative "yes."

"Oh!" exclaims Rocia. "Do you have Father Daly's phone number?" Maria nods yes, and relieved, Rocia exhales, "Good. Well, then let us walk across the bridge." The walk takes about 20 minutes. Rocia and Maria Elena walk side by side conversing over the sounds of engine noises and the shifting gears of the big rig trucks. The four children walk in pairs behind the adults. They are not alone, as other adults and children journey across on foot in front of and behind them.

As they approach the terminal building in the United States, the intense emotions of love and fear wash over everyone in the traveling group. They gather for one last long hug. The three girls are overcome and crying because they know they will not see Rocia for a long time, if ever. In such a short time, she has become a significant person in their young lives.

Finally, Rocia pulls herself apart from them. "And one more thing, Maria Elena," she remembers, almost businesslike to compose herself. "I will work to get the police documents of your husband's murder from the authorities in Tegucigalpa. God be with you." Then she turns, almost sharply, and walks away from the family to enter a line for U.S. citizens and green card holders.

Maria Elena and her children enter the border station, along with several other families, and are herded into a large waiting room inside the Border Patrol Building. The building is large and open, with few walls, exuding an air of coldness and bureaucratic indifference. Maria feels as if she and her family are being treated as herded cattle on their way to the slaughterhouse. Almost no one in the building is smiling or conveying any warmth.

Miguel and Rocia had told Maria that she would be handed some forms as they entered the building, and so she gathers the children around her by some benches they find unoccupied. She begins filling out the necessary information. Once they are completed, she hands them to a middle-aged man who is walking around the large room collecting forms.

Now they wait.

After a long morning and afternoon of sitting anxiously and patiently, Maria Elena hears her name called. The family stands up and goes to the counter. They are taken into another room and fingerprinted. Maria's children have seen this process on television, so they know enough about it to realize it's not a welcoming sign of friendship. Their first act in the United States is an adversarial one. After Camilla rolls her thumb and fingers over the ink pad, she wonders if this means she is now branded for life as a bad person.

Next, they are taken into a small office, which makes Dio and Camilla think they are being taken to the principal's office at school. It is scary. The border official behind the desk appears to be about Maria Elena's age. He is dressed in a white collared shirt and a tie with a pattern of horses printed on it. His shirt sleeves at the cuff are rolled one fold up giving him an image of authority and productivity. He does not smile, and he is clearly a man who has seen many children. His indifference to them is unnerving to Maria Elena.

In Spanish he questions Maria Elena, "Why have you and your children come to the United States?"

Maria Elena takes a deep breath and in a strong voice tinged with sadness tells her story. "Our home and neighborhood in Tegucigalpa are not safe. My husband was murdered by the drug gang called Barrio 18 when he refused to join them and sell narcotics. He was executed with a bullet to his head as he lay face down on the ground near the market where he worked. Then, about one month ago, this same gang severely beat my son and told him he would end up like his father if he did not join the gang. Then this hoodlum told my son, Jose, that they would harm his family. That is when we decided to leave our home and seek asylum in the United States."

Maria Elena knows this is not the full "credible fear" hearing Rocia had told her to expect. Abruptly, after five minutes, the man ends the interview. The border official tells them, "It will be about a month before the full 'credible fear' hearing can be scheduled. In the meantime, you and your children will be bused a hundred miles to the South Texas Family Residential Center where you will live together until the hearing and the disposition of evidence."

The younger children are confused as they board the bus to take them to the Family Residential Center, which is really a renovated campsite that had once been used by oilfield workers. The bus is filled primarily with children and their mothers. Once out of McAllen, the bus passes by endless miles of South Texas scrubland. The wind's whining sound penetrates the bus as the kids gaze out their windows at the tumbleweeds that bump along the desolate landscape. Maria thinks that their lives are being swept away like the scrub blowing in the wind.

Dio asks her mother, "Where are we going, Mommy?"

"To a place we can stay until we learn whether we can remain in the United States," Maria answers

Dio stares at the bleak landscape out her window, then pleads, "Mommy, I don't want to stay in the United States. I want to go back to our home."

Maria Elena puts her arm around her youngest daughter's shoulder and draws her near to kiss her forehead. "We are close to Christmas, so I will tell you a story about the baby Jesus and his mother and father who were also far away from their home.

"Dio, the baby Jesus was a refugee just like we are—and like the others on this bus. Jesus's father, Joseph, and his mother, Mary, walked for days from their small house in the village of Nazareth to reach Bethlehem, a place where the government demanded they come. When they arrived, there wasn't a place for them to sleep, so they found a barn with animals—goats, chickens, and their own donkey. And that was where the Blessed Mother had her baby, and they called him Jesus.

"They wrapped Jesus in swaddling clothes to keep him warm and to make Him feel safe. There was no bed or crib, so they placed Him in a manger. A manger was a trough where the animals sometimes ate. But this manger was empty of feed, so they cleaned it and laid their baby down.

"They lived in the barn and baby Jesus slept in the manger. After two weeks, three kings, who had travelled very far to see this newborn holy child, arrived with presents for the family. Then the Holy Family made their way back home to Nazareth. Mary rode on the donkey holding baby Jesus and Joseph guided the donkey along the road to their home."

Maria Elena looks down at Dio to let her know that she is concluding her story. "Soon, Dio," she said "We will arrive at our new home. Just like Jesus arrived at his new home."

• • •

That same day, about six thousand miles away at the Vatican, Pope Francis meets with pre-teen members of Italy's Catholic Action program for his annual exchange of Christmas greetings with them.

"I'm giving you some homework," the pope tells them. "On Christmas Day, pause in prayer with the same awe as the shepherds who looked upon baby Jesus. Remember that He came into this world to bring the love of God. With His birth Jesus became a bridge between God and humanity, reconciling earth and heaven, restoring the unity of the whole human race."

The pope pauses to let this sink in with his listeners before he continues, "And today he asks you, too, to be little bridges where you live. You know that there always is a need to build bridges, right? What is better, building bridges or walls?"

"Bridges," they shout.

"Being bridges, bringing people together, is not always easy," the pope tells them. "But if we are united in Christ, we can do it."

• • •

Maria Elena and her children do not know that Dilley, as the center is known, is considered the best of the detention facilities in the United States. Unlike many of the others, they are not locked in cages cramped together, and they are given blankets for sleeping.

Dilley is named after a nearby small town. It is a large campsite with buildings that can house more than 3,000 people. There are also eighty cottages, each with two bedrooms, a bathroom, and a small kitchen. However, most of the refugees are boarded in large communal rooms, with bunk beds and community bathrooms, providing none of the privacy offered in the cottages. Still, the shelters are clean, and the occupants are given three meals each day. The migrants are mostly children from Central America who share each other's loneliness for the homes they have left.

To keep the children busy, the center has a school, basketball courts, and soccer fields, as well as a library with a selection of books for children. The migrants are not fenced in, because there really isn't any place they can escape to. They are surrounded by large swaths of Texas scrubland and the small town of Dilley, where they would be obvious to the authorities. If they choose to flee and are apprehended, they will be deported and any attempts at re-entry into the United States would be virtually impossible. They all know this, and so they wait.

When Jose and his sisters are not playing soccer, they choose books from the library, take them back to their bunks, and read. Maria Elena, Teresa, and Jose enjoy reading to the younger girls, Camilla and Dionysia.

Maria Elena is spending her time trying to allay the new fears her children are picking up at the center. Fears of separation and the unknown have begun to occupy her children's minds. Maria also is spending time talking with many of the other mothers in her shelter, who share with each other ideas of where next to live, assuming their "credible fear" interviews go well and they are released. In the evening, she writes down the information she picks up from the other mothers and staff at the facility, about places to live, schools, and job opportunities.

Soon after the Gonzalez family arrives at Dilley, an artificial Christmas tree and a crèche are set up in the commons area. A social worker helps organize a tree-decorating party with the kids making all the ornaments out of paper and other odds and ends. For the next few nights, they gather around the tree in the evening and sing *villancicos* (Christmas carols) like "Feliz Navidad" and "Blanca Navidad."

On Christmas Day, a Mass is said in the commons area, and the priest's homily is mostly directed to all the children present. He talks about the Holy Family and the Nativity and ends with the Angel Prayer, commemorating the Incarnation—when the angel Gabriel, a messenger of God reveals to the Virgin Mary that she will conceive a child to be born the Son of God. During the Offertory, the congregation sings with great gusto a stirring rendition of "Venid, Fieles" (Oh Come, All Ye Faithful):

Venid, adoremos (Come, let us adore Him)
Venid, adoremos
Venid, adoremos
a Cristo el Señor (Christ, the Lord)

While the Mass is in progress, the staff at the center stuffs stockings, donated by Catholic Charities, with an orange, three pieces of hard candy, and a pencil. They then place one on the bunk of each child.

A month into their stay at Dilley, Maria Elena receives a notice on her bunk that her "credible fear" hearing will take place at the center in three days. She is excited but also anxious. Each family at the center is given two phone calls a week, and she uses hers to share the news with Miguel and then with Father Daly.

Each night on her bunk, before she kisses her children good night, Maria Elena goes over her notes for her testimony at the hearing. She wants to have her thoughts so embedded in her mind that they flow naturally and with emotion. On the morning of the hearing, Maria and her children walk outside of their lodging and then several blocks to the Administration Building where the hearing is to take place. Before they walk into the hearing room, the children hug their mom and encourage her.

"You'll do great, Mom" says Teresa.

Even Dio, who has not given up returning to Honduras, tells her mother, "You are like the Blessed Mother, so I know you will do well, and then we can find a home." Maria is touched by her youngest daughters' words and sentiments, and tears well up in her eyes.

For the hearing, Father Daly is on the phone, and an interpreter is in the room with Maria Elena. She faces a man and two women, and she believes as she tells her story that they understand it and are moved by it. Afterward, Father Daly praises her and encourages her, while also cautioning her not to get her hopes up too much. The family is not free yet.

Finally, three days later, Maria and her children receive a release order into the community. How happy they are! But they are also instructed to notify ICE officials of their next residence so they can be alerted to the date, time, and place of their asylum court hearing.

The family takes a bus from Dilley back to the bus terminal in McAllen, and from there, with their small backpacks, walk the three blocks to Sacred Heart Parish, where Sister Norma's

Respite Center is located. Maria Elena is yet again searching for a place where her family can rest their heads for the night. The past month has been quite different for the children from Tegucigalpa. their own home the only place they had ever slept.

"Welcome, Maria!" exclaims Sister Norma, with her arms wide open and her broad smile. "Is this your family?"

"Yes, Sister. My son, Jose, and my daughters Teresa, Camilla, and Dionysia. Thank you for receiving us. You are so busy. We are honored by your graciousness."

"Maria, I have heard from our friend Padre Melo, who wrote to tell me that you and your family were crossing, and that you would be coming here. You are fortunate to have such a wonderful patron."

"He was my pastor, and he looked after my family. Jose used to serve as an altar boy for Father Melo," beams Maria with pride.

After being warmly greeted at the respite center, Maria Elena and her children decide to stay in the parish of the Sacred Heart. They are overjoyed by the kindness and love they experience at the center. The day after they arrive, a counselor guides them through the options for housing and talks to Maria Elena about work opportunities. Schools are discussed, as are English language classes at night.

The center is not meant to be permanent, and the Gonzalez family is allowed to spend only three days there while they line up housing and work opportunities. Maria does have a little savings from her work in Tegucigalpa, but it is not enough to rent an apartment, so Miguel wires her a small loan to help the family get started.

"Hello, Miguel," she excitedly says. "This is Maria."

"Maria!" an effusive Miguel replies, "Congratulations!"

"Oh Miguel! Isn't it wonderful?" she exclaims. "I always

thought we had a good case, but I always worried that something could go wrong. During these last two days after we arrived in McAllen and the respite center, I have been busy looking for work, an apartment, and schools for the children. The Lord must be with me because I have found them!"

"How wonderful! Please tell me about your search."

"We like Sacred Heart Parish so much that we have decided to stay in this neighborhood. The people here have good and generous hearts. Someone at the respite center told me there was a clothing factory that was a fifteen-minute walk from the church, and they were hiring seamstresses. I went there and got a job as a seamstress!"

"Maria, do you mind if I ask how much they will pay you?"

"No. Not at all. I will make the minimum wage of $7.25 an hour for eight hours a day, which is two less hours than what I worked at home. So, I will earn $60 a day, $300 a week and $1,300 a month. For me, that's a lot of money. On the walk back to the respite center, I stopped at an apartment building near the public school. The advisor at the center suggested I try this place. He said it is clean and not too expensive. I found a one-bedroom for $650 a month, which is half of my monthly pay. The advisor later told me it will probably be more than half of my pay after taxes and energy are also paid."

"Maria, you are incredible!" Miguel says.

"Our lives will be centered in the parish, and we will be able to walk to work, school, and church. I just can't believe it."

"How are the children?" Miguel asks, with concern in his voice.

"They are better, but I still think they are traumatized by the past months. I especially worry about Dio. She still wants to go back home to Honduras. But even she has changed since we arrived here in McAllen."

"And Teresa?"

"She is strong like her brother, but I am keeping a close eye on her. Rocia has called and talked to Teresa twice. They are very fond of each other. It is good, but I am a little jealous. I have not had competition for the love of my children. She is a good woman, so I am reconciled to sharing Teresa with her."

"Maria Elena, I miss you very much," Miguel says. "Give my love to the children."

"I miss you too, Miguel. Please call again."

"I will. And I will sleep well tonight dreaming of your happy news. *Buenas noches.*"

"*Buenas noches*, Miguel."

• • •

Jose begs his mother to let him find a job to supplement the money she is earning. He tells her he is the man of the family now and wants to do his part. Maria Elena is impressed by his maturity and recognizes how he has been shaped by the role he played during the attack on the bus. She also knows Jose is still a boy in many ways and should not have to assume the role of an adult yet.

"No," she tells him. "I want you and your sisters to enjoy your childhood as much as possible and focus on your schoolwork. I am very proud of you."

At Sacred Heart Church, Jose becomes an altar boy, and begins to serve at weddings and funerals. He earns a little tip money while doing these jobs and saves the coins until they accumulate into a few dollars, which he gives to his mother. Jose also joins the neighborhood's Catholic Youth Organization (CYO) soccer team and plays up front as an attacker, while his three sisters play together in the girls' league.

This pleases Maria Elena very much, and each weekend, she looks forward to watching her children's soccer matches. Before the matches, Maria, often accompanied by her children, goes to the respite center and volunteers her time for others.

Jose and the girls begin attending the neighborhood public schools. On Wednesdays after school, they attend catechism class at the church. And on Tuesday and Thursday evenings, the church offers an English language class for newly arrived parishioners. Maria Elena insists that the whole family take advantage of this opportunity.

Slowly, they develop a new rhythm of work, school, church, and recreation. Their neighborhood is gang-free, much safer than in Tegucigalpa. Their neighbors are also refugees. Spanish is spoken openly by most, which makes it easier for them to find friends and to start becoming part of a broader community. Time passes, month after month. Nine months after they arrived in McAllen, Father Daly calls with some good news.

He has been monitoring the Gonzalez family's petition for asylum. Father Daly belongs to a large Catholic network called the Catholic Legal Immigration Network or CLINIC, which is a loose group of about 330 organizations that provides legal services to migrants and refugees. Of the 177 Catholic Charity agencies in the United States, 168 of them provide some level of legal assistance. They have trained lawyers and paralegals on their staffs to represent their clients in immigration courts and proceedings. They are indispensable in shepherding their clients, many of whom do not speak English, through the complex legal system. Part of being Catholic is welcoming the stranger and defending the weak.

Father Daly takes note of an article in the monthly Clinic bulletin that mentions a way to ease the long waiting periods for a hearing by having the agency pull out applicants who might qualify for expedited hearings and moving them up on the court calendar. This new pilot program has just gone into effect. Father Daly seizes the opportunity. His petition on behalf of the family is granted, and their hearing is moved up to January 2020. He marks the date on his calendar so he will be sure to be there.

Father Daly calls Maria Elena to tell her the good news, which she shares with her children. After nine months, the family is settled in their new home and community. They have stopped thinking that it might just be temporary. Still, Maria is excited that the hearing is sooner than she expected, although that doesn't mean she isn't also nervous.

• • •

Father Daly takes a cab from the McAllen airport to the respite center, where he is met by Maria Elena and her family. Maria Elena has also called Rocia to tell her the news and to share with her friend how anxious she is about the hearing. Rocia responds with positive excitement and tells Maria not to be nervous, that she will do well.

Rocia also knows Maria Elena's story could be the final piece in her four-part series for the *New York Times*.

Maria Elena tells the good news to Miguel and not surprisingly he wants to be there with her and the children. But he has no papers to enter the United States. Instead, he will be available on the phone from Mexico in case he is needed.

Father Daly gathers them all together in the front lobby of his hotel, so he can describe for them how their case will unfold in front of the judge.

"The judge is a woman who has a great deal of experience

handling these types of cases," Father Daly explains. "She will be aware that this case was put on an expedited calendar because a legal screener looked at the evidence and has determined it is solid."

Father Daly then takes a deep breath before he says, "But it is ultimately her decision to grant asylum or to deny it. The judge may try to poke holes in the assessment she was given to fast-track this case."

He then turns directly to face Maria Elena. "She may ask questions about your fears—and she may try to determine if they are real." He shifts his attention to Jose. "She may talk to you about your beating." Father Daly moves around the circle and faces Rocia and says, "The judge might ask you about your story and the threat against you and Teresa on the bus. The judge may also ask you about the death certificate and other documents regarding Maria Elena's late husband."

A letter to the court from Cardinal Moreno Coto will be read into the record, explaining how he counseled Maria after her husband's murder and describing how Jose looked the day after his beating by Barrio 18. Father Daly concludes with words of confidence. "We have nothing to fear. The truth and the law are on our side."

At the asylum hearing, the judge listens intently to the testimony from Maria Elena, her children and Rocia. Unlike the first five-minute hearing at the Border Patrol Station, this judge is paying attention and is engaged and asks questions in a calm, nonaccusatory manner. She is patient when the children testify and encourages them throughout the process.

At the end of the hearing, the judge asks Jose why he wants to come to America. Jose responds, "I want happiness for my mother. She deserves it. We will be safer here, and we will have a chance for a good education and then a job. Our father, if he were here, would be proud of us."

Thirteen months after the Gonzalez family crossed the border and began seeking asylum, the immigration judge grants asylum to Maria Elena Gonzalez and her four children. The judge concludes that the evidence in their favor is "overwhelming and credible." After an additional year's wait, Maria and her children will be eligible to apply for green cards, and if they are granted, they will be able visit Miguel in Mexico and still return to their new home in the United States.

BOOK FIVE

THE VATICAN

CHAPTER ELEVEN

The Dream

Francis customarily rises at 4:00 a.m. He begins his day with prayer and meditation. His day most often ends with prayer at 9:00 p.m. But on this day, Francis is more fatigued and finds himself craving the quiet of the night.

In the bedroom of his simple Vatican apartment, a cross with the crucifixion hangs on the wall near the foot of his bed where Francis dreams the dreams of an old man. It is where he has dreamed of sitting in his grandmother Rosa's lap as she reads stories to him from the Bible. His favorite is the Good Samaritan and his act of mercy. This room is also where he dreamed about chasing after his sixth-grade classmates through the schoolyard.

Francis also dreamed of serving Mass and feeling the splendor of Christ during the transubstantiation as he rings the shaker bells when the priest lifts above his head the unleavened bread (the body of Christ). This happens again when the priest repeats the miracle by holding up the golden chalice, a gleaming cup reflecting light and altar images. The cup is filled with red wine (the blood of Christ). These acts are followed by the priest's words, "Do this in commemoration of me." Francis believes these words are his invitation into the priesthood.

On this night, Francis has just finished polishing his black shoes, a habit he picked up during his boyhood when he polished his father's shoes. It is a ritual he loves. Removing the lid of the can, he inhales the distinctive aroma of black wax that seals the shoe leather for another week. He applies the wax in circles in a hypnotic exercise. Then with a soft-haired brush, he buffs the wax into a shine that shows the pride he felt when he performed this humble task for his father.

Now this weekly ritual of shoe shining brings his father, Mario, into his life again. His father has been gone for many years, and Francis is now twenty years older than his father was when he passed. This causes Francis to think to himself, *And soon I too will be gone from this life.*

Francis clasps the lid to the can that holds the wax and, with a click, seals it for another week. He then washes the wax from his hands, brushes his teeth, and moves over to his bed, where he says his final prayers of the day. Sleep at his age can be fitful, but this evening he is tired and drifts into a deep slumber—a sleep that reveals images that portend a significant change.

In his dream this night, Francis is a child of ten, like Lucia, Jacinta, and Francesco in Fatima. He is back in Argentina, in Córdoba, peering through magnificent iron gates at the Jesuit Block and Estancias. He stares intently at an apparition that hovers over an open green space. The larger and clearer it grows, the more it draws young Jorge's full attention. It is Our Lady of Solitude, dressed in black satin, with her arms extended as if trying to embrace other images now becoming clear to Francis in his magical dream.

On Mary's right side under her outstretched arm is Mother Teresa of Calcutta, holding hands with Harriet Tubman, whose other arm is interlocked with the Nigerian Sister Veronica Openibo, the scolder of bishops for their failures. Next to Sister Openibo is Saint Clare, founder of the Poor Clares and ally of Saint Francis of Assisi. Alongside Saint Clare is Sister Norma Pimentel, who is listening to Francis's grandmother Rosa, who is speaking loud enough for all the world and heavens to hear, when she proclaims: "He was such a good boy, sometimes naughty, but mostly a loving child and kind child." Behind Rosa and Sister Norma, and trying to join the conversation, is Francis's sister, Maria Elena.

On Mary's left side, under her other outstretched arm, is Francis's favorite Carmelite, Saint Theresa of Lisieux, who is holding hands with Dorothy Day, whose other arm is interlocked with Mary Magdalene. Next to her is Malala Yousafzai, now grown but once a child who was shot in the head by the Taliban for defying their ban on education for girls. Nearby Francis sees Anne Frank and Gertrude Weil, interlocked in unity. Behind them are the women martyrs of recent times: murdered Maryknoll missionary nuns Maura Clark and Ita Ford, also Ursuline nun Dorothy Kazel and her lay missionary friend, Jean Donovan. These martyrs are joined by Elba Ramos and her 16-year-old daughter Celina, both murdered in 1989 at the Catholic University in San Salvador, along with six Jesuit priests. Rising behind them all is Saint Veronica who demonstrated courage and mercy by wiping the bleeding face of Jesus as He made His way up Calvary.

The women are humbly and simply dressed, with no rings, staffs, miters, or pallium. Just their persons and their veils of mercy. In the dream, Our Lady of Solitude is not the one who speaks, but rather Rosa, who tells Francis how proud she is of his accomplishments but admonishes him that he needs to finish his work.

"Jorge," she pleads. "Look to women, for they can be the salvation of the Church."

As the vision begins to fade, the pope is startled awake and sits up in his bed, his arms outstretched. "Don't go. Stay a while longer," he begs. He wants more time with Rosa, Maria Elena, and the lonely figure of Our Lady. But they are gone—even though their vision is still clear in his mind.

Francis has already been thinking about ways to bring more women into the Church leadership. He has recently added several women to his team of counselors and appointed the Benedictine Joan Chittister to lead the Truth and Reconciliation Commission. As well as appointing a commission to study the question of women becoming deaconesses, he has invited ten women to join the bishops' summit.

Perhaps this will lead to the priesthood for women, but tonight, after his haunting dream, a new idea comes to him that will advance the cause of women bringing new energy to the Church.

· · ·

Father Soto places the letter from the late Italian Cardinal Carlo Martini on top of the stack of mail he has left for Pope Francis to read.

Soto knows the pope is an avid admirer of Cardinal Martini, who had been a renowned and respected liberal voice in the Church. Also a Jesuit, Martini had been an expert on scripture and the early church, and his views sometimes ran contrary to Church doctrine. Father Soto hopes the pope will be inspired by rereading this letter.

Cardinal Martini's letter had been made public after his death in August 2012. Seven years later the letter's contents haunt Francis as powerfully as his dream last night about Our Lady of Solitude and the other women of courage.

Martini's views express a willingness to have women ordained as deacons. He supported the use of condoms in fighting AIDS. The cardinal from Milan also supported a patient's right to die when terminally ill, and he brought together Catholics, agnostics, and atheists for group discussions. In 2005,

Cardinal Martini was seen to be a candidate to be elected pope, but after 27 years of Pope John Paul II, the Conclave turned to the more conservative candidate, Cardinal Joseph Ratzinger, who took the name Benedict XVI.

Cardinal Martini's letter draws attention because it reads in part:

> The Church is tired, in the Europe of well-being, and in America. Our culture is aged, our churches are large, our religious houses empty; the Church's bureaucratic apparatus is growing, and our rites and vestments are pompous. Do such things really express what we are today? Well-being weighs us down. We find ourselves like the rich young man who went away sad when Jesus called him to become a disciple. I know that it is not easy to leave everything behind. At least we could find people who are free and closer to their neighbors, as Bishop Romero was, and the Jesuit martyrs from El Salvador. Where among us are our heroes to inspire us? . . . How can the embers be freed from the ashes in order to rekindle the flame of love? . . . I advise the pope and the bishops to look for twelve people outside the lines and give them leadership positions, people who are close to the poorest and surrounded by young people and trying out new things. We need that comparison with people who are on fire so that the spirit can spread everywhere.

Francis knows the Church in Europe and North America is tired, sluggish, and without its evangelical soul. And, like Martini, Francis is an admirer of Bishop Oscar Romero of El Salvador, who was assassinated in 1980, as well as others from poor countries who live their faith and are committed to the poor and the working poor. Now the pope feels that through this letter Martini has come back to life and given him a gift, a path forward.

Francis is especially inspired by the vision of twelve to reignite concerns for those with basic needs and the passion to be missionaries for Christ.

• • •

It is early August 2019, and for the past three weeks Francis has been meeting with Cardinal Ouellet and Father Soto to discuss a sixth consistory, during which he will anoint a new class of cardinals. The pope has called a consistory in each of the past five years to confirm the appointments of new cardinals. A consistory is a formal meeting between the pope and his cardinals where newly chosen prelates are ceremoniously elevated to the rank of cardinal.

During a recent meeting Francis turns directly to Cardinal Ouellet and drops a bombshell. "I am going to break precedent and appoint women as well as men to the rank of cardinal. Marc, I want you to hear me out before you respond," Francis announces in a soft but determined voice.

Father Soto sits quietly as the cardinal and the pope confront an issue that has the potential to either break the Church apart or re-invigorate it. Soto is aware that over the last six months, since the Synod of Bishops meeting in February, Francis has been contemplating this groundbreaking idea. Now Soto feels complicit with Frances since he has never suggested to the pontiff that he reconsider the idea. Soto knows there will be vigorous kick back from the conservative traditionalists and even from some moderates.

Additionally, Juan Soto knows that Francis does not just want to dip his toe into the water but is instead determined to take a full plunge into the depths of the unknown. The pope intends to name not just one woman cardinal but five, along with four new male cardinals. Soto can not stop himself from marveling at the transition from the pope who earlier in the year lamented to him, "Juan, I am a man who was raised in the Italian, Argentinean, and Catholic cultures that all undervalue women. You and I together have struggled to bring more women into the Church leadership. We have personally worked to raise the stature of women in the Church while still wrestling with more questions, 'Is this not enough for one pope to take on? Can I go further without tearing the Church apart? Shall I go forward?'"

Now, Soto is listening anxiously as Francis makes his case to the powerful Canadian cardinal for "going forward" with his controversial proposal. Francis and Soto have discussed the importance of having Ouellet on their side—or at the minimum to neutralize his opposition—when the pope appoints five women as cardinals.

The debate today between Francis and Ouellet is focused on the theological questions centered on the sacrament of Holy Orders. Francis argues that a cardinal's position does not fall under Holy Orders, and instead is a rank of honor. Cardinal Ouellet counters that since 1917 cardinals are first required to be priests, which in itself is one of the three positions in Holy Orders along with deacons and bishops.

"Yes, Marc," Pope Francis retorts, "but the pope in 1917, not that long ago, brought about that restrictive change, and the present pontiff can also change canon law to expand eligibility."

Their discussion becomes increasingly rigorous as the pope and the cardinal argue the history of the rank of cardinal. Francis reminds Cardinal Ouellet that the rules for becoming a cardinal have changed many times over the centuries, depending upon the wishes of the current pontiff and the needs of the Church. "Marc, there have been instances when cardinals were not priests, when they were married, and, for heaven's sake, Marc, one pope even named a boy as a cardinal. Cardinals had high ecclesiastical or government positions. Four cardinals, including Cardinal Richelieu, ruled France in the 1600s. King Henry in Portugal was a cardinal-king, as were other rulers of city-states. Others worked in finance and other important administrative positions."

Pope Francis, Cardinal Ouellet and Father Soto keep up this respectful give-and-take for another hour before they agree to resume the discussion at their next meeting.

That evening Father Soto and Sister Mary meet for dinner at their favorite Italian restaurant near the Vatican.

"Sister. It's so good to see you"

"Father, you as well," says a smiling Mary. "How have you been?"

"Busy as usual. For a very sick man, Francis is still deeply engaged in many issues." And smiling in return, he continues, "That means I have many balls to juggle at one time. I do however have one piece of news to share with you. You know the Martini letter you suggested I show again to Francis?" Mary nods. "Well, I put it at the top of his inbox mail to read, and I am pretty sure he re-read it, although I am not certain. We know each other's ways, and he does not to tell me what he reads or what he ignores. But, without breaking his confidence, I think I can tell that it has influenced him. Francis is looking for a new significant way to energize the Church, and of course that is what Cardinal Martini is calling for in his letter."

The waiter arrives, and they each order their usual: the ravioli for Sister Mary, and the three-cheese pizza for Father Soto.

"And to drink, Sister?" inquired the waiter.

"Water is fine. Thank you"

"And you, Father?"

"A glass of Brunello, please." The waiter collects the menus and leaves.

"Well, Father Soto, this time I have brought a couple of articles that speculate about the next consistory. You know, the annual parlor game of who will be chosen cardinal."

"Sister, there is much I cannot disclose for the obvious reason of my position and access to the pope. But it is no secret that, in this next consistory, there will be nine cardinal vacancies to fill to maintain the number of cardinal electors for pope, who are under 80 years of age, at 120. In addition, with this new group of nine, the number of cardinals appointed by Francis will be at more than the 50 percent mark of 120. This is obviously significant, because they are more likely to uphold the pope's reforms."

"Father, I respect the need for confidentiality," Sister Mary says. "Those of us who care deeply about the pope's choices and the legacy that results because of his picks are hoping that Francis continues to be diverse in his choices." She looks at Father Soto coyly.

"Well, you know the pope's record on diversity," he counters. "For centuries, the majority of cardinals came from Europe, with Italy having the most representation. Even Pope John Paul II and Pope Benedict had moved away from Europe and the Italians. They had begun considering members of the clergy from Africa, Asia, Latin America, and North America to become cardinals. Francis has been the most unorthodox in his picks, more often appointing cardinals from the growth continents of Africa and Asia. Now there are countries with cardinals never before included, such as Myanmar (Burma), Central African Republic, Bangladesh, and even Tonga."

With a sly smile on her face Mary says, "Father, this conversation feels like we are both dancing around the issue of breaking precedent, but not the example you have just cited."

"Sister Mary, I know where you are going with this. And I also know you know that I am constrained in what I can and cannot divulge from my meetings with Francis. So let me answer you this way. Francis believes that his appointments should reflect his concern for, finally, seriously addressing the sexual abuse scandal. But more than anything, Francis is eager to have cardinals who are on fire, who regularly work with the poor—a message he intends to send to clerics and laity alike. The pope believes that Mass should be an experience of passion and elation; that providing for others is the path to salvation. And it starts with leaders who are already caring and administering to the poor, the shunned, migrants, and refugees, to those who are disabled and are God's special children."

Soto takes a sip of his Brunello, and they both begin laughing over the dance they are engaged in.

"Mary, you once strongly told me that, if women had been in the Church's leadership, the sexual abuse scandal would not have reached such a repugnant level. Well, Francis and I have had that discussion. We too have concluded that the abuse of children and nuns would not have been tolerated and would have been handled differently. That is not to say, of course, that women do not ever abuse their power or positions. But much less so. Women are more often the ones who take the lead on questions of morality."

"Father, have you seen this *New York Times* interview between Nicholas Kristof and Cardinal Joseph Tobin?" Mary asks.

"Oh yes, we have all seen it," he says. "And we have heard from many others about it!"

"Well," says Mary, "the journalist has posed an excellent

question, and, in my mind, Cardinal Tobin has given him an excellent answer. The question was, 'If Jesus trusted women like Mary Magdalene, if Phoebe could be a leader of the early church, then why can't women be priests or cardinals today? So will we see women cardinals soon?"

"Believe me, Mary," responds Soto. "We know the courage it took for Joe Tobin to stand up for the nuns in the United States when the Curia and the Vatican wanted him to lead an inquiry to have them disciplined. By defending and supporting their cause and good works, he became their champion. And again, he has not disappointed them. To the cardinal's answer to Kristof—'I don't believe there is a compelling theological reason why the pope could not name a woman cardinal'—I would say that Tobin cannot stand alone. We need other voices to support his position."

Sister Mary pulls out a newspaper she has been holding in case their conversation moved in this direction. She hands it to Father Soto, who begins reading it.

In June 2004, in Dublin, Sister Joan Chittister, gave a talk entitled "Discipleship for a Priestly People in a Priestless Period," in which she posed this question: "What do people really need in a period when the sacraments are being lost in a sacramental church, at the same time that all questions about the nature of the priesthood are blocked, obstructed, denied, and suppressed?"

Father Soto continues to read. "In diocese after diocese, churches are being turned into sacramental way stations, served by retired priests or married male deacons, both of which are designed to keep the Church male. . . . The number of priests is declining, the number of Catholics is increasing, the number of lay ministers being certified is rising in every academic system, even though their services are being restricted, rejected, or made redundant in parish after parish.

"The Church may assert its changelessness," Sister Chittister wrote, "but it is certainly changing. It is a far cry from the dynamism of the early Church in which Prisca and Lydia and Thecla and Phoebe and hundreds of women like them opened churches in homes, walked as disciples of Paul—'constrained him,' the scripture says, to serve a given region—instructed people in the faith, and ministered to the fledgling Christian communities with no apology, no argument, no tricky theological shell games about whether they were ministering 'in persona Christi' or 'in nomine Christi.' What do people really need? Christian community, not patriarchal clericalism."

When Father Soto finishes reading the newspaper clip, Mary says, "the gender issue is why many Catholics in the United States are thinking about leaving their faith. My older sister is a nurse, and I have always looked up to her. She has two daughters. How can she look at them with a straight face in answer to their questions? 'No. You can't be fully yourself in the Catholic Church. Girls and women cannot become priests.'"

CHAPTER TWELVE

The Vatican Releases the List of Newly Appointed Cardinals

Pope Francis issues the names of nine new cardinals who will be appointed at a consistory on October 4, 2019, the feast day of Saint Francis of Assisi. Being honored with the title of cardinal are:

Sister Norma Pimentel (U.S.A.)

Sister Norma is a sister of the Missionaries of Jesus. She is the director of Catholic Charities of the Rio Grande Valley, and she holds a master's degree in theology from St. Mary's University in San Antonio, Texas, as well as a master's degree in counseling psychology from Loyola University in Chicago. Sister Norma has been active in helping to establish migrant shelters along the Mexican/U.S. border. At her Humanitarian Respite Center in McAllen, Texas, she welcomes migrants with a smile, a hug, a shower, clean clothes, meals, a bed, and counseling. The daughter of Mexican immigrants, she is the recipient of the prestigious Laetare Medal from Notre Dame University.

Sister Sudha Varghese (India)

Sister Sudha, or Didi, which means elder sister, is a Sister of Notre Dame. As a social worker and social activist, Sister Sudha has devoted herself to the Dalit, one of the castes that are considered the "untouchables" in India. She is also the CEO of Woman's Voice, a nonprofit that provides education, literacy, vocational training, healthcare, and life skills for the Dalit girls and women. They operate 50 centers in India. Sister Sudha received the prestigious Padma Shri Award, bestowed by the Indian government for her care, work, and leadership on behalf of the poor and shunned.

Sister Veronica Openibo (Nigeria)
Sister Veronica is the first African to lead the Society of the Holy Child of Jesus. She holds a master's degree in pastoral ministry and a degree in social work from Boston College and was also a past president of the Nigerian Conference of Women Religious. Her leadership and articulate voice led Pope Francis to ask her to give one of the major talks at the Synod of Bishops in Rome in February 2019.

Sister Joan Chittister, O.S.B., Ph.D. (U.S.A.)
Sister Joan is a Benedictine nun, a noted theologian, and the author of more than fifty books. She lectures and writes a column for the *National Catholic Reporter*. Highly regarded in religious, academic, and activist circles, Sister Chittister has held many leadership positions, including past president of the Leadership Conference of Women Religious. She is co-chair of the Global Peace Initiative of Women. In 2001, the Vatican directed the Benedictines to stop Sister Chittister from speaking about discipleship at a conference in Dublin, but, with the support from her religious community, she defied the orders and spoke anyway. In 2018, Pope Francis asked her to chair the Truth and Reconciliation Commission.

Mother Yvonne Reungoat (France)
In 2008, Mother Yvonne Reungoat was elected as the new superior general of the Salesian Sisters of Saint John Bosco, after having held numerous leadership positions with the orga-

nization as a teacher and administrator. Founded in 1872, the Salesian Sisters' mission is to educate the young and the poor. With 13,000 members that do missionary work in ninety-four countries, they are a growing order, with approximately 700 novices worldwide.

Father Ismael Moreno Coto (Honduras/Central America)

Better known as Padre Melo, Father Moreno is an African-Honduran priest who works with the poor, mostly in Honduras, El Salvador, and Guatemala. A human rights advocate who speaks truth to power, he has been threatened with death by repressive government leaders in Central America. His Radio Progreso program reports regularly on human rights abuses, especially in Honduras, where an illegal coup in 2009 replaced the elected government. Padre Melo was recently named to Pope Francis's advisory council.

Archbishop Sviatoslav Shevchuk (Ukraine)

At age 49, Archbishop Shevchuk will be one of the youngest cardinals in the college of cardinals. He has been the patriarch of the Ukrainian Greek Catholic Church since 2011 and has been the president of the Synod of the Ukrainian Catholic Church as well as the grand chancellor of the Ukrainian Catholic University. Shevchuk has sought meetings with the Russian Orthodox Patriarch "to bind old wounds," and he has publicly expressed his views that the best way to communicate is through "open and brotherly dialogue, the purification of our memory, and the ability to ask for forgiveness and to forgive."

Archbishop Michel Aupetit (France)

Before his training in the seminary, Michael Aupetit was educated in medicine and worked as a doctor for twenty years, twelve of them specializing in bioethics. In 1990, he entered the seminary and earned a bachelor's degree in theology. After serving as bishop for the Diocese of Nanterre, he was appointed by Francis as the archbishop of Paris and installed in January 2018. Archbishop Aupetit has written extensively, and he has become a leader in the efforts to restore the Cathedral of Notre Dame.

Archbishop Wilton Gregory (U.S.A.)

Much of Archbishop Gregory's service has been in the Chicago area where he was raised. He was ordained as a priest in 1973, and in 1980 earned a Ph.D. in sacred liturgy at Sant'Anselmo in Rome. In 2001, he was elected president of the U.S. Conference of Catholic Bishops, where he led the implementation of the "The Charter for the Protection of Children and Young People." In April 2019, he assumed the position of archbishop of Washington D.C., the first African American to do so.

• • •

These choices for cardinal by Francis are universally applauded. As might be expected, the main headlines are about his selection of five women, which has never been done before. Many in the Church's more conservative hierarchy are quick with their strong and negative reaction. But they don't grasp how out of touch they are with much of the world community.

The reaction in Europe and North America is overwhelmingly positive, especially from women in all regions and religions. Many are saying they are stunned by the news. Priests and bishops report parishioners sending notes and emails of thanksgiving for what one woman describes as a "game changer" and a reason for her to stay in the Church. Clerics also report an uptick in their offertory giving. Two weeks after the announcements,

Pope Francis's poll numbers almost recover from the dramatic drop they took in 2018, after the sexual abuse scandals were resurrected in the news.

The reaction in Africa and Asia does not match the enthusiasm in North America and Europe, but even there it is more positive than negative.

The media coverage is distinctly supportive. Major newspapers lead with the story, carrying front-page photos of the new cardinals and their biographies, focusing on their work with the poor and refugees. Radio, television, and online stories fill the airwaves with banner headlines extolling the victory for women and reformers. One major headline reads "Woke—Francis's Big Surprise!"

In the nations where their fellow women and countrymen are being elevated to the rank of cardinal, there is great pride. Religious workers and laity in the Catholic shelters along the Mexico/U.S. border celebrate Sister Norma and, through her, their own communities of mercy. At the St. Oscar Romero Church in San Pedro Sula, Honduras, Father Ramirez's homily at Sunday Mass praises the courage and goodness of Francis. In the Franciscan shelter in Tenosique, Mexico, Friar Tomás announces that their weekly Saturday evening party is now dedicated to Pope Francis who has given them heroines to emulate. At the kitchen table near the Honduran/Guatemalan border, Captain Menendez tells his wife and four daughters that he admires the strength and generosity of Pope Francis, who has just broken through the thickest of institutional glass ceilings ever constructed by man.

In Africa, Sister Openibo is feted by her fellow sisters and women throughout the continent. Their cry is "The men will follow." In India, Sister Sudha receives an outpouring of support that is similar to the adulation showered upon Mother Teresa, the Albanian/Indian nun and missionary. And even in France, the elevation and recognition of Cardinals Reungoat and Aupetit lead to a renewed pride in the Church. Members of the Salesians celebrate in all ninety-four countries where they are active. Others in France declare their determination to recommit to their faith.

Catholics in Chicago, Atlanta, and Washington, D.C., praise the new American cardinals, and there is special pride in the African American communities where Cardinal Gregory is one of their own. Ukrainians are overjoyed to have their patriarch now made a cardinal. Ukrainians in Winnipeg, Detroit, Cleveland, New Jersey, and other diaspora communities join in the celebration. Benedictines around the globe shelve their practice of humility for this one day and sing the praises of their champion, Sister Joan, who is being recognized for all the gifts she brings to her religious community and to the broader church. They also understand that her enhanced stature will help her as the leader of the Truth and Reconciliation Commission.

• • •

The first order of business for all the new cardinals is to hold a press conference and pledge their support for renewed efforts to report, monitor, and punish those engaged in sexual abuse. Many editorials and stories about the female cardinals focus on the very argument that, if more women had been in the top leadership of the Church, sexual abuse may not have raged out of control for thirty-four years, dragging the Church down to its present discredited level.

In a press briefing, Father Soto points out, "No one should be surprised by Pope Francis's choices, because, before assuming the papacy, Francis spent a good part of his life honing his political skills navigating the politics of his Jesuit community and also the ruthless body politic of Argentina. He did it, for the most part, with great skill and compassion."

The skills Francis burnished in Argentina now serve him well in his intramural bouts with the Curia and with the "blame game" of the sexual abuse scandal. Francis has been masterly in his selection of bishops and cardinals. Many of his appointments have been outside the traditional "box," and they reflect the Church's openness to progressive ideas and change.

Francis's early, consistent, and strong criticism of clericalism helped to create a bridge to the laity and to women. His own views on women were shaped in the sexist cultures of his life. But they are not so embedded that all light is blocked. Rays of illumination touch him and change him. Francis is strategically brilliant in appointing not one woman but five, each from a different continent, all of whom are held in high esteem by their governments, religious leaders, the media, and the general public.

Many of the conservative traditionalists are livid and challenge the pope's right to name women as cardinals. But they rest on the weak end of the sacramental argument, and what they are saying carries little weight in the court of public opinion.

At Catholic University in Washington, D.C., a group of conservative traditionalist funders and supporters create a "Red Hat" scorecard to rate the qualification of each prospective cardinal and papal candidate. It is derived from something that Washington, D.C., interest groups do when they rate members of the House and Senate. The purpose is to check each politician's ideological credentials and call out and embarrass those who do not adhere to the group's positions.

Not surprisingly, the Red Hat brigade issues a negative report on all the woman cardinals as well as Cardinal Moreno or, as he is derisively referred to, "Cardinal Melo." They claim that all six are insufficiently experienced and are weak on Catholic orthodoxy. Some even attempt to use canon law to disqualify the women.

But their criticisms ring hollow and are easily refuted by history.

In the United States, opposition to the pope's reforms surface from the political far right when Donald Trump's former campaign manager and White House Chief of Staff, Steve Bannon, proclaims that he wants to bring Francis down. Bannon is aligned with Cardinal Raymond Burke—both of whom are radical extremists. Bannon also associates himself with far-right parties in Europe and white supremacist groups in the United States.

Pope Benedict XVI, the conservative predecessor to Francis who has been relatively quiet in his retirement, now speaks out against the liberalism of Vatican II, charging that the so-called "reforms" set the table for sexual abuses in the seminaries as well as in the parishes. Benedict is a firm and resolute defender of an all-male priesthood and begins to speak out against any changes, aligning himself once again with his most recent predecessors, Pope Paul VI and John Paul II, who share Benedict's position against women.

Most of the opposition is particularly irritated by what they describe as Francis's stacking of the College of Cardinals with "his kind." They also worry that the next pope will most likely follow in Francis's footsteps on reforms, including the ascent of women in the Church.

All of this takes a personal toll on Francis. He is feeling the chest pain and fatigue of his illness and is surprised at his own strength to push ahead with his agenda. Now, more than ever, he knows it is time for him to retire. But he needs time for the celebratory part of his selections to play out and to take root. Perhaps after the Christmas season he may have something more significant to say.

• • •

In February 2013, Pope Benedict XVI had been pope for almost eight years. On the 11th of that month, in the Consistory Hall, in front of a handful of cardinals, he made history. Tired and worn out, and with an empty voice, the pope read in Latin words that took the few who were present by complete surprise: *"ingravescente aetate non iam aptas esse ad munus Petrinum aeque ad minisrandum. . . .* I have come to the certainty that my strength, due to advanced age, is no longer suited to an adequate exercise of the Petrine mystery." Benedict then announced that his resignation would take effect on February 28.

Benedict was the fourth-oldest man to serve as pope. He was the first to resign in more than 600 years and the first to resign voluntarily since 1294. Benedict's reasons were that he no longer felt he could manage the Curia, and the burden of the long-looming and ever-present sexual abuse scandal.

When the news of Benedict's resignation breaks, Cardinal Jorge Bergoglio in Argentina issues a statement of praise for Benedict's decision to step aside. Bergoglio calls the decision a "revolutionary act" that has been thought out in the presence of God. This is not the only time Cardinal Bergoglio will praise the decision. Once Bergoglio becomes pope, he sees Benedict's resignation as a gift that has broken the precedent of popes hanging on past their physical and mental abilities.

Seven years later, on Tuesday, February 11, 2020, Francis announces his own illness after his morning Mass in the chapel at the Santae Martae. "My doctors tell me I have advanced degenerative heart disease, a congestive heart. I therefore think it best that I follow the decision of my predecessor Benedict and resign as pope. My resignation will take effect two weeks hence on the 25th of February 2020. The Church will then be *in sede vacante* and will be governed by the College of Cardinals until such time as a new pope is elected."

The announcement does not come as a surprise to many who follow the affairs of the Church. One year earlier, in February 2019, at a press conference on a flight home from the United Arab Emirates, the pope was asked if he would be visiting other Arab nations.

"Let's see if next year I or another Peter (pope) will go," he replied.

When a journalist asked the pope what he meant, Francis said, "I think a pope emeritus should not be an exception. You can ask me: 'What if one day, you don't feel prepared to go on?' I would do the same. I would pray hard over it, but I would do the same thing. I am a bishop, and I too must take my leave and step down."

Francis firmly believes that Benedict's decision to retire should not end up as an aberration, and he hopes it will become a precedent that will lead to the institutionalizing of retirements of future popes. Francis had been forceful in support of his predecessor's decision to retire. He sees it as a good thing and a realistic approach to aging. It is also an act of humility by Benedict, and now for Francis, acknowledging that the world will carry on without them. More than one hundred other popes preceding them had not been able to bring themselves to take this step. It also stands in stark contrast to Pope John Paul II, who stayed too long.

John Paul's insistence that he hold to tradition and serve as Pope until his death caused the Church to suffer through too many years with a growing and dysfunctional Curia and a raging and expanding sexual abuse scandal. Though Cardinal Bergoglio never made these observations of his in public, they did cross his mind.

Staying too long may be the epitome of clericalism. And Francis feels strongly that clericalism is poisoning the Church.

CHAPTER THIRTEEN

Electing the Pope

In 1985, Tim Russert was an inside-Washington, D.C., political power player even before he took a job with NBC News. The network was in a slump, with falling revenues and ratings. The future moderator of *Meet the Press* pitched his executives an idea to broadcast the *Today* show in Vatican City during Holy Week and proposed that he would get a live interview with Pope John Paul II. The executives agreed he could give it a try. Russert wrote a letter to the pope, had it translated into Polish, and took it to Cardinal Krol of Philadelphia.

Krol was the longest-serving cardinal in the United States and was, like Pope John Paul, of Polish descent. More importantly, he had been instrumental in bringing the future pope, Cardinal Karol Wojtyla, to the attention of others in Vatican political circles. Popes don't become pope by luck. There is often a careful plan and strategy to get the necessary two-thirds vote in the Conclave. Some cardinals are key advisors and others play the roles of strategists and whips for their candidate. When Cardinal Wojtyla became a candidate for pope in 1978, Krol delivered the votes of all ten U.S. cardinal electors for Poland's favorite son.

Russert took his letter to Krol, who said he might give the letter to the pope, but first he wanted Russert to go with him to hear a concert by the Archdiocesan Boy Choir. "My dream is one day to have these young men sing for the Holy Father," Krol told Russert.

This prompted Russert to rewrite his letter to say that "if the pope accepted NBC's invitation, he would be accompanied by the Archdiocesan Boy Choir of Philadelphia."

Pope John Paul II remembered how good Krol had been to him; he would do just about anything for this cardinal. The deal was done, and Russert's interview with the pope for NBC was a smash, drawing increased attention and ratings to the *Today* show. Krol was once again a kingmaker—this time for Russert.

In the late 1970s, a group of reform-minded progressive cardinals had begun to meet periodically to talk about coalescing around a candidate for pope. The group became known as the St. Gallen Group, named after the university town in the northeastern part of Switzerland near the German border where they first met.

Some members of this group included Cardinals Godfried Danneels of Belgium, Karl Lehman and Walter Kasper, both of Germany, Achilles Silvestrini of Italy, and Cormac Murphy-O'Connor of Great Britain. In 2005, they campaigned for Jorge Bergoglio, though he lost to Cardinal Ratzinger. They came together again in 2013 after Pope Benedict announced his resignation, and this time they succeeded in helping Cardinal Bergoglio become Pope.

No cardinal who had previously been a runner-up had ever been elected pope. In 2013, when Cardinal Bergoglio was asked by the St. Gallen Group if he would accept their support and then serve if elected, he responded, "At this time of crisis, no cardinal could refuse if asked."

The cardinal had provided an answer in keeping with the philosophy of the Society of Jesus, not sounding too overly ambitious while giving his assent. His response also effectively gave the St. Gallen Group the assurance they needed to get busy selling Bergoglio at the dinners where much of the politicking took place. In addition, Cardinal Bergoglio aided his own candidacy at the Synod by giving a compelling three-minute speech that captured the substance and tone many of the cardinals wanted to hear.

According to Austen Ivereigh, Francis's biographer, "Bergoglio was a once-in-a-generation combination of two qualities seldom found together: he had the political genius of a charismatic leader and the prophetic holiness of a desert saint."

It is forbidden to release the speeches and votes to the public, but after Bergoglio's captivating three-minute speech at the Synod, Cardinal James Ortega of Cuba asked his colleague for a copy of it. Bergoglio had spoken in Italian from his notes. He later did his own translation to Spanish, using a fountain pen, and gave it to Ortega, who then put it on his diocesan website. Part of the speech reads:

> The evils over time that appear in Church institutions have their root in self- referentiality, a kind of theological narcissism. In the Book of Revelations, Jesus says that he is at the door and calling, and evidently the text refers to Him standing outside the door and knocking to be let in. But sometimes I think that Jesus is knocking from the inside, for us to let Him out. The self-referential church presumes to keep Jesus for itself and not let Him out.

When news of the resignation makes its way around the globe, few are surprised, because Francis had said earlier that he would follow his predecessors' example. The cardinals direct their staffs to book plane reservations to Rome. Beyond electing a new pope, they are also responsible for running the affairs of the Church in *se sede vacante*.

Angelo Sodano, the 92-year-old dean of the College of Cardinals, is responsible for bringing all the cardinals together for their Synod and then the Conclave. Cardinal Sodano, who was previously the Vatican's powerful Secretary of State, was once considered papabile. However, he was too much of a Vatican insider and therefore too associated with scandal in the minds of many other cardinals; and, of course, his age worked against him. Now his time has passed, and his role is limited to calling others together.

When the papacy is vacated—*se sede vacante*—by the death or resignation of the pope—two interlinking events follow: the Synod and the Conclave. The cardinals from around the world gather at the Vatican in Synod Hall to discuss what is foremost on their minds for the Church to function and grow. Also, at the Synod, cardinals begin looking among their colleagues for candidates who might ascend to the papacy. These meetings can last for up to two weeks, depending on the state of the Church and the stamina of the cardinals. For these older men, being on the road and away from their own beds is not easy.

After the Synod is completed, it will be time to vote. This is called the Conclave. The 120 or so cardinals eligible to vote (those under the age of 80) will in procession enter the Sistine Chapel and begin the selection process with short speeches and then votes.

Eight years earlier, the Synod discussions centered on the corruption in the Church and the needed reforms of the Curia. Today there is a wider split in the Church, and the conservative traditionalists are keenly aware that their powers and ideas have eroded during Francis's papacy. The sexual abuse crisis and the role of women are topics the cardinals may vigorously discuss while they search among their peers for the next Vicar of Christ.

They will also discuss evangelization, which in previous Synods had been squeezed out during conversations centered on scandals and the need for curial reform. Everyone seems hungry to get out from under the terrible weight that has brought down the Church, the sexual abuse scandals. There is a desire to break away into the land of evangelism, to be on the offensive and divorced from defending the indefensible. A desire to "let Jesus out of the House"!

The cardinals begin arriving, most of them landing at Fiumicino Airport. Almost half of them are from Europe, so the train station is busy as well. The red hats are everywhere in and around Synod Hall, where the meetings are held. Most of the politicking is done at the Synod and at mealtime in the two weeks leading up to the Conclave in the Sistine Chapel.

The Vatican's Synod Hall is where most of the same cardinals met a year ago when Pope Francis requested their presence to discuss the sexual abuse crisis. During that week, each cardinal took careful notice of Francis's health. Their general impression was that the pontiff was tired and might not stay much longer. So, in a delicate but nonetheless real way, the politicking for the next pope had begun a year ago with words of praise for so and so and whispers of indiscretions and weakness about another. Unseemly as it might appear, it was real, and the jockeying had already begun.

A steady stream of journalists arrives. In 2013, approximately 4,000 journalists came for the election, and more are expected this time. There is a buzz and excitement about the selection of arguably the most important religious leader as well as the election of the leader of the most powerful nation on the planet. While the progressive Catholics in the United States are opposed to their Trumpian government at home, the conservative Catholics want to defeat the Francis-led wing of the College of Cardinals in Rome.

Almost 200 cardinals come to Rome, 120 of whom are under 80 years of age, thereby qualifying as electors. A two-thirds vote—eighty votes—is required to elect a candidate. Rarely does this occur on the first ballot. Some cardinals might vote for a friend or a beloved figure within the college as a gesture of respect. This also gives them time after the first ballot to see who emerges as the main candidates.

To quote an old political maxim, "You can't beat somebody with nobody." Most of the cardinals break into two camps, the "Progressive Reformers" and the "Conservative Traditionalists," to find their "somebody." A number of them walk a line somewhere in the middle between both camps. These cardinals very often hold a key to who is elected.

Another political maxim made popular in the United States by former speaker of the house Thomas P. (Tip) O'Neill, himself a Catholic, was, "All politics is local." In the context of a papal Conclave, that means regional voting will once again be an important factor. The Italians have controlled the papacy for centuries because they have had the most voting cardinals, and they stuck together. John Paul II broke this dominance by putting together a coalition of regional votes, such as the ten U.S. cardinals, who had supposedly voted en bloc for Cardinal Wojtyla in 1978. Likewise, in 2013, Cardinal Bergoglio benefited from the Latin block of cardinals whom he had led in the CELAM (Conference of Latin American Bishops), while he was the archbishop in Buenos Aires.

Now more than 50 percent of the 120 voting cardinals have been picked by Francis over the last seven years. The question most commonly asked is whether those cardinals chosen by Francis will cast ballots for a progressive reformer who will follow in the footsteps of Francis. Not all, but a significant number of them more than likely will.

The philosopher Seneca once said that loyalty is "the holiest good in the human heart." And there is no doubt that loyalty is a significant factor for those cardinals who have been made a prince of the Church by the pope.

The London oddsmakers were wrong in 2013 when they predicted that Cardinal Peter Turkson of Ghana, the odds-on favorite, would be elected pope. With thousands of journalists hungry for inside information on the frontrunners, the election once again takes on the spectacle of a rumor mill gone wild.

However, one thing is clear. Cardinal Bergoglio's candidacy accelerated the move away from Europe and Italy. In 2020 there is a greater likelihood the next pope might come again from South America or even, as a first, from North America. This also makes it more possible for an African, like Cardinal Turkson, or an Asian, like Cardinal Luis Antonio Tagle of the Philippines, to be elected a pope.

In 2013, more than half of the voting cardinals were from Europe. In 2020, 104 cardinals are from Europe, but of that number only fifty-one are eligible as electors. They still make up 42 percent of the voting cardinals, though the Italians are now down to twenty-two electoral cardinals, just 20 percent of those eligible to vote. The Iberian block is well represented, with Spain having fourteen cardinals, five of whom are electors; and Portugal has four cardinals, two of whom are electors. France has eight cardinals, five of whom are electors; Germany has eight cardinals, three of whom are electors; and Poland has seven cardinals and four electors.

The North American delegation—broken into five sectors, made up of the United States, Canada, Mexico, Central America, and the Caribbean—continues to grow, with the addition of cardinals Joan Chittister, Norma Pimentel, Moreno Coto and Wilton Gregory. Their numbers increased to thirty-six cardinals, of whom twenty-two are electors. The United States has seventeen cardinals, of whom ten are electors, next to Italy, the country with the most cardinals. Mexico has seven cardinals of whom three are electors. Nine other Central American and Caribbean countries have one cardinal each. Canada has three cardinals and three electors, but, most significantly, they have Cardinal Marc Armond Ouellet, considered by many Vatican experts as the most papabile.

South America is a fast-growing Catholic area. Worldwide, the north and south have flipped dominance in their Catholic populations. In 1910, 70 percent of the world's Catholic population lived in the north, mainly Europe, and only 30 percent in the south, whereas in 2010 it was exactly the reverse. In the Latin American Catholic Church, an amazing 70 percent of the Catholic population is 25 years of age or under, the opposite of an older Europe and North America. As Austen Ivereigh, author of *The Great Reformer,* noted, ". . . the Church of this continent leads the world in energy, passion, and missionary zeal."

South America has twenty-seven cardinals of whom thirteen are electors. Brazil leads the way with ten cardinals, of whom four are electors, followed by Argentina with four cardinals, of whom two are electors. Chile has three cardinals and one elector, as does Columbia. Peru has two cardinals, and both are electors.

The only country on the Asian and African continents with more than three cardinals is India, with five who are all electors. Together the continents have twenty-seven cardinals, and seventeen of them are electors. Nigeria leads Africa with three cardinals and one elector. The rest are spread among many nations in those two regions. China, which has only six million Catholics, has cut a deal with the Vatican on who controls future appointments. The country's Catholic population is expected to increase, but for now Hong Kong has two cardinals, one of them an elector. The mainland has many bishops and archbishops, and some are likely to be made cardinals soon, but not before this Conclave in 2020. Australia and New Zealand have two cardinals and one elector each.

The conservative traditionalists realize that they do not have the numbers to elect one of their own. They need to draft a cardinal who has a chance to win. Marc Ouellet of Canada is the closest to their views on Vatican II, which according to Ouellet has been interpreted "too liberally" and disconnected from the doctrine of Catholicism. He is in many ways conservative.

Ouellet has opposed abortion for rape. He opposed same sex marriage, referring to it as a "pseudo-marriage." Yet in 2005, the progressive *National Catholic Reporter* described him as "friendly, humble, and flexible." His flexibility was exercised when he became Pope Francis's chief defender during the Vigano/McCarrick scandal.

Originally appointed cardinal by John Paul II in 2003—and elevated to Archbishop of Quebec and Primate of Canada—Ouellet is seen by many older cardinals as "one of their own." He is an old hand at Vatican politics, having served as head of the powerful committee, Propagation of the Faith. As the Prefect of the Congregation of Bishops, he is an influential voice in elevating bishops around the world, and he has also served as the president of the Pontifical Commission for Latin America. Earlier, Cardinal Ouellet was a missionary in Latin America, where he made many friends in the Latin American religious community.

Ouellet speaks English, Spanish, Portuguese, Italian, and German and can communicate in the language of most cardinals. His motto as a cardinal is "Ut unum sint," which means "That they may be one"—the perfect campaign slogan to keep the Catholic faith unified. Cardinal Ouellet is clearly a frontrunner to be the new pope and will be a formidable candidate. He is 75 years old and appears to be in excellent health. This is likely his last chance to be elected pope.

Other contenders are Cardinal Peter Turkson of Ghana, a favorite last time; Cardinal Blase J. Cupich of the United States, who is close to Francis; Cardinal Joseph W. Tobin, who is also close to Francis and relatively young at 67; and Cardinal Luis Tagle from the Philippines, who is even younger, at 61.

And, of course, there is the possibility of a dark horse like Cardinal Angelo Giuseppe Roncalli, who came out of nowhere in 1958, was elected, and took the name John XXIII. Today he is called Pope Saint John XXIII.

The Synod meetings, where the Church's business is discussed, last a full two weeks with the cardinals dancing around the subject of women in their ranks, trying not to offend, especially before the Conclave when the election ballots are cast.

Cardinal Joan Chittister is 82 years old, and she is ready to defend Francis's choice of the first five women cardinals. The male cardinals who disagree with her are unwilling to challenge her because they are so intimidated by her historical and theological expertise on the role of women in the Church. This of course helps make one of her points. It was a collegiate without courage living off its not so noble past—in its comfort zone.

BOOK SIX

FROM
THE VATICAN
TO
THE BORDER

CHAPTER FOURTEEN

Francis's Retirement Dinner,
February 25, 2020

S ister Mary, this is Jorge Bergoglio," Pope Francis says, casually into the phone. "How are you, my friend?"

Mary is surprised to get a call from the pope, even though they have known each other for six years and have become friends. She has never heard the pope refer to himself as Jorge Bergoglio.

"I am fine, your Holiness, but I am saddened by your announcement."

"Sister Mary. First, I am no longer Pope Francis or even Your Holiness. I am your friend Jorge, or if you prefer, Padre Bergoglio. Second, let us not be sad but joyful for the blessings we have received in this life. It is time. We were both chosen to heal. For me, souls. For you, minds, bodies and souls. But that is not why I am calling. I have something urgent I need to share with you."

With that, Francis pauses in what he is saying, giving Mary a few moments to wonder what is so urgent that the pope, or Padre Bergoglio, would call to tell her about it.

"For the past six years," Francis continues, "you and Father Soto have been raving about the trattoria in your neighborhood. You say it serves the best pizza and ravioli in Rome. Well, I would like to treat you and Juan to dinner there tonight, if you are free."

Mary responds with an enthusiastic "yes." She is honored to be invited.

"You are free?" Francis answers, with surprise and delight. "Wonderful! But you must promise me that I can have a generous helping of everything. This is my retirement dinner, and I choose to dine with two of my favorite people. I will see you there tonight at seven."

The three of them know to meet behind the restaurant and to enter through the kitchen, where the chef, her sous-chef, three kitchen prep workers, and a dishwasher are all busy preparing for tonight's guests. Francis may no longer be the pope, but he still draws crowds on the street as if he is.

The restaurant owner greets Father Soto and Sister Mary, his two regular customers, warmly, and when he spots the pope, his eyes fill with tears. He tries to kiss the pope's ring, but Francis pulls his hand away and instead gives the owner a gentle affectionate hug.

Francis then moves from worker to worker, asking their names and smiling at each one. He kiddingly asks them all to give him extra filling in his ravioli and heavy cheese on his pizza. The kitchen staff all laugh, then break into applause as Francis, Mary, and Juan exit the kitchen and are shown to their table at the back, where they find privacy.

It is still early for dinner by Roma standards, and there are only a few guests at the other tables. Francis is afforded security protection by the Swiss Guards, who are not in their traditional puffy uniforms, but instead in civilian clothes to blend in with the rest of the clientele. Six of them are at two separate tables, near Francis and his guests.

The owner brings a bottle of his best Brunello to the table.

Francis wants to talk about his grand-nieces and -nephews, whom he follows regularly on Instagram. He is fascinated with their young lives—school, soccer, arts, music, their latest electronic gadgets, and of course their first communions and confirmations. It is the kind of conversation grandparents enjoy sharing with friends.

As it turns out, Mary and Juan both have siblings who have children, and they have also kept up with the lives of their nieces and nephews. Francis smiles as Mary tells him amusing stories about what her nephews have been up to lately. Mary has downloaded photos of her nieces and nephews on Instagram.

The food arrives family style, with all the Roma aromas that the kitchen staff can muster.

Once they have filled their plates, Francis asks Sister Mary how things are on Lampedusa. But before she answers, she asks Francis a question. "I like 'Padre'—is that OK?"

With a smile, Francis says, "Padre Jorge or Padre Francis is also acceptable."

"Padre Francis, as you know, the number of refugees on Lampedusa has fallen from 180,000 in 2016 to around 10,000 last year. Most European governments have closed their borders, dramatically narrowing migration into those countries. Italy takes just a small fraction of the migrants it took three years ago. Now it seems that only Spain is showing compassion and generosity. Still, 10,000 lives are significant for us—it is more than our island population of 6,000. The larger question is, what will the international community of nations do to ease this crisis for refugee families? I hope the Church follows your leadership and support and stays involved."

"Before I stepped aside," Francis responds, "I directed church funds for refugees from Africa, the Middle East, Latin America, and Asia. But, as you both know, to effect significant change, we need new leadership in many countries. Mexico seems to have a compassionate new president, Obrador. I hope to meet with him soon. He has shown leadership by providing a donor country plan like the United States did after World War II with its Marshall Plan."

Juan notices that Francis is not eating very much. He doesn't know if he and Sister Mary should compliment the pope on his restraint and will power, or if perhaps Francis doesn't like the food, and they have oversold this restaurant.

"You are not eating, Padre Francis," Mary says. "You don't like the pasta?"

"To the contrary, Sister, I love it all. The pizza is tasty, the crust crisp, and the cheese magnificent! Also, the ravioli is delicious, just like my grandmother Rosa's ravioli. I will take some back to my apartment. But I am old and do not eat as much, especially at night before bed.

"But you Sister," Francis teases, smiling to let her know he is kidding, "have admonished me about my diet. I am obeying my physician just as you obey your confessor. So, we are even."

Sister Mary asks Francis where he plans to live in his retirement.

"I will go home to Argentina and Buenos Aires where I was raised and worked most of my life," he replies. "I look forward to seeing more of my family, taking my nieces and nephews to see San Lorenzo play soccer, and also attending musical concerts with them. But I have a big problem that I have not handled very well."

"What is that, Padre?" Mary inquires.

"I have put off visiting Argentina during my papacy. Many Argentinians are not happy about that. They think I have ignored them or even snubbed them. So now, as I am not the pope, the reception upon my return may not be as warm as I would hope.

"Since you ask where I will be living, I will tell you. In Buenos Aires I plan to stay temporarily with my sister, Maria Elena.

But before I arrive in Argentina, I must make a stopover to visit the border between Mexico and the United States.

"What will you do there?" Mary asks.

Francis looks knowingly at Father Soto. Obviously, the two men have been discussing what the former pope will do at the border during this unofficial visit. "Sister Mary, before I answer, I am going to ask you in your role as a physician to accompany Father Soto and me on this trip. I know there are others who are senior to you on the staff, wonderfully dedicated doctors. But they have their hands full with all the cardinals in town for the Conclave. So will you please join us?"

"Of course, it will be an honor to accompany you, Padre Francis."

"Now to answer your question. I am going to the border to visit refugees, especially the little ones and teenagers who have been separated from their parents and guardians. Also, I am also going to celebrate the two new cardinals from the region, both very special people—Cardinal Norma Pimentel and Cardinal Ismail Moreno Coto. Both of them have told me that there is another Maria Elena they would like for me to meet."

CHAPTER FIFTEEN

Francis Goes Home

Francis sleeps very little the last night in his small apartment at the Vatican. He tosses and turns, knowing that when he rises in the morning his papacy will be over. Tormenting him is his memory of his visit to Lampedusa and the haunting images of the refugees there. At 3:00 a.m., he gives up on sleep, dresses, and says his morning prayers.

He walks down the hall of the Santae Martae and into the small chapel where he has celebrated daily Mass for the past seven years. Next to a pew at the rear of the chapel, he bows to the altar and takes a seat in the near darkness. The plaster figures of Mary and Joseph, occupying places of honor on each side of the main altar, are haloed by candles powered by batteries.

In this solitude, Francis thinks about leaving his papacy. He is feeling the relief of the absence of his powers and responsibilities, yet melancholy about saying farewell to the joys and sorrows being pope has afforded him. Ahead for him now is the community of his aged and retired brethren.

• • •

Aboard the Air Italia charter jet, are Francis, Father Soto, and Sister Mary, who is serving as the former Pope's physician for his flight home. Their first stop is twelve hours away in McAllen, Texas. As the jet lifts off the runway at Leonardo da Vinci Airport, Francis strains to look out the window to catch a last glimpse of St. Peter's Basilica, the renowned Roman Catholic edifice that has recently been at the center of his life.

Alitalia has been the host airline for Francis during his seven-year papacy.

Today his flight is, as usual, filled with reporters who expect Francis to hold a press conference, as he usually does, sometime during the flight. Today's flight is very long, and Francis will work with Father Soto before catching up on his sleep in his refitted compartment furnished with a bed. Then, before dinner, Francis will speak with the reporters, giving them time to write and file their stories prior to landing.

Francis and Father Soto sit next to each other so that Soto can describe how they will spend the two days along the border between the United States and Mexico. Turning to Francis, Soto says, "We will be greeted at the airport by Cardinals Pimentel and Moreno Coto, Father Daly, and Monsignor Torres, the pastor of Sacred Heart Parish. We will then drive twenty minutes to the parish and take you to the Respite Center where you will address the workers, volunteers, and refugees. It will be late, so our visit at the center will be limited. It is our only event, so we can play it by ear. The rectory where we are staying for the night as guests of Monsignor Torres is right next door to the Center."

When Soto finishes, Francis takes a nap, sleeping soundly for two hours until he is wakened by Father Soto.

• • •

Often on these trips, Francis and Soto prepare an announcement for the press corps and then take questions about the announcement or anything else the reporters are interested in discussing. Today, the two men anticipate that the press corps will be most interested in discussing the luncheon meeting tomorrow with Mexican President Obrador.

During the transition with retired Pope Benedict, Francis came to realize there can be only one Pope. Francis is determined to keep his distance from whomever the Conclave chooses as his successor. Even so, as a former pope, he knows he still has a public profile that he can use to promote peace and justice. He is not about to surrender those opportunities. Francis admires Jimmy Carter's work during his years after leaving the White House—especially the efforts Carter made on behalf of the poor with the Habitat for Humanity program and his work to eradicate guinea worm disease in Africa. Francis is committed to work with President Obrador and others to create jobs and educational opportunities in Central America while also tackling the scourge of drug and gang violence, especially in the Northern Triangle countries.

Francis splashes his face with cold water, reviving himself after his sleep. He and Father Soto then go over their last-minute notes before they enter the section of the plane where the reporters are seated.

"*Buenas tardes*," Francis warmly greets the reporters. "It has been a great honor for me to share my papacy with all of you. Your job is challenging and at times very difficult and stressful. I have tried to honor the vital role you perform in the public interest." Francis pauses before continuing. "This may seem strange to some of you, but I will miss you. I will miss the challenge of answering your questions and commenting on your observations. I have always thought that the most important job in a society is that of a teacher. Well, in many ways, that is what you do. By your writings you inform and teach your community of readers. A noble calling indeed."

Francis sees an editor among the reporters and lightens his remarks. "Ah, I see we have an editor here as well." With a teasing smile, Francis continues, "You know what they say about editors. Editors separate the wheat from the chaff and then print the chaff."

The reporters have heard this joke about their bosses before, but they still roar with laughter and appreciation for how well Francis understands their jobs. Francis walks over to the editor, who is seated in an aisle seat, and with a playful smile blesses the editor with the sign of the cross in the manner that a priest uses to absolve a sinner in the confessional. Another roar of laughter bursts throughout the plane. To "make up" to the editor, Francis kisses him on the top of his head and says, "I owe you the first question."

The editor, who has been a good sport about all of this, asks, "Pope Francis, what will you do in your retirement?"

Francis thinks for a few seconds and says, "As many of you know, tomorrow I will meet with President Obrador to discuss the refugee crisis. The Mexican President has proposed something like the Marshall Plan that helped Europe recover after World War II. I think he is onto something here. After our meeting tomorrow, we can talk more about this idea on our last leg of my flight home. So, if my health allows, I will be engaged but will not get in the way of the new pontiff. There can only be one Vicar of Christ at a time.

"I will also try to enjoy the remaining time I have left. I look forward to sitting under a shade tree with a cool drink." Francis pauses again and then adds, "There was a time when I loved to tango. Who knows?"

• • •

Cardinals Norma Pimentel and Moreno Coto along with Father Daly and Monsignor Torres greet Francis at the airport.

Rocia is also there covering the visit for the *New York Times,* and she joins the reporters who have been on the plane. The reporters board a chartered bus while Francis and the other clergy drive by car to the parish, where a throng of supporters are waiting to see and hear the former pontiff.

When they arrive at dusk, it is still light enough for them to see from their cars the structures that make up the complex. There, of course, is the church, which is the center of any parish. Next to the church is a small building where catechism and English classes for non-English-speaking parishioners are held. On the other side is the rectory, and behind the church and rectory is a playfield lined for soccer. Abutting the playfield is the Humanitarian Respite Center and long communal tents, erected by the city of McAllen.

The cars drive up to the main entrance of the Respite Center where above the double-wide doors a sign reads: "Catholic Charities Humanitarian Respite Center." Inside there is a feeling of hope and love. As Francis and the others enter the center, they are greeted by a children's area filled with colorful plastic toys and small red and blue chairs. The chairs are near low, accessible bookshelves filled with books for the children and a higher shelf holding books for older kids. The walls of this room are covered with children's paintings and drawings. Two girls, maybe 7 and 8 years old, are seated next to each other, taking turns reading their book out loud.

Sister Norma—which she is still called here, rather than Cardinal Pimentel—escorts Francis into the center and motions for him to go to the reception area, where the children and adults are sent to be processed when they first arrive. But his attention is immediately drawn to the colorful children's room, lifting his spirits. He stands quietly, enjoying all the pleasure in this room where the girls are reading. Francis waits to see if the girls will look up from their book, and when they do he smiles and waves to them. They wave back, and then he turns his attention to Sister Norma.

The center is filled with staff, volunteers, and refugees who have recently arrived from their long journeys. During Sister Norma's tour, she describes for Francis the function of each room. There is a food pantry that provides staples and even some fresh food during the growing season. There is a shop where refugees can choose clean secondhand clothes. Another large room is filled with refugees, maybe seventy-five people, who rest on mats that cover the space wall to wall. Sister Norma tells Francis and the others that in addition to this room there are long tents out back that have beds, cots, and communal bathrooms.

"Pope Francis," Sister Norma says, "when refugees arrive many are in a state of bewilderment and some suffer depression. They have been on the road for months. Their desire is for rest and stability for themselves and their families. When they walk in for the first time, they are cheered to make them feel welcome and appreciated."

Francis is taken aback by how young they all are. They're mostly children, but even their parents or guardians look as if they are only in their 20s. Francis, Soto, Daly, and the two new cardinals stand out in this sea of youth. Suddenly, a young mother hands her squirming toddler to Francis. As Pope, he was used to people handing him their children, and he gently and kindly, with two hands, receives the child and softly embraces the boy, who is surprised and with a quizzical frown wonders: who is this old man?

"*Como se llama*?" Francis quietly asks his mother.

"Antonio," she beams.

Francis kisses Antonio's forehead, then cradles him in one arm and with his other blesses the boy. His mother has tears of joy in her eyes. Photos are taken, and a significant moment for Antonio and his mother is captured forever. Francis then gives the child back to his mother and asks for all to gather around to hear what he has to say. He waits as those in other rooms make their way into the main commons room of the center. The pool of reporters and photographers scramble for a place in the crowd so they can do their jobs. Finally, all settle down, and Sister Norma comes forward to introduce her special guest.

At the end of her introduction in Spanish, Sister Norma calls Francis a "pope of mercy," and everyone in the room nods their heads. Mercy is well understood and appreciated in this room at this moment. Loud applause and cheers fill the center, and the former pope takes the hand microphone from Sister Norma and waits for the room to quiet itself.

Continuing in Spanish, Francis begins. "I will have many wonderful things to say about Sister Norma and Father Melo tomorrow when we celebrate the work of these two new cardinals." When those in the center hear the word, "cardinals," they explode into cheers of appreciation, recognizing the great honor the pope has bestowed on their beloved nun.

Francis again waits for the crowd to settle. "But tonight it is getting late, and many of you have made a long journey. For me, I just sat on an airplane for twelve hours. But for you, many have walked more than a thousand miles to be here in order to breathe new hope and freedom into your lives and that of your children. There is much love and hope in this room. I can feel it. Can you?"

Shouts of "Si! Si!" ring out from the crowd.

"As children" Francis continues, "Catholics are taught the Acts of Faith, Hope, and Love. We memorize it as children, and it stays with us throughout our life. Before we finish tonight, I want to say something about faith.

"Faith is not a light that scatters all our darkness, but a lamp that guides our steps in the night and suffices for the journey. For some of you, your faith has sustained you and brightened the way in your struggles to reach freedom and safety. Always remember that, even in your darkest hour, Jesus is with you holding a lamp, lighting your way. Go with God, in peace. My friends, I will see you tomorrow.

• • •

On this early Saturday morning, Francis rises, dresses, and walks next door to the church to say the 6:00 a.m. Mass. He is stunned to find the church packed and many parishioners assembled near the front of the church ready to participate through a broadcast that will be seen on a large screen set up next to the steps leading to the church doors. Father Soto has not told Francis about this, and it is a lovely surprise. The size of the crowd and their celebratory mood lifts Francis's spirit.

Francis had not prepared or even thought about a homily for a 6:00 a.m. Mass. But now he is spiritually on fire. This turnout inspires him to focus on a theme that will revolve around community. He remembers the conversation he had last night in the rectory with Cardinal Moreno Coto about the cardinal's former parishioners in Tegucigalpa, the Gonzalez family.

Francis begins his homily by talking about the Church and his vision of what it should be. "I prefer a Church which is bruised, hurting, and dirty because it has been on the street, rather than a Church that is sanitized from being confined and clinging to its own security. I invite each of you to spread your faith by loving and caring for each other. Cardinal Moreno Coto has shared with me the story of one of your families, who migrated here to Sacred Heart Parish. They sought asylum, because of the violence that befell them in Honduras. Because of this violence and the threats against them, they were forced to move. They were able to do so only with the support of Catholic Charities and the generosity of their fellow parishioners in Honduras. It is a poor parish, but they aided each other with what little they had, and the Church stood with them by helping this family, who has suffered so grievously at the hands of gangs and drug lords. Our Church needs to be more about your families, especially your children. Our Church needs to be talking with governmental and community leaders about making every parish, every neighborhood, and every school safe and nourishing. Let us give thanks this morning for the leadership of Monsignor Torres and Sister Norma who have created here at Sacred Heart a place filled with good Samaritans."

• • •

After Mass, at breakfast in the rectory, Father Soto briefs Francis on their next event this morning at the immigration detention center, also called the Customs and Patrol Processing Center. This is where Maria Elena and her family were brought after they crossed the border and first asked for asylum.

"This is where tens of thousands were taken once they crossed the border," Soto tells Francis. "This facility received notoriety last year for horrendous living conditions. It is also where children were separated from their parents and where today, over a year later, a thousand children have not been reunited with their families. The international media, human rights organizations, and child welfare agencies and organizations exposed the unacceptable conditions. As you recall in the report that Sister Mary and I presented to you, the refugees were locked in caged enclosures and forced to sleep on cold cement floors. It was reported that often the refugees were denied basic sanitary objects like toothbrushes or clean water. These were inhumane and demeaning conditions. Rather than recognize the dignity of those who walk great distances each day for months at a time to escape terror and seek asylum, the Trump administration treats them as criminals. The spotlight recently has been on this facility, and it is better, but it still needs improvement."

Cardinals Pimentel and Moreno Coto, along with Father Daly, meet Francis at the Customs and Patrol Processing Center for their tour, and they are followed by a pool of reporters. Prior to the visit, Father Soto arranged for Francis to speak to an assembly of staff and workers. After a short tour of the facility, Francis joins a room of about 200 staff in the building's auditorium. He is graciously introduced by the manager of the center.

Francis begins by thanking them for their work. "All work has value" he says. "And your work is most difficult. You see families and little ones who have been for months without a home. It must break your hearts. You may wonder why the refugees don't remain in their own communities. You are puzzled as to why this has not happened. I also share your concerns about why so many come. And I think we all know the answers to that—they don't feel safe and secure, and they want better economic opportunity for themselves and their families.

"After I leave this meeting, I will go to Reynosa to meet the Mexican president. We have pledged to work together to try to do something about this question of 'Why do they come?' If there is safety and economic opportunity in their home countries, we believe that most would not come and would prefer to remain among their relatives and friends.

"Sister Norma has told me personally how demanding your jobs are. She has told me about the good people who work for the Border Patrol and that most of you treat the migrants with respect and dignity while also trying to uphold your laws. I thank you for that. And, if you see your brothers or sisters abuse the refugees, it is important for you to speak up. Remind them that every human being has dignity and the vast majority are good and decent people often trapped in a corrupt and dangerous environment. Let us all work together to solve our border issues so that safety and justice work for all. Please pray for our success at our meeting this afternoon."

When Francis finishes, the crowd rises and applauds his remarks. They are touched that he recognizes them with his kindness and understanding.

• • •

On the International Bridge leading to Reynosa, Francis stares out his window at the refugees making their way in the pedestrian lane. Sitting next to Francis, Soto wonders what his boss is thinking as he watches the stream of weary migrants, many carrying backpacks, as they trudge their last quarter-mile into the United States.

At the Cathedral of Our Lady of Guadalupe near the central Plaza, President Manuel Lopez Obrador waits at the curbside ready to receive his distinguished guests. Parts of the neoclassical cathedral are the remains of a Franciscan mission built in 1789. The president is hoping to add to its legacy today with this historic meeting.

Francis, who practices what he preaches about the environment, insisted that he, Soto, and the two cardinals be driven in one car. He even asked Father Soto about the possibility of their taking public transportation, but Soto convinced him that taking a bus across the border would eat up valuable time that was better spent discussing the aid package. The three prelates are squeezed into the back seat of the Ford Lincoln MKZ that had been assembled in Hermosillo, Mexico. After an uncomfortable forty-five-minute drive, they arrive at the cathedral and are received as dignitaries by Obrador and Mexican Cardinal Carlos Aguilar Retes, who is a longtime friend of Francis.

During the lunch, which is served in a conference room attached to the cathedral, the well-prepared Obrador presents a list of world leaders he has talked with who are interested in, and even excited about, the idea of creating a development and recovery fund for Central American countries with emphasis for those from the Northern Triangle—Guatemala, Honduras, and El Salvador.

"I have talked with Oscar Arias, the former president of Costa Rica, Michelle Bachelet, the former president of Chile, and former Brazilian President Lula, and they have all pledged their support to participate in this endeavor. In the United States, there is great interest from former president George W. Bush and Senator Mitt Romney. Also, I have talked with former President Obama, Speaker Pelosi, and Senator Schumer, who have also expressed their willingness to work toward this goal.

"I am of course open to your suggestions of who should participate, and it is my hope that the Catholic Church will play a major role in our discussions and eventual implementation. We are deeply honored that you, Pope Francis, have spoken positively about the concept and have done so publicly. We will all miss your leadership in Rome. Thank you for the courage and decency you have demonstrated during your long and distinguished service. And, oh yes! We will need your help to convince your successor to support our vision."

Francis thanks President Obrador for his extraordinary work and pledges to stay active to try to make this idea a reality. After lunch, more details are discussed, and then the participants depart, each having a list of assignments to perform before they come together again.

Father Soto listens carefully to the conversation between Francis and Obrador, takes good notes, and responds when called upon by Francis. The priest knows that this project is another chapter in his life of service to the Church and specifically to his boss. Soto's admiration and loyalty for Francis is his lifetime commitment. Soto views this next assignment as a continuation on the road to justice and mercy. He thinks to himself, *Building the beloved community, exactly what Francis talked about in his homily this morning.*

The afternoon is sunny and mild. It is seventy-six degrees, perfect weather to play or watch soccer. Maria Elena sits on the sidelines near midfield with her three daughters, who have just finished their game. Teresa is especially elated after scoring a goal that helped her team to a victory over a neighboring parish team. The girls and their mother are watching Jose's team warm up with stretches and footwork drills.

Thirty minutes before the match is to begin, Maria and her daughters see in the near distance flashing red lights and sirens from police cars. Normally, that is not a welcome sight or sound in this parish of refugees. However, this afternoon the motorcade is bringing Pope Francis and his colleagues back from their luncheon meeting in Reynosa. The car drops off the former pope and the new cardinals in front of the rectory next to the soccer field.

Rocia and several other reporters jump off their bus and rush toward the clerics, trying to get a comment about the meeting with President Obrador. Father Soto intercepts them and reports on the meeting as Francis and the two cardinals enter the rectory.

Rocia listens for ten minutes to Soto's give-and-take with the reporters until she suddenly notices three familiar girls staring at her with big eyes and smiles. She immediately breaks away, runs to the girls and tightly embraces Teresa and her sisters.

Inside the rectory, Francis and Cardinal Moreno Coto are watching all this through the dining room window.

"Those three girls are part of the family you preached about this morning at Mass," Cardinal Coto explains to Francis. "Their brother, Jose, who helped to restrain the armed abductor on the bus, served Mass for me in their parish in Tegucigalpa. He is playing a CYO soccer match this afternoon."

"Where?" asks Francis

Somewhat surprised, the cardinal points in the direction of the field and says, "Right here, on the parish field."

Excited, Francis says, "Let's go watch for a little while. I would like to meet their mother."

"I was just going to suggest that we do that," Cardinal Coto interjects. "It has been more than a year since I have seen Maria Elena, and she will be thrilled to meet you."

With a furrowed brow and somewhat puzzled look on his face, Francis asks, "That reporter with the girls—she must be the one who was on the bus, don't you think?"

"Yes. Her name is Rocia Marquez, and she works for the *New York Times*. She has been covering Central America for many decades and is excellent at her job."

Sister Norma, Father Daly, Sister Mary Vernard, and Monsignor Torre are in the rectory kitchen discussing the meeting with Obrador when Francis walks in and surprises them. "Let's all go to the field next door and watch a kids' soccer match. We will be meeting the Gonzalez family, former parishioners of Cardinal Moreno Coto."

With that, all six religious leaders walk to the nearby field.

The three girls and Rocia follow with Father Soto, who is now finished with his briefing.

Maria Elena sees the group headed for the field and recognizes Padre Melo. She jumps up and rushes over to greet him with a hug. There is no kissing of rings here. For many years, Padre Melo had been Maria's confessor and counsellor. Francis stops and waits while the new cardinal and Maria Elena renew their friendship. Francis is confirming to himself: *It is a good thing to have made him a cardinal.*

Padre Melo introduces Maria Elena and her daughters to Francis. The girls crowd close to their mother. They are not used to all this attention from such important people. Teresa seems to enjoy it more than her younger sisters, who partially hide behind their mother's skirt.

Before Maria Elena is able to say anything, Francis says, "I am pleased to meet you and your children. And I am so sorry for all the sadness you and your family have suffered. Padre Melo, Father Daly, and now Sister Norma have all shared your story with me. I am pleased to hear that you and your family were granted asylum."

In a hushed and humble voice, with words that could have been spoken by an ambassador, Maria Elena responds, "Thank you, Pope Francis, for your kindness. You have given me and my children inspiration and hope for a better future. We wish you a good retirement and happiness."

Sister Norma joins the conversation. "Pope Francis, Maria and her children are some of our best volunteers. Each Saturday morning, they are at the respite center doing whatever work that they are asked to do. Maria is a wonderful example for her children. Our parish is grateful to have them."

Pope Francis notices Jose, who now has become part of the

group. "And I see, Sister Norma, that the parish has inherited some promising young soccer players. I heard walking over here that Teresa scored a goal in victory earlier today, and now I would like to meet Jose. Padre Melo tells me that this young man had put a dent in the wall of the church in Tegucigalpa from all his soccer kicks.

Everyone laughs at Francis's complimentary joke.

"Jose," Francis says, "we are all grateful for your courage on that bus and for your leadership in your family and now again at this parish. Padre Melo and Monsignor Torres have told me that you are also an excellent altar boy. You and your sisters have made your mother very proud. You have given her a lovely gift in return for the care and love that she has given to you. Now go play—they are waiting to start the game."

Rocia is mentally memorizing these exchanges so she can recreate this scene for the final article in her series for the *New York Times*.

Francis beams, watching Jose as he runs out to join his teammates on the field.

• • •

The choice of venue for the celebration of the two new cardinals is no fancy ballroom but instead a place of the people, the Humanitarian Respite Center. Volunteers spend the afternoon cleaning and decorating so it will look its best. Sacred Heart Parish is expecting most of the parishioners to be there to see and hear Francis. The two new cardinals insist that children be part of the celebration, to have the experience of being in the presence of Pope Francis. In addition, labor and business leaders are expected to attend, along with the mayor and city council of McAllen. Other politicians and religious leaders from Brownsville, an hour's drive away, will be coming. From across the border, in Matamoros, Father Anthony, the pastor of Our Lady of Refuge Church, who has been a courageous leader on issues of immigration, and Cardinal Retes, Francis's good friend from Mexico City, will make the journey to attend.

At the celebration, Francis talks about how unique and special the two new cardinals are. "Tonight," he says, "we celebrate their lives of sacrifice and courage. We honor them with a new title, but to you, in your hearts, they will always be Sister Norma and Padre Melo. I look around this room, and it is filled with beautiful people, and more than half are girls and women. I think to myself that the children here tonight, no matter their gender, race, or station in life, can aspire to leadership in our church. I think this is what Jesus would want.

"Sister Norma and Padre Melo are true shepherds of their flock. A woman and this priest elevated to high leadership fill my heart with joy. The Church is changing from its bureaucratic self and evolving into a pastoral church. By becoming a church of the people, it is facing up to its derelictions and sins of the past.

"In the morning, the cardinals here tonight will fly to Rome for the Vatican Synod and Conclave to choose my successor. I will fly to be with my sister in Buenos Aires, Argentina. My home. But I will always remember this special parish and those who have made it so.

"St. Ignatius taught us, there are two things to know about love. The first: Love is expressed more clearly in actions than in words. The second: There is greater love in giving than in receiving. Thank you for sharing your love."

CHAPTER SIXTEEN

The Synod and the Conclave

The general congregation Synod is now completed. Several grievances and issues were expressed, but the only conclusion reached was that bishops need to exert more vigilance regarding accountability in their dioceses on the matter of sexual abuse by priests. Some like Cardinal Blase Cupich, of Chicago, continued to encourage his colleagues to include lay persons within the accountability structures. Beyond that, the congregation was reluctant to risk offending undecided voting cardinals, with the papal election just days away.

On the morning of the Conclave, the cardinal electors celebrated Mass at the Basilica, then ate lunch back at the Santae Martae before gathering in the afternoon to begin the Conclave. Santae Martae is a relatively new part of the Vatican complex that has a modest hotel for visitors. It was built in 1996 so that it could afford some comfort to the cardinals, mostly old men. Before it was built, the cardinals slept on cots in a large partitioned room and used a communal bathroom. It also has a modest dining area and a chapel. This is where Francis lived in lieu of the palace. It is also where he said his daily Mass in the small chapel.

This is the first Conclave that includes female cardinals, and there is great interest from religious orders of nuns as well as the throng of journalists about what the women will wear. Will their dress be distinct or identical to that of their male colleagues? Indeed, the five women cardinals have met to discuss this issue.

Over the two weeks in the Synod leading up to the Conclave,

they gathered for several discussions and finally agreed on how best to approach this very public event as a group. They have chosen a practical middle ground, deciding to show respect for the institution by blending their dress with that of their male colleagues, yet also reserving the right to stand out and make a statement about who they are and who they represent.

All five of the women wear scarlet silk cassocks (their robes), covered by white lace surplices, and also scarlet mozzettas, which are short capes, around their shoulders. On their heads, they wear small red zucchettos which resemble yarmulkes. Unlike the men, they will not wear the usual stiff red biretta, a hat traditionally worn by cardinals on top of the zucchetto.

Father Peter Daly observed (referring to the previously all male cardinals) in his novel *Strange Gods* that "individually, they looked ridiculous. But together they were strangely impressive."

The five women cardinals have also agreed to make their dress distinct in three other ways, each one to symbolize their respect and affection for Francis and their devotion to Mary. The first is a veil like the one Veronica used to show mercy by wiping the face of Christ on his way to his crucifixion. Each woman cardinal will carry the veil draped over her left forearm. The second is a veiled head covering, similar to what Mary is customarily depicted wearing. This will be worn instead of the biretta, covering the zucchetto and flowing down beyond their shoulders.

And finally, each woman will wear boots to symbolize the Sisters of Mercy, the walking nuns whose first steps led them through the streets of Dublin and other Irish towns, in search of the sick and poor living in hovels. They walked in slum alleys, through snow and mud, and any place people were suffering. They reflect the teachings of Jesus and Francis, who today still call us to walk in the shoes of another. Each woman cardinal has sown up the hem of her cassock, making the boots visible to all. A simple cross of mercy is hung around their necks and rests exquisitely on the lace surplice.

That afternoon, the cardinals follow the custom of lining up by seniority outside the Sistine Chapel. All electronic devices have been surrendered so there can be no contact with the outside world. The choice they are about to make is to be between them and their God.

In the line-up of 120 cardinals, the women are in the back, accompanied by the four new male cardinals in their class. They stand out as the most diverse class in the history of the Church. In addition to the four women—with Cardinal Chittister, who at 82 years old is not eligible to be an elector—the four males include two of the youngest cardinals, Cardinal Michel Aupetit from Paris and Cardinal Sviatoslav Shevchuk from Kiev. There are three of African descent, Cardinal Wilton D. Gregory from Washington; Cardinal Moreno Coto from the Northern Triangle countries; and Cardinal Veronica Openibo from Nigeria. And of course, there is the additional ethnic diversity of Cardinal Norma Pimentel (Hispanic) and Cardinal Varghese (Indian).

While they are waiting for the procession to begin, the four new male cardinals slyly catch the attention of the women cardinals by hiking up their cassocks. Low and behold, they too are wearing their own boots in an act of solidarity. The women's faces brighten in expressions of great joy!

Hundreds of thousands of people have assembled in St. Peter's Square, where a large video monitor displays the procession of cardinals as they walk into the Sistine Chapel. The choir chants the names of the saints, and after each saint's name the cardinals answer with the simple chant of "Ora pro nobis" (pray for us).

When the camera zooms in on the women at the end of the procession, a huge roar of approval swells from the crowd in rolling waves of rejoicing. The cheers are so loud, it sounds as if the next pope has already appeared on the balcony above them.

Amen.

Writing a novel with Pope Francis as a lead character calls upon the writer to take some leaps of imagination. As much as I wish I could have sat down in conversation with His Holiness, this did not occur. The private scenes I have created are fiction, though they are based on readings I have done about Francis and observations of him during his papacy. In particular, I was informed by these major sources.

The first was Austen Ivereigh's compelling biography of Francis, *The Great Reformer: Francis and the Making of a Radical Pope.* Dr. Pietro Bartolo's *Tears of Salt* is the heartrending story of the refugee migration to the island of Lampedusa, written with Lidia Tilotta. I also found *A Shepherd's Diary by* Archbishop Oscar Romero insightful as well as inspirational. Tom Robert's book, *Joan Chittister: Her Journey from Certainty to Faith,* was helpful in understanding the theological arguments for gender equality. And the novel, *Strange Gods: A Novel about Murder, Sin, and Redemption,* by Father Peter J. Daly and Monsignor John F. Mylinski, opened my eyes to the political and competitive side of Vatican politics. Stephanie Spinner's short but exceptionally clear book *Who Is Pope Francis?* inspired me to dig deeper into the life of the pope. And, speaking of inspiration, the Reverend Dr. William J. Barber II's book, *The Third Reconstruction,* underscored for me the significance of the intersection of politics and faith in our lives. Jacob Soboroff's recent book, *Separated: Inside an American Tragedy,* is an excellent and detailed exposé of how the U.S. government separated immigrant children from their parents and guardians.

I also express my deep appreciation to the staff, reporters, and columnists of the *National Catholic Reporter* for their incisive and analytical reporting and opinion pieces. Their persistent advocacy on behalf of progressive church reform is a much-needed voice. *NCR* has helped push the Church toward reform and accountability for its actions. *NCR* is also there to report on the outstanding and courageous work of Catholic nuns, missionaries, and other progressive reformers who continue their magnificent work despite the pall that is cast upon them by others in the Church. I also relied on readings in *America, The Jesuit Review, Crux,* and the *Catholic News Service.*

And finally, my appreciation to John Carr and his staff at the Initiative on Catholic Social Thought and Public Life at Georgetown University. Their informative lectures and panel discussions have allowed me to see and hear many of the leaders of the Church discussing important church issues that became part of this novel.

I have used fiction to tell this story about Pope Francis, but Father Juan Soto, the character who has known the pope for many years and comes with him to the Vatican as his closest confidant, is a purely fictional character, though in many ways he is a composite of a number of people who fit that description in real life. Sister Mary Vernard is also a character I created, though I believe there are many Dr. Marys out in the world.

Maria Elena and her children are fictional characters, including Miguel, their courageous guide. Rocia, the reporter, is also a fictional character, though she is inspired by a reporter who in real life has covered similar stories. The challenges faced by the Gonzalez family on their journey north are undertaken by thousands of families, and these events were inspired by a few specific stories I have heard or read.

The majority of Pope Francis's public moments in this book actually happened and below are descriptions of my sourcing, not only for what occurred but also what the pope and others said at the time.

PREFACE

The story of Francis and the boy who asked if his dad was in heaven took place in a working-class neighborhood near Rome on April 15, 2018. Reporting about this event can be found in Cindy Wooten's article for the *Catholic News Service* on April 16, 2018. It can also be found on YouTube.

BOOK ONE

CHAPTER ONE

Information about Father Peter Daly's confrontation with Cardinal McCarrick in April 2002 can be found in Father Daly's August 20, 2018, column in the *National Catholic Reporter*.

CHAPTER THREE

Information about the Franciscan Shelter La 72 in Tenosique, Mexico can be found in *America: The Jesuit Review*, July 2, 2019. And they do celebrate every Saturday night. I relied on reporting in the October 25, 2018, *Washington Post* for details about President Donald Trump and the caravans, the MS-13 gangs, the Hebrew Immigrant Aid Society (HIAS) rabbis and their travel to the Mexican/U.S. border, as well as the words about Mexicans some believe triggered the killings at the Tree of Life Synagogue. The quote from Mark Hetfield can be found in an October 29, 2019, article by Mariam Jordon in the *New York Times*.

CHAPTER FOUR

The story of the women of Las Patronas, who dedicate their lives to feeding the refugees, especially those on La Bestia, is indeed true. A good report about them is by Will Grant on BBC.com; there is also a documentary feature about Las Patronas. The prayer offered by Sister Vivian at the shelter in Saltillo, Mexico, can be found on Beliefnet.com. For Mexican crime statistics, see James Frederick in *Vox*, August 2018. For Sister Clare's prayer, see Lesli White on Beliefnet.com

BOOK TWO

CHAPTER FIVE

I learned more about Joe Tobin from reporting by Sharon Otterman in the *New York Times* on December 22, 2016, and January 7, 2017. Additional information about the refugees at Lampedusa and Dr. Bartolo's work there was found in *Tears of Salt: A Doctor's Story* by Pietro Bartolo and Lidia Tilotta (W.W. Norton & Company, 2018).

CHAPTER SEVEN

The story of Cardinal Marc Ouellet's exoneration of Francis can be found in an October 8, 2018, article in the *National Catholic Reporter* by Thomas Reece of the Religion News Service. The results of the Dallas Charter can be found in a November 14, 2018, article in the *National Catholic Reporter* entitled, "Psychologist: Communication Failures Obscure U.S. Bishops' Progress on Abuse" by Dan Morris-Young.

BOOK THREE

CHAPTER EIGHT

Sister Veronica Openibo's remarks can be found in an article in the *New York Times* and the *National Catholic Reporter* on

February 23, 2019. See also, "Nigerian Sister Asks Bishops: Why Did the Church Allow Atrocities of Sex Abuse to Remain Secret" by Michael J. O'Loughlin, February 23, 2019, in *America: the Jesuit Review*.

BOOK FOUR

CHAPTER NINE

My information about Sister Norma in the jail with small kids comes, in part, from a July 9, 2014, *Texas Monthly* article entitled "Faces of the Border Crisis: Sister Norma Pimentel" by Eric Benson. Sister Norma's moment in church via satellite with Pope Francis appeared on ABC News video on September 4, 2015, by Teri Whitcraft. The details and information about Casa Padre, the previous Walmart in Brownsville, Texas, are from a *New York Times* article on July 14, 2018.

CHAPTER TEN

For the meeting in the Vatican between Francis and the preteen members of Italy's Catholic Action Program, I relied on Rome Reports, December 16, 2019. Rome Reports is an independent international TV news agency based in Rome.

BOOK FIVE

CHAPTER ELEVEN

The Martini letter is on pages 344–345 of Austen Ivereigh's biography of Pope Francis entitled *The Great Reformer* (Henry Holt, 2014). For thoughts on Cardinal Martini's liberalism, see Gaia Pianigiani's *New York Times* article on August 31, 2012. For Sister Joan Chittister's remarks on an all-male clergy, see page 170 of Tom Robert's excellent biography, *Joan Chittister: Her Journey from Certainty to Faith* (Orbis Books, 2015).

CHAPTER THIRTEEN

The story of Tim Russert contacting Cardinal Krol of Philadelphia to help him gain an interview with Pope John Paul II was told to me by journalist and friend Mark Shields. Further details about this are in Jennifer Hewko's story in *Morning Call*, April 3, 1997. The story on the St. Gallen Group is on page 257 of Austen Ivereigh's *The Great Reformer*.

BOOK SIX

CHAPTER FIFTEEN

The quote by Pope Francis about faith was taken from "Lumen fidei I," Encyclical Letter of Pope Francis, co-written with Pope Emeritus Benedict XVI, June 2013. Francis's thoughts on the Church, in his quote saying he, "prefers a church which is bruised, hurting, and dirty . . ." is from his Apostolic Exhortation "Evangelii Gaudium," November 2013. The St. Ignatius quote on love is from Morning Meditations in the chapel of the Domus Sanctae Martha, June 2013.

ACKNOWLEDGMENTS

It was noon on January 20, 2017, and Donald Trump was about to assume the presidency. I was troubled and verging on distraught. Since the November election I had given considerable thought to how I was going to cope with the next four years in what, predictably, turned out to be the worst presidency in our country's history. Philip Roth, one of my favorite writers, captured my feelings about Trump when he labeled him "a massive fraud and a boastful buffoon." I needed an antidote to Trump, so I poured myself into reading about Pope Francis, whom I admired from afar. With Trump there is despair, deceit, and boastfulness. With Francis there is hope, honesty, and humility.

I had just finished writing my congressional memoir, *Whip,* and was looking for another writing project. While I was sickened by the sexual abuse crisis within the Church and the harm it had caused the victims, I also felt sorrow for those in the Church who were not predators and who were doing courageous Christlike work in their parishes and in faraway environs around the globe. It was not long before I was immersed in the Church controversies and enthralled with the mercy shown by Pope Francis. From all of that, the idea of a novel took root.

My long history of engagement in Central America and my distain for the Church's sexist exclusion of women from the sacrament of Holy Orders were themes that I wanted to explore. I could not imagine the sexual abuse scandal running for thirty-four-plus years if women were priests and inherited powers of leadership. It would not have been tolerated. We are all on a journey. For the Gonzalez family it was 1,425 miles from Honduras to the Texas border. For the Catholic Church it has been a journey of 2,000-plus years. For me, the question is whether an individual, family, or institution is maturing and growing. For me, the Catholic Church is moribund. It is a venerable institution led by too many old men who are tired and unimaginative—many spiritless. The Church at almost every turn has denied women equality and by doing so has limited their futures as well as the future of the Church. Men of quality embrace the struggle for equality.

• • •

This book would not have been possible without the guidance and editing skills of Henry Ferris, a senior editor (*Dreams from My Father* and *Eyes on the Prize),* who helped me understand the novel form. Henry gave me valuable insights into dialog, plot, and character development. He was always available, and always considerate in his teaching. From our work together we developed a friendship that I cherish.

My dear friend Sarah Flynn, an editor in her own right, (also *Eyes on the Prize,* as well as co-editor of *Voices of Freedom)* guided me to Henry Ferris. Sarah helped in many ways, including reading the manuscript and reaching out to others in the publishing world.

Tom Fox, the former publisher at the *National Catholic Reporter (NCR),* was amazingly generous with his time in reading the manuscript in its first cut and provided guidance, especially on voice tense. *NCR* was often my go-to source for material and ideas. Tom's fantastic leadership as publisher of that award-winning publication is an inspiration to me and many others.

Thank you to Kitty Burns Florey for the excellent job on the final copy edit. She was great to work with.

This is the third book for which I have partnered with David Wilk. As my publisher he has been amazing in incorporating all the pieces that make a book work and making it accessible. I thank David, City Point Press, and Simon & Schuster for helping produce the book and for distributing it.

Dr. Kathryn Dreger, my physician, generously tutored me in the abnormalities of the physical heart, information I used in describing Pope Francis's health problems.

My appreciation to Lynne P. Brown, Ph.D., professor of political science and senior vice president at NYU, and her colleague Ellyn Toscano for directing me to the series *Women and Migration*, which under Ms. Toscano's leadership and direction helped me to understand better the significant roles women play in their families' migration stories.

As always, my sister Nancy Bonior, an artist and teacher, has been there to support her older brother. She not only read the manuscript but produced a very useful map of parts of Central America that includes the routes taken by the Gonzalez family and Jesus Aguilar. Nancy's map of the region helps to bring clarity to the journeys taken.

Andrew Bonior, my youngest son, was immensely helpful to his technologically backward "old man" by providing generous amounts of his time tutoring him on the changing world of computer technology. Andy was also one of the first readers of the manuscript and shared with me ideas for improvements as well as his enthusiasm for the stories I told.

I was introduced to Father Peter Daly's wonderful novel, *Strange Gods: A Novel about Faith, Murder, Sin, and Redemption,* by my neighbors Dan and Jane Head. In addition to the spirituality of Father Daly's novel, I was intrigued by the political aspects of the Church. A seed was planted, and my writing adventure followed. Over a series of breakfasts at a favorite neighborhood restaurant, I learned from Peter about the politics of the Church and also about Peter's new work as an immigration attorney for Catholic Charities. Father Daly's story of his confrontation with then Cardinal Theodore McCarrick, as written in Peter's *NCR* column, was my springboard into understanding the sexual abuse scandals.

Miguel Cabrera and I have been friends for about ten years. He has become part of the family. I have learned from him and his family the many nuances of Mexican culture and of the hardship working Mexicans face at home and in the United States. His character in the novel is a significant dramatic persona who reflects the goodness and generosity of the real Miguel Cabrera.

One of the pleasant surprises in writing this novel was linking back up with Colman McCarthy, a former editor and columnist at the *Washington Post*. In the late 1970s and early 1980s Colman helped me and my co-authors with our book *Vietnam Veterans: A History of Neglect*. It was Colman's columns and editorials that prompted us to write the book. Colman read the manuscript for *When Mercy Seasons Justice* and provided me with encouragement to go forward. In addition to his literary and teaching background, Colman continues his life-long work and passion for peace and justice.

I met John Carr when I first arrived in Congress in 1977. He was then working for the U.S. Catholic Bishops' Conference. Over the years John grew to be an important architect of ideas and policy at the conference. Like Colman McCarthy, his specialty was peace and justice. Today John's program at Georgetown University, the Initiative on Catholic Social Thought and Public Life, offered me an opportunity to see and hear church leaders, scholars, social workers, journalists, and other social and religious actors, several of whom are characters in the novel. I thank John and his partner at Georgetown, Kim Daniels, for their conversations and for reading the manuscript.

Geoff Thale is the president of the Washington Office on Latin America (WOLA). We have travelled together to El Salvador and Cuba and have collaborated for several decades. Geoff is one of the best minds on Latin America Policy. I thank him for reading the manuscript.

Another WOLA senior person is Kathy Gille who worked for me for over two decades in Congress as my top leadership aide. We both grew up on Detroit's Eastside in Catholic families and neighborhoods. Her passion for peace and social justice has been a significant value she has carried throughout her life. Together we fought many legislative battles to end wars and grow justice. I thank Kathy for reading the manuscript and for her always thoughtful suggestions.

Doug Tanner was the Founding Director of the Faith and Politics Institute in Washington, D.C. The institute is best known for its Congressional Civil Rights Pilgrimages to Alabama, led from 1998 to 2020 by the late Congressman John Lewis. A progressive Methodist Minister, Doug also once served as Chief of Staff for former U.S. Congressman Charles Robin Britt of North Carolina. Thoughtful and reflective, Doug has a keen understanding of the dynamics of how public policy and religion intersect and how that intersection affects politicians, policy makers, and the general public. Doug read the manuscript and provided me with valuable insight into spirituality and its impact upon the issue of race.

Jeanne Zulick is an award-winning writer of children's books (*Ruby in the Sky* and *A Galaxy of Sea Stars*). She is also a volunteer in Connecticut with IRIS—Integrated Refugee and Immigrant Services. Jeanne not only read the manuscript but offered valuable suggestions on the text as well as reaching out to others in the publishing community. We found that we both shared an interest in the Church as well as the immigration crises that abound around the world. I also thank her for her kind and reflective words about the book.

Lydia Chavez and I have known each other for almost forty years. We first met when she was covering El Salvador for the *New York Times* in the 1980s and I was working on Central American issues of war and human rights. Years later our paths crossed at the University of California at Berkeley where she was a professor of journalism and where we participated with other scholars, journalists, and policy makers from the United States. and Latin America in a series of forums in the United States and Mexico. Lydia's coverage of El Salvador in the 1980s was amazing and helped us get to a point to end the civil war there. I thank her for reading the manuscript and for her thoughtful comments on the novel.

The following individuals were also helpful, and I thank them: Larry Cohen, Tom King, Tom Birch, Sidney Lawrence, Bill Mitchell, Heidi Schlumpf, Decker Anstrom, Ken DeBeaussaert, Gary Lytle, Drew Hammill, Dan Gleason, Martha Pope, Fred Miller, Michael Collins, Karen Tumulty, E.J. Dionne, Jane Dystel, George Kundanis, Tim and Lisa Morse, Denise Breitburg, Julie Sutherland, Julie Matuzak, Warren Tolman, Chris Koch, George Hager, and Tom Downey.

And finally, a few words about two extraordinary women, Speaker Nancy Pelosi and Judy Bonior.

On December 20, 2019, a *National Catholic Reporter* editorial read: "For steady and thoughtful service to the nation at a time of extraordinary challenge and for exemplifying, in all its complexity, a public and, in this case, political role in which her Catholicism acts as a kind of moral bedrock, *NCR* names Speaker Nancy Pelosi as our Catholic newsmaker of the year."

I served with many good legislators during my twenty-six years in the U.S. House of Representatives. But two stand out: John Lewis, who was my Chief Deputy Whip, and Speaker Pelosi, whom I endorsed to replace me as Whip when I left Congress in 2002. Both were the "moral bedrocks" of the U.S. House of Representatives.

When I was first elected to Congress in 1976, in a Democratic class of 49 new members, only two were women. In total there were only seventeen women out of 435 members of the House, just four percent. The Senate was even worse, with three out of 100 being women. One of the accomplishments I am most proud of during my service was promoting women to leadership in the House. The country was fortunate to have Nancy Pelosi ascend to the highest perch on the hill. She is smart, savvy, compassionate, and accomplished. But the nation learned something I knew early about her: she is also courageous and tough, and she knew how to handle bullies. Also, under Speaker Pelosi's leadership, the number of women in the House of Representatives has risen to 101 and the percentage in the House from 4 percent when I arrive to 25 percent. It's not enough, but it is an impressive and marked improvement that is moving in the right direction. Much of the credit for the ascent of women rests with Speaker Pelosi's leadership. So, Catholic leaders, take note.

I am honored to have the Speaker's kind words of support for *When Mercy Seasons Justice*.

Judy Bonior has been my bedrock. My wife's editing skills, general sound advice, and unfailing encouragement made this writing exercise enjoyable. As with Henry Ferris, without her there would be no book.

041120-650-1-60W